Mama's Boy

Hammer & Sharpe Noir Mystery Thriller, Book 3

Eface Media

68 Barnes, Street
Long Beach, N.Y. 11561
DavidEFeldmanAuthor.com

CW01500546

ISBN 979-8-9926798-1-6 soft cover
ISBN 979-8-9926798-0-9 eBook

Cataloguing in Publication
Names: Feldman, David E., author.
Title: Mama's boy / by David E. Feldman.
Description: Long Beach, N.Y. : Eface Media, [2025] | Series: Hammer & Sharpe
                 noir mystery thriller ; book 3
Identifiers: ISBN: 979-8-9926798-1-6 (softcover) | 979-8-9926798-0-9 (ebook) |
                 979-8-9926798-2-3 (audiobook)
Subjects: LCSH: Mothers and sons--Fiction. | Prostitutes--Crimes against--Fiction. |
             Private investigators--Fiction. | Murder--Investigation--Fiction. |
             Missing persons--Fiction. | Organized crime--Fiction. | Elections--Fiction. |
             Substance abuse--Fiction. | LCGFT: Thrillers (Fiction) |
             Detective and mystery fiction. | BISAC: FICTION / Thrillers / Crime. |
             FICTION / Thrillers / Suspense. | FICTION / Mystery & Detective /
             Private Investigators.
Classification: LCC: PS3606.E3858 M36 2025 | DDC: 813/.6--dc23
Printed in the United States of America

For those who believe in clowns

MAMA'S BOY

Hammer & Sharpe Noir Mystery Thriller

Book 3

by David E. Feldman

Eface Media
Long Beach, NY

Table of Contents

Prologue

On a Wednesday night in mid-September, a scruffy 45-year-old man sat in a wooden chair next to Detective Abraham Gold's desk at the Towson Police Station. Twenty-five pounds overweight, with receding brown hair going gray and in need of a shave, he looked desperate and exhausted as he handed the detective his phone.

"That's the most recent picture I've got," he said. "It's about a year old, so Becca'd be"—he hesitated—"twenty-three."

"Okay if I text it to myself?" The question was rhetorical, so the detective didn't wait for an answer, but took the phone, tapped in his number and hit "Send." Then he took a good look at the photo.

In his mid-30s, bald with uneven teeth and a heavy mustache, Detective Gold set the phone on his desk, where he could see its screen, and began typing into his computer.

Hamilton's daughter had wide green eyes, neatly trimmed eyebrows, long, fine auburn hair, a slim nose, and a hint of a smile showing subtle dimples on either side.

"When's the last time you saw her?"

Jason Hamilton's eyes wandered while he thought. "Last night. We had dinner together." He gave a faint smile. "Shared a bottle of wine."

Gold looked at Hamilton and his eyes widened. "Have you been drinking today, Mr. Hamilton?"

Hamilton looked embarrassed and turned away. "I had a beer." He turned back to the detective. "One beer." When the detective didn't look away, he thrust his face toward him. "Hey, my daughter's missing. Gimme a break."

Gold asked, "Rebecca lives with you? Is there a Mrs. Hamilton, siblings, or other family there too?"

"Becca lives with me and it's just the two of us."

"Young women sometimes stay out all night."

Hamilton grimaced, then shook his head. "Becca always comes home. Or calls."

Gold said, "Tell me about her habits, schedule, her friends, other family…"

Hamilton took a breath, shrugged, and shook his head sheepishly. "She's a young woman. You know how they are."

"How are they, Mr. Hamilton?"

"Private, that's how they are. She goes to community college during the day and is out with friends at night."

"Every night?"

Hamilton nodded.

Gold took a yellow pad from his desk and passed it along with a pen and the man's phone to Hamilton. "Write down her friends' names, phones and addresses if you have. Then I want to know where she goes at night."

Hamilton looked back helplessly. "I don't know much."

"Well, write what you do know."

What Jason Hamilton didn't know was that his daughter was less than a half mile away. And a quarter of a mile away. And a mile away. They say you can't be in two places at once, but Rebecca Hamilton was in five, because she was in five suitcases. Four were within the town of Towson. Her torso was beneath the side of the road at a construction site. Her arms were in a rusty green dumpster behind a row of stores. Her legs were in a hole in a strip of lawn that bordered a parking lot in a dangerous part of town, and her head was in a cake box mixed with other garbage behind a bakery.

The person who had killed her and cut her body into pieces was just getting home from spreading her around town. He was exhausted but satisfied. He made himself a cup of peppermint and chamomile tea, and sat back on the couch with the TV turned to a romantic comedy. He loved romantic comedies that ended with happily ever after. He was a big fan of love and was, in fact, in love right now—with the girl he'd just buried all over town.

Chapter 1

Sam Sharpe arrived at his office at 10 a.m. on Thursday morning. His assistant, Robin Mendoza, looked up from her computer screen, her eyes scanning his face. He knew that she wanted to see if he was hung over, or worse, drunk.

He gave her a smile that was far cheerier than he felt. He'd been more or less sober for a year and a half—depending on one's definition of sober and who one asked.

"What've you got?" he asked, his tone matching his smile. Maybe he could throw her off. Robin's scrutiny along with her incessant cheeriness were like looking at the sun. She could be overwhelming, especially early in the morning. But she was good at her job, and she tolerated him, which was saying something.

Sharpe Investigations hadn't had a new client in weeks. They did have ongoing work provided by lawyers, two of whose companies, Charlson, Bain, & Woods and Marks & Marks, were responsible for more than half of Sharpe's income. The work was routine and included verifying prospective employees' backgrounds, tracking down witnesses for lawyers, surveilling disability cheats for the government, and cheating spouses for their soon-to-be exes.

Fewer marital cheating cases had come in recently and Sharpe wondered why that was. Was it a trend? Were people cheating less or were spouses less suspicious? And if spouses were less suspicious, was it because their marriages were better? And if marriages were better, was there less cheating or were the marriages more open and forgiving?

Sharpe's mind chewed obsessively on these and other questions. He had a mind with a motor, a monkey mind his NA sponsor had told him—a mind that drove him more than a little bit crazy. It sunk its teeth into an idea and wouldn't let go, keeping him up at night thinking, thinking, thinking.

Which was overrated.

Not thinking was what he was after.

He struggled to find ways to retreat from his thinking.

Drinking had worked, but then he'd had to get away from the drinking. He went too far down and had to come up.

So … cocaine or crystal. But then, too far up. So, shooting or snorting dope. But all came with obvious drawbacks—financial, physical, emotional and spiritual. And the drawbacks were bottomless.

For a while, those had been the days. His days.

But his days were over. Yes, over.

He was happier now.

He was.

He really was.

Really.

While they paid the bills, the routine work didn't satisfy Sharpe. He'd been involved in two murder investigations, and those had been the best days of his life. He had felt truly alive in a way he'd never felt before.

The problem with these cases was that they awakened his addiction—which was a beast, a monster, and the monster craved the chase of a murder case. With each case he'd battled not only the challenges of the case itself, but his reawakened addiction. Along with the thrill of the case he'd come to crave both the utter numb oblivion of heroin and the intense drive of crystal—a combination commonly called speed balls.

But all that was in the past. He was doing his best to attend 12-step meetings and follow their instructions—which seemed a bit much. Today, he had bought and nearly finished an enormous coffee on the way to the office from his tiny apartment. He drained the cup, threw it in the office garbage, and walked around Robin's desk so he could look over her shoulder to see what she was working on.

Her hair smelled nice, some new shampoo or conditioner. Strawberry. He liked looking over her shoulder. She was scanning police and newspaper reports for crimes, with separate windows displaying two paid databases to which Sharpe subscribed. She also had her computer's photo app open to several dozen images Sharpe had taken and uploaded the day before for one of the lawyers.

He could feel her awareness of him in her sudden tension, and looked toward her face, but her Afro was in the way. She must have been aware of this and turned her head to the left, trying to catch his eye, but Sharpe moved farther behind her, foiling her attempt. Robin was incredibly intuitive and able to anticipate his every action, word and, perhaps, thought.

"Who's that?"

"Who's what?" Sharpe peered at her screen, but Robin was looking beyond her computer, at the street-facing window.

"The guy looking through the window, his hand cupped over his eyes. There." She pointed to the left side of the window. "There." She pointed to the right, closer to the door. "Here he is now."

The door had opened and a middle-aged man in a brown corduroy jacket shuffled in. He stopped several feet in front of Sharpe and his tired gray eyes looked at the investigator with despair.

Sharpe strode to the man and put out a hand. "Sam Sharpe. How can I help you?"

He choked on his words. "I need you to find my daughter."

"Have you been to the police?"

The man gave a faint nod. "Yesterday." He looked about to cry. "Nothing. I know it's soon, but…they say after twenty-four hours…" His eyes filled and his breath caught.

"When did you last see her?"

"Tuesday night. She never came home."

Finally, a possible case.

He said nothing for a moment, and Robin got up and stood between them and the office couch. "Why don't you have a seat, Mr.—"

"Hamilton. Sorry. Jason Hamilton."

"Coffee, Mr. Hamilton?"

"That'd be great." Hamilton gave a grimace for a smile and sat down on the couch.

Robin went to the closet for a third coffee mug, giving Sharpe a severe yet somehow still cheerful look as she went by.

Sharpe sat down on one of the two chairs beside the couch.

"What's your daughter's name, Mr. Hamilton?"

"Becca—Rebecca. She's twenty-three. I have a picture." He withdrew his phone and showed Sharpe her picture. "I can text it to you."

Sharpe looked at Robin, who was busy making coffee. "I'll get it," she said, without looking back, then dictated a phone number and said, "How do you take your coffee, Mr. Hamilton?"

"Black, please."

"Coming up."

Hamilton texted Robin the photo.

"Tell me about Rebecca," Sharpe said. "Everything you can think of." He took out his iPhone and held it up, showing the voice recorder. "Do you mind if I record this?" he asked.

"It's fine," Hamilton said, holding his own phone up so that Sharpe could see his daughter's photo. "I wish I knew more. I know so little about her life." He looked away.

"I take it you've tried her cell?"

"At least ten times. That was the first red flag. She always either picks up or calls back. Not this time." His expression hardened. "Something's wrong, and the police haven't done a thing."

"Does she work?"

"She goes to community college during the day."

"And at night?"

"She's out with friends."

"I'd like to get any contact information you have for the friends."

"Don't have."

"What was she doing when you last saw her?"

"We had dinner together on Tuesday."

"Did you argue or fight?"

Hamilton huffed a breath. "Not any more than usual."

Sharpe pursed his lips. "What did you argue about?"

Hamilton blinked and his expression went blank. "I don't remember. I was probably letting her know I disapprove of the way she lives her life. That's what we always argue about."

"What is it you disapprove of?"

Hamilton gave Sharpe a tormented look. "Everything. The hours she keeps. The girls she hangs out with."

"Please give Robin whatever names and contact information you have for them."

Hamilton shook his head and shrugged. "Like I said. Don't have. Sorry."

"Tell me about these girls."

"The girls she knows now, they're a bad influence. When she was in grade school and high school she had nice friends. You gotta understand, Becca's a quiet girl, a good girl—or, she was. Her friends are loud and wild and I don't know what else, but it isn't good."

"Okay. Who else lives with you?"

"No one. It's just the two of us."

"She has no siblings?"

"She has a sister, Mary. Lives in New Jersey. They don't speak. I don't know why—some argument I wasn't privy to."

"Do you get along with Mary?"

"More or less. I visit." He suddenly smiled. "She and her husband, Kevin, have a boy—my grandson, Max. Best part of my life, Max is."

"Tell me more about your relationship with Rebecca. Did whatever conflict you have ever go beyond verbal arguments?"

Hamilton's expression darkened. "Why would you ask that?"

Keeping his expression blank, Sharpe looked steadily back at him. "Just trying to get as full a picture as I can."

"The answer is no. Absolutely not. I never put my hands on her in any way. I'm her father. Our relationship is like every father and daughter, where the daughter's a young woman. She wanders off the right path and I try to steer her back, and she … resists." He spread his hands. "She does what she does." He leaned toward Sharpe. "Gotta say. I'm hiring you here, and you're kind of insulting, maybe even accusing, me."

17

"Just gathering information. No insult intended. I apologize if it seemed that way."

"All right."

"Does she have a source of income? You didn't really answer whether she works or not."

Hamilton hesitated. "I didn't answer because I don't know. She might work part time somewhere—at a store or a coffee shop."

"So, you don't know?"

Hamilton shrugged. "Sorry. Like I said, she's pretty private."

Robin, who had been standing beside the shelf that held the coffee machine turned toward them. "Coffee's ready." She walked over and held a mug out to Hamilton, who rose and took it from her.

"Thanks." He sipped and gave Robin a grateful look.

She handed another mug to Sharpe, who stood, took the mug and sipped.

"Is there any reason Rebecca would want to avoid coming home?" he asked.

Hamilton's expression was bleak. "I don't know. I don't think so. Not on my end. She never tells me anything. I never know what the hell she's thinking."

"Does she have a boyfriend?"

Hamilton shrugged. "Not that I'm not aware of. It's these women she's out with mostly."

"Does she drink or use drugs that you know of?"

Hamilton sighed. "She drinks some I guess, but not any more than other girls—women her age." He looked baffled. "I guess that could mean anything. I don't know about drugs. None that I know of. A little weed, maybe. But that's a guess. I think I've smelled it on her when she came in a time or two."

"Does she have a Facebook page, Instagram, an X account?"

Hamilton shook his head. "I don't know. She might. They all do, don't they?"

Sharpe gave him an encouraging look. "Robin will figure that out." He paused. "I'd like to come by and have a look around her room. Do you live in a house or an apartment?"

"A three-bedroom home on Doyle Street. Come by anytime."

Sharpe stood. "I think I have what I need for now. If you'd like to hire us, Robin has a contract for you. We ask for sixteen hundred down, which is a two-day retainer, and we do pay as you go from there."

From her desk, Robin held out a clipboard with a multi-page contract. Hamilton took it from her, setting his coffee down on the edge of her desk. He took the pen from the surface of the clipboard and scanned the contract, then signed and handed it back. He took his wallet from a back pocket and slid out a credit card, which he handed to Robin.

He said, "Let's get this show on the road."

Sharpe said, "How 'bout we take a look at her room now?"

Robin ran Hamilton's credit card and handed it back.

Hamilton returned his wallet to his pocket and took out his keys. "Let's go." He met Sharpe's gaze and blinked back tears. "Isn't it true that if she's not found in the first day, then…."

"Let's take a look at her room, Mr. Hamilton, and go from there," Sharpe advised.

• • •

Rebecca Hamilton's bedroom was painted pink, and Sharpe could see that this had been her bedroom since she was a little girl. Her bed was layered with six pillows and three comforters: one pink, another done in multi-colored stripes, a third displaying peace symbols of various sizes and colors. A dozen picture frames were attached to one another on the wall at the head of her bed. Together they formed a kind of cross, with the frames spreading outward in four directions—upward, downward, to the left and the right.

Sharpe sat on the bed and leaned close, examining the photos. Most featured the same dimpled, green-eyed girl with straight hair of varying lengths. In some, she was with other girls. In one she was with a boy. In another she was with her father. In another she was of grade school age and with both parents.

"Does Rebecca visit her mother?" Sharpe asked.

"When she does, it's at the cemetery," Hamilton said. "It's been three years. Breast cancer."

"Oh, I'm sorry. Just to confirm, you don't have the names and numbers of any of her friends."

Hamilton had remained in the doorway, leaning with a shoulder on the door jamb. He looked at the floor and then back up at Sharpe. "I'm sure they're in her phone, which is with her. Otherwise, no."

Sharpe nodded and looked through the books, coins, tiny figurines of frogs and swans, and bits of paper on her shelves.

Hamilton had turned and was profiled in the doorway, his back against the jamb, staring at the other side. "I pushed her to get a job to have enough of a career to be self-sufficient. She was studying accounting, getting good grades too."

On one of the shelves, Sharpe came across a half dozen birthday cards that were standing, half open. He read each one and then stood them up again carefully. He held one open and asked, "Any idea who Maya Louise is?"

Hamilton's mouth set in a hard line. He shook his head, then paused and said, "There's a dive downtown called John's Bar. You might try there."

• • •

John's Barroom was a dive bar between private homes on a side street that looked to Sharpe as though it was not zoned for business. The sign was painted on pine wood and had been faded by decades of sunlight until its once green block letters and red fleur-de-lis were barely visible.

Inside were the bare bones of a tavern that might have existed during the Civil War era. A spare bar featured two taps and a few bottles on shelves in front of a dirty mirror on the wall behind the bar. Simple stools graced the scuffed wooden floor. Two tiny tables, each with a single chair, sat in opposite corners of the back area.

Three men of indeterminate ages were more or less evenly spaced along the bar. Two women sat along the short side of the bar to Sharpe's right. They watched him approach the bartender, an elderly man with sparse white hair on the sides of his head, small rheumy blue eyes that were lost in his deeply lined face, and a hard mouth above three wrinkled chins.

"You John?" Sharpe asked.

The bartender looked back at him and said nothing.

Sharpe took out his phone and showed the man the photo of Rebecca Hamilton. "Has this woman come in here?"

"Why are you looking for her?" The bartender's voice was a phlegmy rasp.

"I'm investigating her disappearance."

The bartender shrugged. "Couldn't say."

"Couldn't, or won't?" Sharpe didn't wait for an answer. "What about Maya Louise?" He nodded toward the women at the end of the bar. "Is she one of them?"

"Nobody here by that name," the bartender answered.

"C'mere Mistah," one of the women said.

Sharpe walked to the end of the bar. The woman who had spoken was a full-figured Black woman wearing tight black pants, a frilly purple button-down blouse that was open enough to show a deep décolletage.

"Are you Maya Louise?" Sharpe asked.

"We both of 'em. I'm Maya and this"—she nodded toward the other woman—"this Louise."

The other woman was olive-skinned with long, dark hair and would have been pretty if she didn't look so severe and weathered. Her hard eyes glared from a bony face. With an annoyed glance at Sharpe, she pushed past him and strode to the center of the bar, where Sharpe had been speaking to the bartender.

The bartender leaned toward Louise, and the two spoke in low tones, glancing distastefully in Sharpe's direction.

Maya appraised Sharpe. "I take it you not looking for a date?"

"I'm looking for information about a young woman who comes in here sometimes. Name's Rebecca Hamilton."

"You a cop?"

"I'm a private investigator."

The woman grunted and leaned forward, her elbows on the bar. "Leas' you can buy me a drink."

"I can do that," Sharpe said, and signaled to the bartender. "A drink for the lady," he said, when the bartender arrived. "And ginger ale for me."

Once Maya had her drink and took a sip from it, she seemed to relax. "Becca be thin, too thin. We met here, and Bec, me, and Lou—that be Louise—hung out at night. She drank rum and cokes and never ate, and I mean never. Well, she ate peanuts, pro'ly 'cause they was free. I swear, she lived on fuckin' peanuts and vodka."

"So, the three of you met and just…hit it off?"

"Wasn't like that. Well, me and Lou did, yeah. Becca show up later. She was just some girl was around. Not in the life then."

"How'd she get your trust?"

Maya huffed a breath. "She dint at first. She was just this bitch did her best to look scary. But we say a few words 'cause we all be in here anyways. Me and Maya be working and Becca figured that out, you know?"

"By working, you mean…" Sharpe searched for the right word. "Escorting?"

"Hah, escortin'. You want escortin' you go to the casino lounge. We sex workers, 'kay?" She smiled. "But you can call us ladies." She sipped her drink, put it down on the bar, then picked it up again and drank half. "Becca, she attract men, but not the right kind. She want to meet men, just to be around. But she also broke."

"So you suggested she start working with you?"

She gave Sharpe a cold look. "You gon' let me tell it?"

"Sorry."

"Well, I did suggest it, and Lou said it was okay. Becca didn't want to at first. She was scared. But we said we gotchu, girl. We say we

24

keep a eye out, you know? So, she did one guy and said she thought she could do it."

Sharpe waited.

Maya said, "That was, say, seven month ago. Then I got—well, I got pregnant, and Becca helped me. Lou did too, but Lou got her own problems—problems I ain't here to discuss." She glanced toward Louise. "Becca, she stay with me, brung me soup and shit."

Sharpe said, "Well, now she's missing and her father hasn't heard from her. He says she always calls, and she hasn't, so this is a missing person situation and possibly something worse."

Maya didn't answer right away. "Well," she said finally. "The men we … see are usually the same men. They regulars. We do this like a business. Was myself and Lou, then got even more organized with Becca. Becca smart. We had routines. We met them at the bar. We used an apartment Lou and me shared. No one ever stay the night. I mean ever. And John's bartenders kep' an eye on things and made sure we was safe."

She paused again and Sharpe waited.

"Becca, she was good for business—attract men like fucking flies. Pretty girl. Not used up, like—" She glanced toward Louise and could see she was listening. "Like me."

"So, what about Tuesday night? Was she here? Did she meet someone?"

Maya drank the rest of her drink, put her glass down and pointed to it with a long, orange nail. "Refill?"

Sharpe signaled the bartender and pointed to Maya's glass.

"Becca keep' a burner phone. Guy call her to meet."

"A client? Someone she'd seen before?"

Maya shrugged. "Don't know. She didn't say. She just say, 'I gots to go,' sump'n like that. Maybe she say, 'I got someone.' I don't 'member. I didn't think much 'bout it, tell the trut'."

"Is there anything else you remember? Anything about who she was going to meet, or where? Do you know the number of the phone she had?"

Maya shook her head, then held up an orange nail and said, "Know what? I do." She recited the number, and Sharpe logged it into a Google Doc in his phone. He noticed Louise staring from the center of the bar; her glare's intensity had increased and was now focused on Maya. The bartender was also watching them with impatient displeasure.

Sharpe took out his wallet, slid a card from it and laid it on the bar. He tapped it with a finger. "If you think of anything, anything at all that would help me find her, give me a call."

• • •

Sharpe and Robin spent the next working day searching for any hint of Rebecca Hamilton's whereabouts.

They scoured social media and Googled her name. Nothing.

Sharpe called her cell, but there was no answer and no message.

While Robin continued the virtual search, Sharpe visited local supermarkets, coffee shops, bars, and restaurants, showing employees Rebecca's picture. Several people said they thought they had seen her, but none offered any useful information. He visited the bank associated with Rebecca's credit card but was told that she had not been in for several months.

Her credit cards had not been used that week. Prior usage had been limited to gas and food.

Robin called the community college, and after explaining the reason for her call, was told that Rebecca Hamilton had withdrawn from her program in June, at the end of the previous semester.

Her father claimed to have no knowledge of any of Rebecca's childhood friends, with the exception of several first names: Jan, Rhonda, and Judy. Since Rebecca did not have a Facebook page and her bedroom offered no leads, the names were not useful, for now.

Sharpe began to consider the possibility that Rebecca Hamilton did not want to be found. Her relationship with her father was strained, so he thought it logical that she had run off with someone, possibly a client.

And yet, Sharpe had the nagging feeling that her disappearance was something else. Perhaps she was hiding from someone—a violent client, the police, or her father. Perhaps it was something worse.

For the moment, however, Sharpe's search for Rebecca Hamilton was at a dead end.

Chapter 2

It was Thursday night and Junior was chilling at home with Tim and Tyra, who were cool, easy and fun. Junior was drinking and eating from a plate of boneless wings with the TV on. They were having a good time.

Earlier Mama berated him again about meeting another girl, her tone alternately hopeful and derisive. Her monologue had gone on for some time and grew nastier with every moment.

The pressure began to build behind Junior's eyes; Mama scared the hell out of Junior to the point that he dared not disobey her.

"Whatcha wanna do?" Tim asked.

"Dunno," Junior answered, though he knew very well. "You?"

"Party," Tyra answered, clapping her hands once, then rubbing them together.

"Girls," Mama reminded him, plain as day, from the next room. "You need to meet a girl. Bring her home."

"Where?" Tim asked, and Junior knew that the question was meant for him. Tim wanted to cause trouble—break something, start a fire, steal something. All were appealing ideas, but Junior didn't want to entice Tyra into something that could come back and bite her, though

Tyra would probably be up for anything. Junior thought Tyra was sweet and hot and worthy of protecting—from herself as much as from anything else. He had a tendency to fall in love with whatever girl he was around … until Mama changed things.

"Gotta think on it," Junior said, stalling.

"And how 'bout making a little money for a change," Mama yelled from the dining room. "While you're looking for the right girl to bring home to me."

Junior rolled his eyes and gave a dismissive wave of his hand. "Just ignore her," he advised.

"You haven't worked in God knows how long," Mama continued over the TV. "Not like your daddy. Now *there* was a man!"

"Maaa!" Junior whined.

"Well, it's something your friends should know."

"Fuck," he muttered. He didn't want them listening to her.

"Don't you talk like that to me!" came her bellowing rejoinder.

"But, Ma," Junior begged.

"It's cool," Tim said, beneath hooded eyes. "I get the same shit at my house."

Junior winced.

"I get it," Tyra agreed, then perked up and asked, "Got a bottle stashed here somewhere?"

Junior leaned over the side of the bed and withdrew a half-full fifth of whiskey from between the bed and the wall. "You mean … this?"

"Sweet!" Tim looked impressed.

"I know what you're doing!" Mama called, in her cut-through-iron screech. "Drinkin'!"

"No," Junior answered, trying to sound confident.

"Drinkin'! Don't say you're not! And don't you talk back to me!"

"We're watching TV," Junior answered, which was true.

"And drinking'. Why doncha go out and earn. Earn! And meet a girl, and bring her home, dammit!"

"Fuckin' hell." Junior was breathing hard, a mix of fear and anger roiling in his chest. He feared it would burst through the front of his shirt.

He looked at Tim and Tyra and said, "We gotta get the fuck outta here." He paused, then said, "Casino." He took a pull from the bottle and his features clenched from the whiskey's bite.

His guests looked agreeable.

"Just don't let Coach see us," he added.

Tyra brushed the comment off. "Coach wouldn't be at the casino, silly. He's home, with Tammi."

"I know what you're planning!" Mama accused.

"Yeah," Junior muttered. "I know you do."

• • •

The dance floor at the Towson Hotel Lounge was lit in soft blue with hints of pink. A band at the front was playing a mix of uptempo rock and roll loud enough so that the people at the round tables beyond the dance floor had to lean close to one another to be heard.

Three women, Jennifer, Sheri and Ruby, were dancing together, and several couples had joined them. The long bar was populated by men in their late twenties and early thirties, and was tended by two dark-haired young women and one bearded man.

A handful of attractive young women in tight dresses sat at two corner tables that were pushed together, and now and then one would catch the eye of a young man at the bar and either she would go to him, or he would come to her. A brief conversation followed and often they would leave together.

The women at the corner tables were escorts, as were Jennifer, Sheri and Ruby. All worked for Judah Hammer, the hotel-casino's owner and crime boss for the Towson vicinity.

About half of the men at the bar were watching the dancing women. Some watched in the mirror behind the bar; others had turned their seats to face the dance floor.

Three of the men worked for Judah, and each had his own specialty. Lou Fedorov was slender and attractive, with a brown goatee, matching medium-length hair and an aquiline nose. He was an assassin. When someone needed killing, especially with a gun, the job was usually his. Lou was also expert at stealing expensive cars, a lucrative wing of Judah's business. To Lou, these tasks were not work, they were opportunities, even sport.

Rinny Mallach was a preternaturally gifted fighter, a mixed martial artist with exquisite fighting skills both standing and on the ground. He had been the featured fighter at the weekly "Fight Nights" presented by Wallace North, the local crime boss before Judah. He was the man one had to beat to win the night. No one ever had. Until Judah.

Rinny's fighting skills were often unnecessary, as his appearance was frequently enough to frighten away the opposition. His face looked like it had been made of wax and held to a flame. The skin on his forehead was melted and sagging, his brows drooped over his eyes, and the skin beneath his eyes crumpled over ruined cheeks in bulging, veined sacks of flesh. His ears looked like halves of yellow Brussels sprouts and his sparse hair stood in sandy tufts amid red welts, wheals, and scars on his head. Everyone gave him a wide berth.

Scurge Granville was more conventional muscle. He, too, was a skilled fighter and trained killer, though perhaps not Rinny's equal. He often used a weapon—a knife, gun, or sap. Or whatever was handy. He was an integral part of Judah's loan and collection business, with en-forced collections being his specialty. Recently he had developed a fascination with knives. He had taught himself to accurately throw them and he had an affinity for cutting people, beginning with their fingers and progressing to faces, bellies or throats. He was grateful to Judah for allowing him to occasionally indulge his new obsession.

But at the moment Scurge was obsessed with Jennifer, one of the three escorts dancing several feet away. Like the escorts, Judah's trio of muscle was based at the Towson Hotel Lounge, and fraternizing between the two groups occurred naturally and was permitted, as long as it didn't get in the way of business.

Scurge had been fascinated with Jennifer for the two months since she had come to work for Judah. She was dark, with enormous brown eyes beneath full dark eyebrows, a strong, prominent nose and a mouth with a narrow upper lip and full lower lip. She had long, sleek, luscious hair that fell nearly to her waist. She was intelligent, well read and had a wicked sense of humor.

Scurge couldn't take his eyes off her, but despite being a courageous fighter and willing executioner, he couldn't bring himself to look her in the eye, speak to her or, God forbid, ask her to dance.

Jennifer was aware of Scurge's fascination with her and flashed him faux shy smiles and occasional furtive glances as she danced.

Rinny Mallach was watching Ruby, who had smooth, dark brown skin that lightened slightly around her features. Her neat black eyebrows arched over warm, caramel eyes, a powerful Nubian nose, and sleek cheekbones that surrounded a generous, well-defined mouth. Her hair was done in flat twists that began high on her forehead and lifted into scalloped edges. She danced with herself and appeared unaware of anyone else in the room. She would feel, rather than see, potential clients, glancing up when she felt their eyes on her. But for now, she danced alone and was the object of Rinny's fascination.

Sheri was dark-eyed, with brown brows and blonde hair with bright highlights that fell to her eyes and over her ears. Her small mouth was pursed in concentration as she danced, glancing around now and then to catch the eye of any potential clients that might come through the door.

"C'mon, ask her, Scurgie." It was hard to tell, but Rinny was grinning at him. Rinny's mouth didn't curl into anything resembling a smile. His face looked more like an oval bowl of oatmeal that had been dipped with a ladle on one side. "What's the worst that can happen?"

Embarrassed, Scurge turned from the dance floor, but continued to watch Jennifer with brief sideways glances. She was the most beautiful woman he had ever seen—not conventionally beautiful, but something more substantial, more real, more present.

"She could say no." he said softly. "It'd fuckin' kill me."

Lou's shoulders shook with suppressed laughter and Rinny gave a high-pitched titter. Rinny's voice was unnaturally high—something to do with whatever had befallen his skin. His body, too, had been badly scarred. When shirtless he looked like a biology class model of the human body, his muscles showing raw and red.

"It won't kill you," Lou said.

"You've been shot in the gut, kicked in the balls and punched in the face," Rinny whined. "Little girl sayin' no—what the fuck is that?"

Scurge looked back at Rinny. "Yeah? So go talk to Ruby." He waited. "Didn't think so." He then glanced at Jennifer, then at Lou. Then back at Jennifer.

"He's gonna do it," Lou predicted.

Scurge pressed his lips together and started to lean in Jennifer's direction. Anticipating him, Jennifer turned to face him, her face all innocent expectation.

At that moment, a dark-skinned young man approached and said something to her. He was a shade over six feet tall, had a tight Afro and a focused, confident expression. He wore an expensive navy-blue sport coat, a pink dress shirt with gold onyx cufflinks and neatly pleated slacks that matched his coat.

Scurge looked at the man; he couldn't hear what was said, but watched Jennifer respond politely and give him a charming smile. The man looked familiar, Scurge thought, as he and Jennifer turned away and walked toward the exit. Just inside the door, the man smiled at Jen and left the bar. Jennifer glanced back in Scurge's direction, her lips pressed together with what looked like regret, then stepped toward the exit, as if to follow the man. But something momentarily drew her attention toward the hallway leading to the restroom. She paused, then left the lounge.

Scurge turned back to the bar and signaled Scotty, the bartender, for another drink. "Double," he said.

"That guy"—Rinny was nodding toward the door—"looked just like Frank."

Lou nodded. "You're right."

Scurge was shaking his head and staring into his drink. "She broke my fuckin' heart."

"Ah, come on," Rinny said. "She got a client. Next time. This was an 'almost.' Step in the right direction."

Lou was looking at Scurge with something like compassion. "She'll be back," Lou said quietly. He and Scurge were as near to best friends as was possible in their line of work.

"Yeah, well," Scurge said, then turned back toward Scotty. "Make it two."

"That must have been Frank's brother," Lou said. "Probably looking for Frank."

"Right," Scurge breathed. "Where's he live again—the brother?"

"Atlanta," Rinny filled in.

"Wonder what he's doin' here," Scurge said.

"Long way to come for a date," Scurge said, and looked longingly toward the exit. He sighed as his drinks arrived. Both were the same as the first. Bourbon, rocks—Buffalo Trace. He only drank Buffalo when he was celebrating, or really depressed.

• • •

Junior arrived at the casino alone, having left Tim and Tyra to hang with their usual crowd. He played the slots but was quickly down a hundred and forty dollars. The pressure in his chest was squeezing his lungs, which made breathing difficult.

He switched to blackjack but did no better. After losing another hundred and sixty dollars, he wandered into the lounge and found exactly what he was looking for. She was dancing with two other women, both of whom were attractive enough, but this one—this one was a real princess. A Jewish princess, from the looks of her. He walked past her to the bar, which was crowded with men, and felt her focus on him.

Junior turned and they locked eyes. The ache in his chest made him cough, and he had to look away, then forced himself to look back at her. She was still looking at him. Now she was smiling.

"Here you go," the bartender said, and Junior heard the faint clunk of the beer bottle on the bar in front of him. He paid, leaving a tip, turned, and there she was, barely a foot away.

She was taller than he was by several inches, and her mouth was level with his eyes. When she spoke, he looked directly at her mouth, which had taken on a life of its own.

"Got plans tonight?" she asked.

He tried to speak but no words would come. The thing in his chest was crawling up into his throat and he was overcome by a wave of panic. "I, I, gotta go to the bathroom," he squeaked, his lips pressed together. "Be right back. You—you wait there."

"I'll be here, dancing with my friends." She was still smiling and there was something about her smile. It seemed … kind.

He really had to go. His intestines had turned to liquid. He sat and clenched the muscles in his face and neck. He hated public bathrooms! As he finished, pulled his pants up and left the stall to wash his hands, he wondered if she'd waited.

When he exited the restroom, he found her talking to a big well-dressed Black guy not far from the dance floor. For a moment he was hesitant. Should he return to the bar and buy another beer he didn't really want? He didn't much like beer, but drank it for social accept-ability. What he really wanted was to take this princess home—to Mama.

The well-dressed Black guy was leaving, and, after a glance toward the bar, the princess appeared to be following him. Still in the hallway outside the men's room, which was close to the exit, Junior lifted his head, raised his eyebrows and managed to catch her eye—and there was that smile again! So warm, friendly, inviting, and true.

The Black guy left and she paused, inclined her head, and the look on her face plainly said "follow me," and so he did, through the exit and into the parking lot.

"I'm Jen," she said. "Why don't we get a room in the hotel?"

He couldn't answer; the pressure in his throat was too much, and he was sure he was going to puke right there in front of her.

Finally he said, "Let's go to my place."

"All right," she said.

• • •

Once they arrived at his house, Junior unlocked the door and pushed it open silently. He listened, heard nothing from Mama, but knew she was there. Listening. Waiting.

He put a finger to his lips. "Shhh." He grinned silently at her and Jen smiled back, his co-conspirator.

"Mama," he whispered.

Jen followed him into his room and began unbuttoning her blouse.

He was hard. He was ready; he didn't know if he could wait. He fumbled with the button on his pants.

Jen had stopped undressing. "Could you please pay me now? That's kind of the policy."

He swallowed. He knew this was going to be a problem. He had spent all but twenty-four dollars at the casino and lounge.

"Yeah," he said. "Gimme a sec." He turned, saw what he wanted on the floor a few feet away. She was sitting on the edge of the bed and had begun removing her pants.

He reached for a ten-pound weight and realized that a five would move faster and would hit just as hard.

"Okay," he said, and stepped back toward the bed.

She was still smiling but frowned when she saw the weight in his hand, not understanding.

He heard Mama in the hallway speaking as naturally as if she was telling him to take out the garbage. "Do it, Junior. Do it now!"

And so, he did, whipping the weight up and around, windmilling his arms.

Her eyes were wide with shock and terror and her hands came up involuntarily, partially blocking the weight, which dented her forehead, leaving a gash and a red wound. Desperately she tried to push him away, making little mewling sounds.

The thing in his chest was gone now and there was Mama looking at him from the doorway, screaming. "That's the way! That's my boy! You do it! You kill her. You fucking kill that bitch!"

When he was finished and the blood was thick around her head, Mama said, "I'll wait while you cut her up and wrap her."

He paused. "How will I—?"

"Don't worry," she said. "I'll explain. Your brother's in his room in the basement. He'll help."

• • •

Late that night, Judah's street team pulled up in front of the bar in Rinny's black Escalade. Scurge was in the passenger seat with Lou in the back.

Rinny glanced at the bar. The neon sign above the door identifying it as the Iron Horse Tavern was unlit and the windows were covered with blinds. Around the blinds' edges, faint blue light glimmered.

"You sure this is the popup?" Scurge asked.

"I'm sure," Lou said confidently. "Source says you knock three times, wait, then twice, wait, then once. They'll crack the door and you give the password, which is 'freak'."

Scurge's expression didn't change.

"Give me your piece," Rinny said, and Scurge handed over his Glock 17. Rinny locked it in the glove box. Scurge would be the point man and he would be thoroughly frisked once inside.

Lou and Rinny would carry AR-15 automatic rifles, though Lou was partial to his Glock.

Scurge kept a leather holster of knives under his arm. The knives were thin, their handles flat, and together the holster and knives were virtually undetectable by frisking.

Lou held out a two-inch long hard cardboard cylinder. "This is a tube of testing solution. Drop in a pinch of product. If it turns red, product is cut with fentanyl. If it's tan, it's cut with sugar or talcum powder. If it's black, it's rat poison."

"Okay. Then what?" Scurge wanted to know.

"Then nothing," Rinny said. "It's all bullshit. A smokescreen. We're coming in four minutes behind you, guns blazing. Lou will take out the guy at the door and anyone on the other side."

"Is there a back door?"

Rinny grinned horribly. "Malik and Lubbock will be waiting out back. No one's going anywhere."

Scurge remained expressionless. Rinny slapped him on the shoulder. "Cheer up, man. It's not a funeral. We're giving you point here to forget the girl. She'll be there when you get back." He reached into his coat and pulled out a small, brown paper bag wrapped with rubber bands. "Here's thirty grand for the brick."

Scurge took the money.

"Hey," Rinny said. "Smile."

"Leave me the fuck alone," Scurge growled, and pushed the car door open. He looked around the lot. A black F150 was parked at the other end. He started toward it then angled along the side of the building, looking for other vehicles and a door or window that might be used as an escape route. He thought he saw a black motorcycle but couldn't be sure. It might have been a bicycle.

He went back to the front door and knocked as instructed. The door opened a crack; no one spoke.

"Freak," he muttered.

The door opened and he was pulled inside by rough hands and shoved against the wall next to the door. The barroom smelled like any other barroom, but Scurge could also smell leather and something burning.

He was held by the back of his collar and behind one arm and propelled into a back room that was dark except for a single faint blue bulb. A man was sitting alone at a table off to one side, smoking something out of a small pipe—something that had to be lit each time he hit on it.

At a table in the center of the room sat a Black man in a flowing red cape and a black baseball cap. On the cap was the number one, large and red. The man looked at his oversized Apple Watch, its big, glowing red digits giving the time. The blue light was behind him, so the man's face was in shadow.

Scurge could see rather than feel others around them, in the area opposite the entrance and toward the back door.

"Cash," the man said, in a husky voice.

"Product," Scurge replied.

The man leaned to one side, reached down, and produced a rectangular block, which he laid on the table between them. The block had a gritty consistency and looked like dark green sand.

He pressed a button on a lamp that Scurge had not known was there and the block was illuminated.

Scurge began to reach toward the inside of his jacket.

The man's hand went to his waist. "Don't," he said.

Scurge held both palms up so the man could see them. He was planning what he would do when Rinny and Lou showed up. "Test kit," Scurge explained.

"Slow," the man said, as he brought up a Walther PDP 9mm pistol and laid it on the table, his palm on its stock, his finger on the trigger.

Scurge continued holding up his left hand while reaching slowly into his jacket with his right. He drew out the cardboard cylinder, making sure to keep his jacket open and loose over his chest for easy access. He opened the top of the cardboard and shook out the glass tube.

"I need—"

"I'll do it," the man said, and let go of the gun to reach toward the tube in Scurge's hand.

Scurge heard the series of knocks from the door, then a pause, and then two quick explosions followed by the thump of a body hitting the floor.

Several things happened simultaneously. The man reached for his gun, but Scurge was faster. As the man touched the pistol, Scurge plunged the knife through the back of the man's hand and into the wooden tabletop.

He heard more gunfire and realized that the man's friends had run into Malik and Lubbock outside the back door. The man, who was standing but bent over his pinned hand, was grunting repeatedly in agony.

Lou appeared and put his Glock to the man's head. Scurge pulled his knife from the man's hand and wiped it on the black tablecloth. The man gave one long, deep-throated scream, and then a gasp of horror when he saw Rinny, who had appeared next to him. Scurge returned the knife to its holster as Rinny bent the lamp up and toward his own face, so the man could get a good look.

Scurge smiled at Rinny's sense of humor.

The man's eyes bulged.

"What's your name?" Rinny asked.

"Freak."

"Freak?"

The man nodded; he was whimpering now.

"Makes sense," Lou muttered.

Rinny continued, his voice a whine like a table saw. "And you work for—?"

"Dante."

"Dante?" Rinny asked. "Like the *Inferno*?"

"'Zactly."

"Well, Freak. You tell Dante that no one distributes product in this town or any town it borders."

"Borders?" the man sneered, though he was still in obvious pain.

Rinny thrust his face so close to Freak's that flakes from the dead skin on what had once been Rinny's nose sprinkled onto the man's collar.

"You do business in this town or in the neighboring towns"—Rinny arranged his features in something that approximated regret —"Your guys start losing body parts. That is, the guys who don't end up like your doorman—your dead fuckin' doorman."

Freak blinked.

"Ya hear?"

"Yeah," came the sullen reply.

"What?" Rinny demanded, his voice rising to a wail. "Whaaaat?"

"I hear. I hear!"

Rinny smiled, a terrifying jack-o-lantern smile, and Scurge thought, *Halloween's only a week away.*

Chapter 3

Junior pulled on a pair of sweats, which he covered with a pair of green nylon PVC waterproof chest waders. The waders featured rubber boots, so he was entirely covered, waterproofed, from chest to toe. Next, he wriggled his fingers into disposable plastic gloves, and examined Jen's body, considering what to do next.

"Don't just stand there," Mama said. "Get the black trash bags from where I keep 'em. Get two bags over her top half and two more over her bottom half and do just like the first one. Drag her down the basement by her feet, and Norman will help you cut her up and bag her parts separately. Then spread the parts around, but not in the same places. I'll help you figure out where."

"Okay, Mama."

"You may need to drive a ways. But I'll be with you, and I'll explain."

"Can Norman come?"

She didn't answer right away. "Well, okay. I guess."

Junior slipped a bag over Jen's feet and nearly to her waist. He pulled another over her head and struggled against her weight to slide it down over her shoulders and chest. He had to turn her over and fight with the bag, pulling it over one shoulder and upper arm, then turning her again to do her back.

He took her feet and dragged her down to the cellar, where his brother's bedroom and bathroom sat next to an open area Junior and Norman had used as a playroom when they were growing up. Now, it housed computers and an array of gaming consoles, a dusty, faded red couch and a matching arm chair. Everything in the room had been covered with old tarps. Those that were on the floor were splattered and pooled with dried, congealed blood.

He was about to get to work, but stopped and considered for a moment, then returned to his bedroom and stripped the blanket, sheets and pillowcases from the bed and stuffed them into trash bags.

"Now you're thinking!" Mama said approvingly. "Now, when you're done downstairs, take all that to the dumpster behind the supermarket, along with whatever you're wearing. In fact, take it to a supermarket at least two towns away. Then, come back and take a shower."

"Okay, Mama." He lifted a corner of the tarp from the stereo and put on some music. He was able to control the unit with his iPhone via Bluetooth and he set Spotify to loop his favorite song, Green Day's "Boulevard of Broken Dreams."

His tools were laid out on the painted little red and white unit that had been his childhood desk. He had a new reciprocating saw to go along with his chainsaw, hacksaw, meat cleaver and rubber mallet.

Once she was out of the bags, the girl's head wounds oozed and dribbled blood and the wife-beater T-shirt he'd covered her face with while he did the deed was still stuck to her forehead.

Norman helped Junior position her body in the middle of the room, and pull the tarp, which had been dragged beneath her, back into place.

Junior looked around and noted that his work with the bleach later on was cut out for him. He fit his goggles over his eyes, fired up the chainsaw, and focused on the job at hand.

Afterward, he carefully washed and separated her parts as he had the first girl's, and rolled each of the arms, legs, torso and head into separate tarp packages, which he wrapped in duct tape. He had a line of refrigerators ready and waiting against a basement wall, and in the coming days he would spread the body parts separately around a thirty-mile radius with Norman's and Mama's help and guidance.

Finally, he was satiated and satisfied, with no thought of ever doing anything like this ever again. But that was exactly how he'd felt after the first girl, and yet after a week he'd started to ponder doing *exactly this* again. And within a few days, he'd been obsessed and then *po*ssessed.

So, he was already wondering about next time.

• • •

The next day, Detective Abraham Gold wheeled an office chair from a nearby empty desk to a spot beside his own and motioned for the woman to sit down while he remained standing.

The woman, who was in her forties and had unkempt reddish-brown hair and wore no makeup, wiped her nose with a balled-up tissue she held in her left fist. She held out her right hand. "Harriet Teitlebaum."

Gold shook her hand, which was limp and sweaty.

Detective Barbara Cortez, who was dark-haired and sinewy, stood behind Gold's desk. She reached toward the woman and took her hand, then sat down and began to type.

Harriet sat down heavily. "My daughter never came home last night. She always comes home, even if she's out late, even if she has a date…"

"Slow down, Mrs. Teitlebaum. It's Mrs.?" Gold asked.

Harriet nodded. "Neil, my husband, passed two years ago this August. Heart attack."

"I'm sorry to hear that," Gold said politely. Cortez had stopped typing and was waiting.

Harriet had been looking at her hands, which clenched her thighs.

"Your daughter?" Gold prodded.

She grimaced. "Jen comes home every night. And when she isn't coming home, she calls. But she doesn't need to call because she does come home every night, though sometimes quite late. But I wait up. I'm sorry. I'm getting a little crazy."

Gold sat on the corner of the desk nearest Harriet. "What does Jennifer do for a living?"

Harriet blinked and frowned. Either the question made her uncomfortable or she wasn't sure what her daughter did for a living. "She's, well, she worked as a barista at Smooth Coffee & Scones downtown. Um, she was a waitress at—"

"But right now, what does she do?" Gold repeated.

"She's between jobs."

"It sounds as though she's often out in the evening. Do you know where she goes? Who she's with?"

Harriet took a breath. "She wants to be a singer, and she sometimes sings with this guy at the lounge at the Towson Hotel."

"Towson Hotel Lounge," Gold quietly repeated, glancing at Cortez, who was typing.

"Who's the musician?" Cortez asked.

"I think his name's Izzy?"

Gold and Cortez exchanged a glance.

"Izzy Hammer?" Gold asked.

"I guess. I don't know," Harriet responded, with a shrug.

"What about her friends?" Gold asked.

Harriet's eyes wandered as she considered the question. "Sheri, or Sheryl—I think she's called Sheri, and Ruby is the other one."

The detectives exchanged another look.

"So, is it fair to say your daughter—"

"Jennifer."

"Jennifer—spends time at the Towson Hotel Lounge with two women named Sheri and Ruby?"

Harriet wiped her nose again, then shook her head. "Well, I don't know where they go. But wherever she was last night, she didn't call and she didn't come home." Her features crumpled, her mouth opened, and she began to cry silently, her face rigid with anguish. She began sniffling as her nose began to run. "What I want to know is, what can you do to bring my daughter home—my beautiful, sweet girl? I keep imagining such awful things!"

Gold bent toward the woman, who was crying harder now, and squeezed her clasped hands. His tone was gentle, kind, compassionate. "We're starting with a missing persons report and we'll go from there. I promise you; we will look into her whereabouts and do whatever is necessary to find her. Meanwhile, your job is to give us a call as soon as she calls or comes home." He straightened up, his hands on his hips. "She may be doing the right thing. She might have had too much to drink and stayed overnight with friends rather than drive home while impaired."

Harriet shook her head, and Gold led her to the exit and watched her leave. He returned to his desk, where Cortez had finished typing.

"She's an escort," Cortez said. "Isn't she?"

Gold nodded. "Probably works for Judah Hammer. The women she mentioned as her friends work for him."

"Ties in with the Hamilton girl, don't you think?"

51

Gold sat down in the chair he'd pulled over for Mrs. Teitlebaum. "That, I don't know."

"Just seems like—"

"Key phrase, 'seems like.' Two missing girls. Nothing else in common, fact-wise."

"Both live with single parents."

"So? Teitlebaum's an escort. Rebecca Hamilton's a college student."

"So says her father."

• • •

A 70-foot 18-wheel tractor trailer rolled into the two miles of campgrounds that lay along Towson's eastern border. Painted in bright yellow and red circus stripes, it displayed the face of a grinning man in clown makeup on one side, his head shaved, his face orange with painted white arches outlined in black above his eyes, an open mouth made wider with white and red outlines that extended to his cheeks and below his chin. He wore a round red nose and shocks of bright red hair in a U-shape around the sides and back of his head. His features were laughing with low eyebrows that added a hint of menace.

The other side of the truck was painted yellow with swirling blue accents around enormous red lettering that read "Clowney's Bandwagon."

As soon as the truck came to a stop, the driver climbed down from the cab and went around to the rear of the truck. He wore clown make-up and red pants with matching suspenders, a white shirt and a blue vest. The man sprang the lock on the truck's back door, which immediately opened, revealing another, slightly shorter but wider man, dressed and made up exactly like the driver. The two spoke, and the driver lowered a ramp from the back of the semi to the ground.

Instantly, a small yellow and red striped car rolled down the ramp and settled on the ground a half dozen yards from the truck. Six large men, all in clown regalia emerged from the little car. Another seven men followed on foot, carrying small red and yellow striped tents, which they quickly set up on the grass beyond the parking lot.

Next, two small pop top camper vans rolled from the back of the semi onto the grass between the pup tents and tractor trailer. Four women, also in clown makeup, emerged from the camper vans and connected them to the campground's electricity, plumbing and sewage systems. They began setting up two long electric grills, which soon began to smoke as they were brushed with oil and layered with vegetables and strips of beef and pork.

Several hours later, in front of the BuyAll Supermarket on the corner of Main Street and Broadway, four of the clown-painted men in white shirts, blue vests and frizzy red hair began handing out colorful fliers reading "Clowney for Mayor."

Passersby began to congregate and stare. Many took the fliers and wordlessly walked on. One young man said something along the lines of "Nuh-uh. I'm for Stafford," and one of the costumed men hit him twice in the face with a small heavy metal object held in his fist.

The police were called but by the time they arrived, the costumed men had piled into their tiny car and headed back in the direction of the campgrounds.

When the police questioned the people at the campground, none would admit to handing out the fliers, much less attacking anyone. Since the assault victim's only description was of a man in clown makeup, no identification was possible and the police had little choice but to leave the campground with only a vague warning made to one of the men, a tall, rangy man with a shaved head in clown makeup who claimed to be Clowney himself.

• • •

Judah sat in a chair at the kitchen table, while Dinah stirred something, perhaps soup, on the stove. Whatever it was, it smelled delicious. Dinah had been Judah's favorite of his siblings and probably his favorite person in the world, with the exception perhaps of his Raisa and their daughter, Rachel.

"I heard there was some trouble yesterday," Dinah commented, her eyes on the soup.

Judah looked up at her. "Gang working for a guy named Dante is selling product at popup locations. Probably gets the word out via text chains. We took care of it but probably haven't heard the last of them."

Dinah gave him a look. "Did you get the leader?"

Judah shook his head. "Wasn't there." He changed the subject. "How's Josh?"

His sister snorted a laugh. "Like you when you were his age."

"Uh, oh."

"That's right. Uh, oh."

"Trouble at school?"

"Trouble everywhere. Especially since the kidnapping. Kid's got a mouth and talks back to anyone and everyone."

Judah widened his eyes and gave Dinah a meaningful look. "Well, you're in a position to give him what I never got."

She laughed. "A whipping?"

Judah remained serious. "Love."

She looked at him with eyes that sparkled beneath hooded lids. "He gets that. It's the other he doesn't get."

"Rachel's worse. She's been talking like a baby."

"The kidnapping was worse for her," Dinah suggested.

Judah's mouth tightened and he gave a small nod.

Dinah took a breath. "Lev wants to move Zebby to a home."

"No."

"I know you don't want to, Jude, but Zeb's a handful. He can't do anything. He's in diapers. He has to be changed and bathed, and fed."

"No."

"And we all have schedules. I work for you. Raisa's at the newspaper, though she can work a bit from home, and all our brothers have jobs. Taking care of someone with the kind of disabilities Zeb has is a full-time job."

Judah looked steadily at her. "It would fuckin' kill him. We can figure out schedules, work together."

Dinah gave him a scornful look. "We can't even have dinner together."

She was right about that, he had to admit. The six siblings could agree on virtually nothing, and Zeb's combination of cerebral palsy and a nameless muscle and nerve wasting genetic disorder had left him unable to do much of anything besides watch TV.

"He does want a computer."

Judah was startled. "Who does?"

"Zebby."

"How the hell's he going to use a computer? And what's he going to use it for?"

"I don't know what he's going to use it for, but he says he can use a trackball with the fingers of his right hand, if the track ball's positioned right."

Judah was impressed. "So, let's get him a computer with a trackball." He felt his phone vibrate in his pocket. He retrieved it and took the call. "Yeah, Frank."

"I'm at the lounge. Seems Jennifer didn't come in today."

"Can someone check her place?"

"Already done. I sent Ruby, who has a key. She's not there and it doesn't look like she was there last night. Toothbrush wasn't wet."

"Maybe she had someone."

"She did. Apparently went somewhere with him."

"What do we know about him?"

"Nothing, really. Just some guy caught her eye at the lounge. They left. That's it."

Judah sighed. Dealing with these girls meant dealing with their messy lives. "Well, thanks for the heads up. I suspect she'll show eventually. But she's gotta be made to understand. This is unacceptable."

"Yup. I'll garnish a third of last night's take."

"That should do. See you later."

He ended the call and saw his sister looking at him, waiting.

"One of our girls hasn't come in yet." He huffed a breath. "Par for the course. Frank will deal with her when she gets in."

Dinah nodded. "Good."

· · ·

As he walked from the back door of his house to the garage, Judah's mind was bubbling over with concerns that fell into two categories: business and family.

Business was good, despite the usual issues that included fluctuating prices, maintaining security, and finding good help. He had no control over the price of liquor or hotel supplies. He did have some control over the prices of narcotics, which depended on the stability of his sources and the cost of defending them.

He was worried about Dante, who, he suspected, would not let the killing of his man or the violent warning from Rinny, Scurge and Lou go without retribution. He would be hearing from Dante and he had to be prepared to take some loss in what would inevitably be a surprise attack—and he had to mitigate the surprise.

The casino was in the black, the hotel booked solid, the escorts were seeing clients, and Judah was reasonably confident that his employees could be trusted to the degree anyone could be trusted in his business.

The hotel-casino complex also contained a moderate-sized arena, which seated several thousand. Wallace North, who had owned the facility and run local organized crime several years earlier, had regularly presented "Fight Nights." At ringside at the last of these, Dinah had finally achieved revenge for North's countless rapes by shooting and killing the man, but not before he'd impregnated her with their son, Joshua.

The arena was now booked each Saturday through Election Day by Mayor Stafford's opponent in the upcoming race, an election that would take place the following month. Judah knew nothing of the man or the events he had planned, but the candidate's people had paid in advance and Judah was happy for the business.

His family was the greater concern. Rachel had to have someone with her in order to fall asleep. The kidnapping had been two years earlier and had congealed in her mind until it was a persistent, ongoing nightmare.

Raisa's work at the *Towson Gazette* enabled her to be home many afternoons. On the other days, rather than introduce a new babysitter, Raisa left Rachel along with her cousin, Dinah's son Joshua, in the care of her Uncle Izzy until Uncles Reuben and Lev came home. They were safe in the big Hammer home until then, as long as Izzy didn't get high—a pretty big "if."

Raisa had transcended her own trauma, anxiety, and depression, and was now navigating her work as a journalist, being a mother, her place in their large family, and being his partner in life, all with grace and authority. And yet she hated Judah's work and refused to marry him because of it. She had demanded to know how he could be a good man if his life was steeped in criminal activity. His response had been lighthearted and off-hand. Everything and everyone around us is steeped in crime, he'd said. The government is steeped in crime. Greed is everywhere. What matters is how regular people, citizens, neighbors are affected.

He had expected an argument and was pleasantly surprised when Raisa had looked thoughtfully back at him and said nothing. They had not discussed his work since.

As he strode to the garage, these thoughts were banging around his head like the silver ball in a pinball machine. He thumbed the combination into the lock and opened the door. He smiled. The motorcycle, a brand new "whiskey red" Harley Davidson Street Glide, glinted back at him.

He climbed on, started the bike, and felt the rumbling vibration of the engine below him. Once he left the driveway and ran through the gears on the open road, his jumbled thoughts began to arrange themselves in his mind. What had been confusion assembled into prioritized, structured order.

His mind cleared as he sailed along, banking through turns and accelerating onto straightaways. His neck, shoulders and legs relaxed as he and the bike merged and flew along.

As soon as he parked the bike, his mind was working again. All those jumbled disparate puzzle pieces were now coherent parts of a whole, a tapestry—his family, his business. His world. And his job was to protect that world.

Judah signed in at the front desk, writing "mayor's office" as his destination. He waited as the guard called upstairs, then waved him through.

He stepped off the elevator, put his keys, wallet and phone into the little bowl on the long table, which he slid across to the two police officers on the other side. He walked through the metal detector and was allowed to retrieve his belongings and continue on to the mayor's office.

Mayor John Lee Stafford III was a career politician. In his mid-50s, he had long, dyed, perfectly coiffed blond hair that was flipped up, combed back, and held in place with gel.

He had a handsome, fleshy face, the red, veiny nose of a heavy drinker, and a toothy, boyish grin he could flash at will, particularly in front of any camera that happened to be nearby. He had a habit of rubbing his fingers and thumbs together, as though daydreaming about money.

Stafford stood in the doorway of his conference room, flashed his smile and shook Judah's hand while grasping his forearm with his other hand. His expression was deeply grateful. "Thank you for coming, my friend."

"Of course," Judah said, wondering at the mayor's choice of words. The man was not exactly his friend.

"Coffee?"

"Already had, thank you."

"Come on in and sit down."

Judah followed the mayor into the conference room. The mayor sat in a tall, black leather chair at the head of the table and motioned for Judah to sit in the chair nearest him.

"I called you in to talk about the election," Stafford began. "We're only a month away and I have an opponent this time."

"I've seen the posters," Judah said. "But I thought they were some kind of joke or PR campaign."

The mayor's smile disappeared. He shook his head, his expression grave. "It is a PR campaign, but it's no joke. This Clowney is a real person and he's filed to run against me."

"Who is he?"

"His name is Tagill, and he's…" The mayor searched for a word. "A huckster, a P.T. Barnum." He stabbed the air with his finger. "He's a dangerous man because he makes a joke of every issue, but he also casts blame in ways that catch people's attention. He's a conniving son of a bitch."

Judah looked confused. "Well, you've been running this town for a while. People know you, so why is this guy a problem?"

"I don't know that he will be. I asked you to meet with me because you've been helping me for over a year." He waved a palm in the air. "I've allowed you to run your businesses, some of which are perfectly legal and above board—others not so much—because you've kept the more, shall we say nefarious, elements around here at bay."

Now Judah was beginning to understand. "And you think this Clowney—Tagill guy—is a nefarious element."

Stafford spread both palms. "I don't know, but I suspect we'll soon find out, and I'm counting on you to help us keep the peace and maybe help me maintain an advantage with the public."

Chapter 4

Judah stood in front of the stage in the Towson Arena, which was part of his hotel-casino complex.

"Should I leave these boxes?" yelled one of the four men working in the wings.

"They're bringing their own sets and want the wings and stage as cleared out as possible. So, I'd say no, get rid of everything."

"What about the lights?" another stagehand asked.

Judah thought a moment before answering. "Leave the lights. They might want to use them. Once they're here, we can ask and move them if they want."

Frank James entered the arena through one of the rotunda entrances that led to the restrooms and food courts. With him was a man of similar size, shape, bearing and coloring. The main difference between them was that the man had a dense Afro while Frank was entirely bald. Both men had similar features and beards. Because Judah was facing the stage and was focused on the work going on there, he did not notice the two until Frank spoke.

"Judah, there's someone I want you to meet."

As Judah turned, Frank continued. "My baby brother, Kofi. Kofi, Judah Hammer."

The two men shook hands. Judah's eyes wandered the man's face and he broke into a grin. "Baby brother? You could be twins 'cept for the hair."

Kofi looked embarrassed. "Yeah, I am the junior brother, but I'm blessed. What can I say?" He proudly ran a hand over his thick head of hair.

Frank gave his brother a mock disdainful look. "Baldness is a sign of high testosterone."

Kofi shook his head. "B.S., made up by some bald guy."

"So, what brings you to town, Kofi?" Judah asked.

"I'm thinking about buying the Exxon station over on Park and Towson Boulevard. We came into a few dollars when our father passed away."

"Kofi's named for him," Frank added.

Kofi nodded. "And I thought it would be cool business-wise and to be part of a sort of Nigerian ex-pat community. Quite a few of the local stations are owned by Nigerian-American families."

"I didn't know you were Nigerian," Judah said to Frank.

"I'm American," Frank corrected.

"We were born in Nigeria," Kofi added. "Frank moved here with our mother when we were little and our parents split up. I stayed in Nigeria with Kofi Sr. We moved to a suburb of Trenton, New Jersey, three years ago. Then I moved to Atlanta." Kofi gave a sly smile toward his brother. "But there's another reason I'm here. A surprise."

Frank raised his eyebrows, then said to Judah, "I'm going to introduce him to Sam Sharpe," Frank said. "They have a few things in common."

"Okay then," Judah said.

"Did you want the usual security setup for tonight?" Frank asked Judah.

Judah shook his head. "These guys have their own security. I'd keep half the rent-a-cops on—outside until the doors open, then bring them inside. Keep half in here and the other half patrolling the rotunda."

A giant of a man, six-foot-seven and three hundred forty pounds, lumbered down the aisle toward them. He wasn't quite running but was swinging his massive arms in a barreling speed walk.

Judah saw him first and raised his eyebrows.

"Some cops are here," the man said. "They want to talk to you."

Judah nodded and glanced at Kofi. "Glad to meet you. Make yourself at home."

He followed the giant, whose name was Lubbock and was one of Judah's street team members, out of the arena and through a series of hallways into the massive library that was a combination of Judah's office, conference room, and Dinah Hammer's tech center.

Standing beside the conference table were Detectives Abraham Gold and Barbara Cortez. The latter was holding up a shield as identification. Gold was holding out his cellphone, which displayed a photo of an attractive young woman.

"What can you tell us about the whereabouts of this young woman, anytime since Thursday night?"

"I don't know," Judah said, his tone off hand. "Who is she?"

Cortez answered. "Her name is Jennifer Teitlebaum, and we believe she may work for you."

"Doesn't ring a bell," Judah answered, shaking his head and shrugging. He was aware that the detectives probably knew he was lying, but this was a conversation he did not want to have.

"She's a prostitute," Cortez added, emphatically.

Judah was still shaking his head, his lower lip curling outward. "Well, she doesn't work for us." He put his hands on his hips, squared his shoulders and faced the detectives. "We do not employ hookers. What consenting patrons might do when they're on the premises is not something we can control." This was his standard line with the authorities.

"Okay, not hookers," Cortez countered. "Escorts."

But Gold laid a restraining hand on her forearm; he knew how the game was played. "Do you happen to have video footage of the casino and lounge from Thursday night?" he asked.

"Let's find out." Judah turned and walked toward the glass-enclosed booth at the far end of the room. He paused at its doorway, as the detectives followed. The three crowded into the booth where Dinah was seated at a U-shaped desk in front of two computers and four large screens. The screens showed live feeds from the casino, the lounge, the arena, and parking lots from various angles.

"Di, do we still have video from the lounge and casino floor from Thursday?"

Dinah nodded. "We keep everything a week. So we'd have that until the start of business Thursday, when it would overwrite."

Judah stood to one side, his arms folded across his chest, as the detectives spilled into the booth.

"What do you want to see?" Dinah asked.

Judah looked questioningly at the detectives.

"She spent her time with women named Sheri and Ruby," Gold said.

Judah nodded knowingly and spoke to his sister. "Pull up the lounge. Start at, say, nine-thirty and scrub through to closing. Detectives, maybe get closer to the screen so you can get a good look. Dinah, can you scoot to one side? Yeah, with your keyboard and mouse."

The room was silent as the scenes on the screen began to shift into high gear. They watched people waddle around and move in jerky fits and starts.

"There!" Cortez said, pointing.

"Back up. Now, zoom in," Judah said.

"Pretty sure that's her," Gold announced.

"I'll let it play"—Dinah offered—"while keeping her in view."

They watched for a few minutes more. "Well, now she's left," Gold said. "Let's see if she comes back."

They waited until the video ended as the lights in the lounge came on at closing time, but Jennifer had not returned.

"Can we go back to when she left and get a closer look at what was going on there?" Gold asked.

Dinah scrubbed backward until several minutes before Jennifer exited the lounge.

"So she's dancing..." Cortez said. "And she has some interaction with that guy, and then—see, that guy left, and she followed him out." She looked to Gold for confirmation. He nodded.

"Looks like that guy might have been her client," the senior detective said. He looked at Judah. "Any idea who he is?"

"First of all," Judah emphasized. "This woman does not work for me. Any date, relationship or anything else she might have been doing here, was strictly the activity of a private citizen. We got that?"

Gold huffed and smiled. "Sure it is."

"Okay then. Yeah, I do happen to know who he is. I just met him. He's my employee Frank James's brother, Kofi."

Judah phoned Frank James, and soon he and his brother had joined Judah and the detectives in front of the video from the previous Thursday night.

"Were you this woman's client?" Gold asked.

Kofi shook his head. "I was not. I was asking whether she knew my brother, Frank, and where I could find him."

Detective Gold grunted in either disapproval or disbelief. Judah was not sure which. "Did you happen to notice where she went when she left the premises?"

"As you can see," Kofi said, "I left before her. So, no, I did not notice where she went when she left the premises."

Gold took a long breath and let it out slowly.

"Will that be all, detectives?" Judah asked.

Gold nodded. "For now." He looked at Kofi. "But we may want to talk with you again."

Kofi spread his hands with an agreeable nod. "I'll be around for a little while."

Detective Cortez leaned over and spoke softly in Gold's ear. The senior detective straightened up.

"Mr. Hammer, we'd like to ask you a few questions, if you don't mind."

Judah nodded. "Let's go into the conference room, so my sister can get back to work. Frank, how 'bout giving your brother a tour, if he hasn't had one yet?"

"Good idea," Frank said, and the brothers made their way through the library and out the exit.

Judah led the detectives to the long, polished conference table.

"Can I get you coffee?" Judah asked.

Gold shook his head. "This won't take long." He flashed a look at Cortez, who spoke.

"Late Thursday night—actually, early Friday morning, there was a shooting at the Iron Horse Tavern. The doorman there was killed. Do you know anything about that?"

"Why would I?" Judah asked, shaking his head.

"It's come to our attention that the place was a major drug distribution spot—at least for that night. A kind of temporary dispensary."

Judah gave a half shrug. "Maybe it's come to your attention a little late. I'm not sure they're still in business."

"How would you know that?" Cortez snapped. "And yet you don't seem to know what went on there Thursday night?"

Judah grimaced a grin. "You're the detective."

Cortez took a step toward him. "You," she jabbed a finger toward his chest. "Watch your mouth."

Judah kept his eyes on the finger, but he ignored Cortez and looked at Gold. "Maybe you should thank me, if I was involved—and I'm not saying I was. I mean if they're not a drug spot anymore, that's one less crime scene you need to worry about. Little less work for you, right?"

"You're quite the wise ass, Hammer," Cortez said, pressing toward him, but Gold caught her by the upper arm.

"Let's go, detective."

But Cortez continued to glare at Judah.

"You heard him," Judah said; he was smiling now.

• • •

Gold and Cortez had just returned to the station when Gold's cell rang.

He held it to his ear. "Gold." He listened, glancing at Cortez, who waited, eyebrows raised.

He returned the phone to his pocket, spun on his heel, and walked quickly back toward the door. "Come on."

"What?" Cortez asked, as she struggled to catch up.

"Sanitation truck found something behind the supermarket. I told them not to touch it 'til we get there."

"A body?"

"Nah."

They arrived to find a crowd of people in the lot, whose entrance to the street was blocked by a green garbage truck. Behind the truck was a dumpster, and behind the dumpster were three cars whose irate drivers were waiting impatiently for the truck to move and allow them to exit the lot.

One of the sanitation men was leaning against a rear tire of the truck, smoking. The other must have been in front of the truck. The driver, wearing an orange waterproof suit, was waiting beside the dumpster.

As Gold and Cortez approached, one of the waiting drivers called to them. "Hey! How 'bout getting them to move the truck!"

Gold waved to the man and approached the driver of the sanitation truck, who pointed toward the dumpster.

"This didn't look right, so I called the office and they called you," he said.

Gold looked into the dumpster and saw a blue blanket and sheet twisted together, along with several pillows and some men's clothing.

He looked at Cortez. "Call forensics and have them send someone to collect this stuff to get it analyzed."

As Cortez made the call, Gold addressed the waiting motorists. "I need you all to be patient a little while longer while we have someone from the station come for some of the items these guys found."

Two of the motorists returned to their cars.

The driver who had called to them gave Gold a look of disbelief and spread his palms wide. "Aren't you from the station?" He shook his head. "Fuck's sake!"

"The situation requires forensics," Gold said politely.

"The situation requires competence," the man said.

Cortez had finished her call and overheard. "Hey!" she yelled to the man and walked over until she was nose to nose with him. The man held up two hands, as if protesting his innocence.

"Cortez," Gold said.

"Yeah, Cortez," the man repeated, sarcastically.

● ● ●

Junior was running errands and, as usual, Mama had come along.

They began at the bank, where they waited while a mother with a little girl used an ATM. As the machine emitted a two-tone prompt, the little girl asked her mother where they would be having lunch.

"At the diner. Would you like that, honey?" the mother answered.

"Can I have a milkshake?"

"Eggs would be better, darling."

"But I don't like eggs!"

"Will someone shut that kid's mouth!" Mama muttered.

"Ma," Junior softly complained.

"Don't 'Ma' me!" Mama responded and Junior recoiled, as he often did when Mama turned her harsh light of rage toward him.

Once they were at the teller, Junior was asked how he would like his money.

"What kind of stupid question is that?" Mama whispered.

"Twenties, please," he said to the teller, doing his best to ignore Mama.

From the bank, they drove to the supermarket, parked and pulled a shopping cart from the line of carts out front.

"Don't forget the waffles," Mama reminded Junior, as they rolled along the freezer aisle. "And ice cream. Coffee ice cream!"

"I won't forget, Mama."

They made their way up and down the aisles, with Mama muttering whenever they had to wait for slower shoppers.

In the freezer aisle, a young woman stopped her cart in front of the door to the ice cream shelves and was eyeing different items, not yet ready to make her choice.

The woman turned at the sound of Junior's cart and gave a faint smile.

"Make your damn choice already," came Mama's fierce whisper.

The woman turned back to the freezer. Finally she moved on without taking anything.

"What was the point of that?" Mama demanded. "Stupid cow."

"It's okay, Ma," Junior said.

"It's not okay! These entitled women are everywhere. We need to get rid of them, one girl at a time! And that's what we're going to do."

"Shh!" Junior said, as they approached the frozen vegetables. The same woman had paused there.

"Bang her cart with yours. Go ahead, bang it!"

"Ma," Junior protested, as the woman moved on, and Junior took a bag of mixed veggies from the shelf and dropped it into the cart.

"Follow her," Mama said, insistently. "Follow her out of the store. See where she lives."

"No, Ma. Come on!"

But Junior was a good son and did as Mama told him.

The woman lived in a light brown single-family home in a cul-de-sac less than a mile from the market.

"Now drive two blocks, park, and come back. Then knock on her door, and when she answers, push it open, and pound her head into the God damn floor!"

"With what, Mama? No!" Junior put the car in gear, made a U-turn and drove directly home, refusing to respond to any of Mama's orders, which softened to entreaties and finally to gentle, cooing kindness. He did his best not to listen. He didn't want to do this anymore.

No more. *No more!*

But as he drove, Junior remembered how he had felt after killing the two young women. Mama said he'd feel good, and he had. He'd felt empowered. Satisfied. He almost never felt satisfied anymore, yet killing the two young women had, now that he thought about it, been the most satisfying moments of his year.

He had also been excited—which was also rare—and while he was disgusted by what he had done, there was no denying the rush of excitement, the thrill and exultation at the sight of all that blood.

He was torn—thrilled and excited by this most natural of actions: stalking, and killing, and yet disgusted and nauseated by what he had done.

• • •

As he did at least once each day, Judah made the rounds of his business interests. He began behind a low wall at the back of the hotel-casino parking lot, where the boosted cars were kept. Lou first showed him a dark blue 2024 BMW X5. Together, they walked around the car, and Judah ran a finger over two long scratches on the left rear quarter panel.

"Will detailing get rid of these?"

"Yep." Lou walked to the next car. "Check this out."

Judah stepped back to admire the sleek silver sedan. "Alfa Romeo."

"Stelvio, and it's loaded. Eighty grand, new."

Judah whistled. "I might keep this one for myself."

"Not a good idea," Lou advised, shaking his head.

Judah held up a hand. "I was kidding. I'm not doing that."

The next two cars had taken significant damage. The first was a gray Toyota Camry, its passenger side door crumpled.

"So, what happened here was—" Lou began.

"Don't tell me. I don't want to know."

"Body shop?"

Judah shook his head. "Not worth it. Parts."

Next was a shining black 2024 BMW M5 sedan with a banged up front end.

"Sorry about this," Lou said.

Judah was shaking his head. "Fuck. This is a hundred twenty grand."

"I know."

"Body shop," Judah said.

"Figured," Lou agreed.

Judah returned to the Hammer suites in the hotel, where he found Scurge in the Loans and Collections room, poring over an Excel list called Debtors, Debts and Circumstance.

Judah pulled a chair up beside his athletic, blond soldier with a broad nose and began pointing at names.

"Tell me about him," Judah said.

"Regular family man, more or less. Works for the phone company, stringing poles. Has a kid in college and another in high school. Wife's a schoolteacher."

"How'd he end up with us?"

"Fell off a pole in July. Gets sick pay and has good insurance but lost out on summer overtime he was counting on for the kid's college bills."

"Sounds like he'll be good for it."

"Agreed."

"Next."

Scurge sat back and scratched his cheek. "Bit of a knucklehead. Been a good customer at the casino but got in over his head. Single guy with a girlfriend. Bets on football, too."

"Job?"

"Stockbroker."

"Lean on him. Bounce him around a little bit but don't break anything. He'll come through. And if he doesn't—" Judah shrugged.

"Got it."

"Next?"

"Taxi driver. Also drives Uber part time."

"Haven't I seen his name here before?"

"You have. Three months ago."

"And he paid?"

"He did, but we had to go at him pretty hard. Broke his right knee cap."

"Aw, man. I hate this shit. We shouldn't have given him anything."

"This is from the blackjack table. Says he's got a sick mother."

Judah pinched the bridge of his nose between his thumb and fore-finger. Finally he looked up at Scurge. "All right. Rough him up good. Give him a week to pay—no excuses. If he doesn't, start with fingers, but leave his legs alone. He's gotta be able to work. And ban him from the casino."

"What if he doesn't pay?"

"Well, he's got ten fingers."

Judah's organization's business suites were set up with an outer living room manned by two armed guards, with business conducted in the bedrooms.

Drugs were separated into pills and powders, each with its own room. The pill room was manned by Malik, a muscular Black man with sharp eyes and quick fists. He supervised two men at a desk and a table who were taking pain pills from a large plastic bag and carefully dropping them into orange vials with white tops.

Lubbock supervised the powder room, where three men were breaking up bricks of brown heroin, mixing it with similarly colored quinine powder and spooning the mixture into small glassine bags, which were weighed and placed in bunches into larger bags, which were then stacked in the suitcases.

Judah went from room to room, watched the work, quietly questioned or commented, and moved on.

His last stop was the lounge, where Ruby approached him as soon as he came through the door. At the bar, a lone man of about sixty with tousled gray hair and matching beard was bent over a drink he held with both hands. He didn't look up when Judah entered. It was early afternoon, too early for the lounge to be full.

"Jen didn't come in today. She didn't call either." Ruby looked worried.

Judah looked at his watch. "It's not even two thirty."

Ruby shook her head. "We have a rule. Call by twelve. And on Saturdays we don't fuck around."

He shook his head. "Still? She never came home Thursday. Her mother called the cops."

"Shit."

"Listen," Judah said. "Just go about your day. We have a business to run. We'll find out where she is eventually." He gave Ruby a supportive smile. "This isn't your problem. She'll either turn up or we find another girl."

Chapter 5

By seven-thirty that night, the arena at the Towson Hotel & Casino complex had been transformed with blue and white lights, streamers, balloons and an enormous screen at the back of the stage on which was projected the face of a grinning clown wearing a blue baseball cap with the letters CUT emblazoned in white on the front. Above the stage and at various spots around the room were these same white initials with smaller letters spelling out "Clowney Understands Towson."

The doors had opened to patrons at seven, and the arena, which Clowney had booked months in advance, was nearly full. At seven forty-five, a half dozen blue and white striped Ford Pintos arrived outside the arena. The doors of each car were flung open and men in clown makeup, white shirts and blue vests emerged, each carrying a blue bag. The men walked through the crowd and handed out free blue baseball caps which featured wide white clown grins and the red letters CUT. More men in clown regalia wandered the crowd carrying computer tablets and asking people to sign petitions supporting the candidate and giving their names, addresses and emails. Most signed; those that didn't were subject to pressure and ridicule.

At exactly 8 p.m. a trumpet blew a heralding blast, followed by the national anthem. The crowd and the clowns all stood at attention and sang, as hats were doffed, and hands were held to hearts.

As the anthem ended, the arena grew silent; after a minute or so, the murmuring began until a figure appeared at the back of the stage.

Clowney waved as he approached the microphone and podium.

"My friends! Fellow citizens of Towson, it is my honor to stand here before you as your next mayor! We are living through a terrible time! Terrible!" He gripped the sides of the lectern with both hands and leaned forward.

"My friends." He shook his head. "There is so much hatred! So much hatred. I don't know where it's coming from, but I can tell you this: Clowney understands Towson!" The letters CUT flashed on the screen behind him and the crowd echoed his words, chanting them over and over.

"But our current mayor." He shook his head sadly. "Well, Stafford is crazy." The letters SIC flashed on the screen in red. "And," he added. "Stafford is corrupt!" The SIC continued to flash.

A man in the third row began yelling. "But Stafford is for law and order!"

Angry shouts erupted around the man and a scrum of clowns converged and he disappeared beneath a sea of orange hair, white makeup and blue costumes.

Clowney continued. "We're having a real problem around here. And it's showing up in the average citizen's bank accounts. One real problem is at the pumps. The price of gas is through the roof. But I'll let you in on a little secret." The crowd hushed with anticipation. "I'll tell you what the problem is, and it isn't the gas. It's the Nigerians. That's right." He nodded as the crowd began to stir; several boos could be heard. "When you leave tonight, drive around. Stop in at a gas station and take a look at who's behind the desk. Nigerians. They've taken over our gas stations."

The crowd was stirring now; people were talking among themselves, shouting, exclaiming, yelling, shrieking. Clowney held up a hand for calm. "Now, it's a free country, and Nigerians—assuming they're legal citizens—are as free as anyone else to own gas stations." He paused as people throughout the crowd looked at their neighbors and nodded in agreement. "But aren't we free to have the gas stations we want serving our communities?" His voice started low and rose to a roar. "Aren't we free too? Aren't we free to run our mowers, tractors, cars, motorcycles, trucks, boats, and planes on the gas of our choice? Aren't we?"

He nodded along with the crowd, his painted-on grin garish and wide. "We've got to retake our gas stations one pump at a time from these Nigerians. Most of them are criminals. It's true. I have this on good authority. They're criminals. They're bad, very bad. Some are rapists. They're born that way. So, if you see a Nigerian, let them know—Clowney wants them gone. Towson is for Towsonians. Not for Nigerians! You can't cure these people. They're Nigerians. Can you cure a child molester? No. And you can't cure these Nigerians. Clowney wants them gone and so do you!"

The crowd began to chant, softly at first, and then louder and louder. "Clowney wants them gone! And so do we!"

A black and white photo of Mayor John Lee Stafford appeared on the screen. He was frowning and the picture had been taken in an unflattering light that emphasized his multiple chins.

"Stafford is—come on, look at him! You can see the dishonesty in his face." The crowd began to boo.

"Stupid Stafford is bought and paid for." Clowney waved a finger in the air. "Let me tell you about a problem we have around here. Every afternoon on Park Avenue we have a traffic jam. Everybody knows it. Everybody sees it, because everybody has to sit in it for an hour or so to travel the two miles from the parkway to the center of town. Has Mayor Stafford solved the problem? No. But I'm going to solve it here and now. Everyone's going to carpool. That's right. Everybody into the pool!" He laughed, then his tone grew serious. He swiped his palms together, up and down, as though ridding himself of a problem. "We're going to ban single occupant cars, which will cut the number of cars in half. If you drive to work, you're going to buddy up with your neighbor or we'll assign someone to your car. That will take care of the traffic problem in the afternoon. And once we see it's working, we'll get it going in the morning."

A man's voice called out from somewhere in the crowd. "And Mussolini's trains ran on time in Italy!"

There was a shuffling in the crowd as people around the man began pushing and shoving. Several clowns converged on the man and began to beat him to the ground, where he was kicked by clowns and a few of the people around him.

Several of Judah's men had been alerted and were rushing to the scene, where a scuffling could be heard and the man yelped in pain. "Hey! Come on! What are you—?"

Clowney was smiling and nodding. "Yeah, they did. Didn't they?"

By the time Judah's men arrived, the man was gone.

As the event ended, arguments that had been taking place within the crowd spilled into the parking lot. Several broke out into fights, and at least one fight escalated when clowns pounced on individuals on one side of the argument.

Judah's security people intervened and when the clowns refused to back down, police were called. More clowns appeared and began pushing Judah's men and the police. Someone off to one side fired a shot, which drew the police away and the clowns melted into the crowd. When the police were unable to identify the shooter, they were left with no one to arrest.

Early the following morning, bricks were thrown through the windows of several local gas stations owned by people of Nigerian descent.

• • •

"Junior, find me that woman we had that problem with that time in traffic."

"What woman? What problem?"

"The one who tried to knock me down—Patrice. It's time we took care of Patrice."

"Okay, Mama. I'll go look now."

He knew just where to look. Mama was smart. She wrote things down and she saved everything. Junior went to the old desk in the guest room, opened the drawer and found it filled with scraps of paper, napkins, old business cards, torn envelopes—anything that had been close at hand when they'd had a run-in with someone. On these scraps were written whatever Mama had been able to learn about the person at the time. Sometimes it was a name, sometimes it was a license plate. Occasionally, when she was really mad, she followed people home and learned their addresses.

Mama knew how to find personal information using people-finder websites and databases. Junior's brother Norman worked for the post office and Mama had worked for an insurance company for five years and knew how to perform DPPA searches based on only a license plate in the Motor Vehicles database.

Junior performed the search with Mama looking over his shoulder, and found that Patrice was Patrice Gamble, who lived with her husband, Clayton, in a modest brown raised ranch with their fourteen-year-old daughter, Marsha, about six miles north of Towson.

"Are we going to take care of her now, Mama?"

"Not yet. I want to have the information for when the time comes. I need to get you prepared first. We need to practice."

"What do you mean, practice?"

"You'll see, Junior, when the time is right. When the time is right."

"Okay, Mama. Just let me know."

"I will. We have a list, and we're working on it. Patrice is just the beginning."

• • •

Raisa was rinsing her hair in the shower when Judah stepped in behind her and enfolded her in his arms.

"We need to talk about what happened last night," she said.

"What happened last night?" he murmured. "Scratch that. Whatever happened—it'll wait."

"Weren't you there?"

"I was going over…" He began kissing her shoulder.

"Jude, this was—" She didn't finish because Judah had turned her toward him and was kissing her, and before she knew it, she was kissing him back.

So it was more than a half hour before she had a chance to explain.

"Clowney started a riot at the arena last night."

Judah was slipping on his underwear; Raisa was already dressed and was watching him.

He looked at his phone. "That explains seven calls from Frank James," Judah said. "I thought it had something to do with the new guys we're bringing on, or maybe his brother."

"Frank has a brother?"

"Kofi. Looks just like him, but with hair."

"Are they twins?"

"I think Frank is older. One of our girls hasn't come in since Thursday and her mother reported her missing, so I showed the cops the feed from inside the lounge and Frank's brother was the last to talk to her as she was leaving."

"Was his brother with her that night?"

Judah shook his head as he slipped on a polo shirt. "He says not. So, what happened at the arena?"

"You'd better play the messages. Clowney said some inflammatory things and people got rowdy."

"Didn't our guys handle it?"

"You'd better play the messages. We had a stringer and a photographer there. There's a blurb up now. I need to write the complete story this morning." She gave him a concerned look. "You might not like what I write."

But Judah had pressed his phone to his ear and was listening. He waved Raisa away. He heard Frank James's voice.

"The rally was a shitshow, Jude. Clowney had his own security, and they aided and abetted rowdy factions in the crowd. It was too much for our guys and the rent-a-cops. I'd think twice about having the guy back."

"We have a contract with the guy," was Judah's firm answer. "And we're going to fulfill it, but we'll do it our way."

• • •

"Where are we going, Mama?"

They were driving the pickup around town, noting the homes and vehicles that were on Mama's list.

"How are we going to get them, Mama?" Junior was trying to imagine how they would coax grown women and several men into their home. Unlike the two women they had done thus far, none would have a reason to be there.

"All in good time, Junior."

The conversation was scaring him, so he time traveled back to a puppet show they'd attended when he and Norman were little and before his father had left. They were sitting in the front row, and as the show ended one of the puppets asked if any of the children would like to come up on stage to sing along with them. He'd been too frightened to raise his hand, but Norman had, and the puppet had chosen Norman along with several other children.

He'd never forgotten the happiness on Mama's face that day as she'd watched Norman up there with that puppet, singing away! His father had looked happy too. That had been not long before Mama changed and his father had decided to leave. The memory was—

"We will have to find a way to get them alone," Mama was saying.

"That makes sense," Junior said.

"Each one will be different, so we will have to figure out a different strategy for each one. But don't worry, Junior. We will. We will."

"I believe you, Mama," Junior said. And he did.

• • •

Frank James and his brother, Kofi, were sitting opposite one another in a booth at the Towson Diner. Frank was sipping from a mug of coffee and looking at his phone. In front of him was a half-eaten plate of scrambled eggs, well done bacon and home fries. Kofi was eating an egg white and turkey omelet and drinking black coffee.

Frank asked, "You been seeing anyone?"

Kofi gave a small smile. "Can't say."

"Oh. The boy has a girlfriend. No shit!"

"Didn't say that."

"You did."

Kofi laughed. "You?"

Frank laughed. "Can't say."

"You can't say 'cause you're not."

"So your can't say means you are and mine means I'm not?"

Kofi grinned. "Can't say." He took another bite of his omelet, washed it down with coffee and added. "Listen, if you was seein' someone, you'd be bragging about it the second you saw me—all pulling out pictures and showing me and sayin', 'you ever seen a girl like that?'"

Frank laughed in agreement.

Kofi eyed his brother. "You always been jealous of me with the girls."

Frank put down his phone, sipped from his mug and looked at his brother. "I don't understand what this guy is trying to do, talking about Nigerians being the problem around here."

"Who 'zactly is he?" Kofi asked.

"Asshole running for mayor."

Kofi waved his fork dismissively. "When it comes to elections, blame can be effective."

Frank pressed a palm to the table and thrust his face toward his brother. "But violence? And having his security guys support the violence? I mean, what the fuck?" He gave a knowing nod. "Judah's not going to stand for it."

"What's he going to do?"

Frank gave a shrug. "Dunno, but you don't fuck with him." He picked up his phone and resumed reading.

Kofi went back to his breakfast.

After a few minutes, Frank said, "So Clowney already posted on social media that he never said the shit he said last night." He put the phone down and looked at his brother. "I mean people saw it. People recorded it and now he denies it? That's fuckin' crazy. You know, for him to put out this denial so fast, he must have known what the paper was going to write and what people were going to say."

Kofi looked thoughtful. "Could be."

A roar sounded from outside the diner and the brothers turned toward the window as three motorcycles sped past. All were black Harley Fat Boys, ridden by black clad men with black helmets with a bit of something red above the visor. All wore red capes that rippled behind them. These were the same outfits they had recently encountered at the Iron Horse Tavern—Dante and his Inferno.

Frank slid out of the booth. "I'll be right back." As Frank ran to his car, and chased after the bikes, Kofi calmly went back to his breakfast.

By the time Frank was on the road, the bikes were out of sight, so he decided to chance a speeding ticket and gunned the Escalade, hoping the riders weren't in too much of a hurry. He was rewarded after five minutes as the bikes came into view. He remained several cars behind; he wanted to see where they were based and report the information back to Judah.

The bikes turned onto a side street, and when Frank turned to follow, he saw them pull into a driveway a block away. As he pulled even with the driveway, he saw that it featured an electronic iron gate between brick pillars, along with a security booth. Beyond the booth were two tall apartment buildings. Dante and his men could be anywhere in the complex.

As he drove away, Frank wondered if Judah knew Dante's last name.

. . .

Sam Sharpe was seated at an overhead press workout station at the Body & Soul Works Fitness Center. He was pretending to fiddle with his phone while watching a yoga class through a window that divided the fitness and cardio room with the weight room. What he was actually doing was recording video of one Adam Lavengello. Adam had been in a fender bender nine days earlier and had since been to an orthopedist and rehab center. He claimed to have severe cervical spine injuries that would prevent him from working, and claims had been submitted to a local insurance company. The company had hired Sharpe to check up on Adam due to the efforts of Sharpe's insightful, proactive office manager, Robin Mendoza, who was proving herself worth every bit of what Sharpe was coming to realize was a reasonable hourly rate.

Sharpe's phone buzzed and he was forced to stop videotaping Adam. He saw who it was and took the call.

"Judah?"

"You busy?"

"Well … what's up?"

"Can you stop by my library? There's something I'd like to discuss."

"Half an hour okay?"

"Perfect."

Thirty-five minutes later, Sharpe was in Judah's library, seated at the long table, a can of peach-flavored seltzer in his hand.

Judah had his own can of the same seltzer, already open. "Let me know what you think of it," he said. "I'm kind of addicted to the stuff, myself."

Sharpe popped open the can, took a sip, and shrugged. "It's okay, I guess. What's up?"

Judah took out his phone, touched it twice, and spoke softly into it. Moments later, Frank James came in with a man who looked exactly like him, but with hair. "You know Frank," Judah said, as Frank put out his hand.

Sharpe rose and shook the proffered hand. "Hey."

Frank said, "This is my brother, Kofi."

Kofi smiled and gripped Sharpe's hand. "Pleasure," he said.

"My brother's in town for a bit, and I thought you two should meet," Frank explained.

"Why's that?" Sharpe asked.

"We'll leave you guys alone," Judah said, and he rose and turned toward the door. "Kofi will explain." Frank had already gone to the door and was holding it open. "Oh, by the way," Judah said. "One of my lounge girls hasn't come in since Thursday and didn't call. You keep an eye on police scanners, don't you?"

"My office does."

"Your office?"

"Robin, my office manager," Sharpe explained.

"Well," Judah said. "If you happen to hear anything. Her name's"—he ran a palm over his mouth, trying to remember—"Jennifer Teitlebaum, but she calls herself Spencer. She was in the lounge Thursday night and then she disappeared. Her mother called the cops."

Sharpe said, "Well, I was hired to find another girl who I believe may be an escort."

"Name?"

Sharpe considered whether to answer the question. "Rebecca Hamilton," he said finally.

Judah shook his head. "Well, if you hear anything—" He followed Frank James from the room.

Kofi was standing beside the table, waiting for Sharpe to sit. He did and Kofi followed suit.

"My brother speaks highly of you," Kofi began politely.

Sharpe's palms rested on the table. He lifted one and spread his fingers.

"My understanding is you might be trying to quit using drugs."

The words were like a slap to Sharpe's face. He was too stunned to answer.

Kofi gave an apologetic wince. "Look, there's no polite way to broach the subject, and since it can be a matter of life and death, I decided to chance it. You want to get up and walk out, or tell me to go fuck myself, I'll totally understand."

Sharpe said nothing. He had been considering doing exactly those things, but the mention of them told him that if he did either one he would feel more shame than he already felt now that the subject was already on the table. So he forced out the only words he could manage.

"I'm listening."

"I used heroin for twelve years. Every day." He huffed a bitter laugh. "Actually, every couple of hours."

"And you stopped?" Sharpe asked.

Kofi nodded, still smiling. "Hundreds of times."

"For good?"

The other man raised his eyebrows. "For *today*."

"Why are you telling me this? Why bring me over here?"

"Because quitting alone is pretty much impossible."

"And you think you can help?"

Kofi nodded.

"I'm already in a twelve-step program."

"Good. How's that going?"

"Okay, I guess. I haven't been high in a while."

"Outstanding. Well listen, I'm here to help." Kofi stood and pulled a wallet from the back pocket of his pants. "Maybe you're doing just fine, but if you ever want to discuss or if you need a sponsor, feel free to give me a call." He slid a white card with black writing from the wallet and handed it to Sharpe. On it was one word, "Kofi," and a phone number.

Chapter 6

After returning to his office, Sharpe carried one of the folding chairs to one side and slightly behind where Robin was sitting behind her computer. She was navigating around Facebook; her hair smelled of vanilla shampoo today.

"Check this out," Robin said. "It's Jennifer Teitlebaum's account but it looks like one of her parents is posting to some local pages." They were looking at a "Towson Moms" page on which Jennifer Teitlebaum's account had posted a picture of an attractive young woman with long dark hair and a dimpled smile along with the words "Have you seen my daughter?"

They spent a few minutes perusing the comments below the post.

Robin navigated to a page called "I Love Towson" which featured the same post. Here, too, were comments from people who knew Jennifer, who had grown up and gone to school in Towson. All were sending thoughts and prayers and hopes she would be found soon.

Sharpe asked, "What do you think about looking up a few of these friends?"

Robin turned to look at him. "Not what we're hired to do."

"No, we weren't. But I'm pretty sure we've got a serial killer here, killing prostitutes."

Robin looked at him, surprised. "Based on what? We've been hired to look into a young woman who's of age, who didn't come home a few nights ago. She might be an escort, or she might be off doing more or less anything. Maybe what we really have is a helicopter dad. And the other girl isn't any of our business. And neither one's confirmed dead." She widened her eyes emphatically. "Maybe you're getting your hopes up."

Sharpe disagreed. "I never get my hopes up for murder. I have a sense for these things."

Robin changed the subject. "So, are you going to talk to Kofi James about your drug problem?"

Sharpe stared back at her. "How do you know about that?"

She raised an eyebrow. "I have a sense for these things."

Sharpe didn't answer but got up and started back toward his desk as the door opened and Jason Hamilton came in, waving something small and beige in his hand. Sharpe met him a few feet inside the door.

"I found this in Becca's desk drawer," he said, and handed Sharpe a business card with fine script lettering that read "Be-You-T Salon," below which were the words, "Hair, Nails, Makeup," along with a Towson address and a phone number.

"This is good," Sharpe said.

"Have you learned anything yet?" Hamilton asked.

"Only that another local girl is missing, and I'm concerned."

Hamilton's expression darkened.

"But I don't want to jump to any conclusions," Sharpe said.

"You'll reach out to them?" Hamilton asked, nodding toward the card.

"Right away," Sharpe confirmed.

Hamilton thanked him and, assured of an update, left the office.

Rather than call, Sharpe decided to drive to the salon. The woman at the lectern inside the door asked Sharpe to wait, while she called for the owner. Soon he was talking to an attractive, 60-ish woman with Scandinavian features in a leather skirt and white blouse, named Dorothy.

Sharpe showed her Becca's photo.

"She was here every Thursday," Dorothy confirmed. "Always with a friend. Let me see if I can find you the friend's name." She walked to the back of the shop and came back with a credit card receipt. "Victoria Sandford. That's the friend. I don't have an address or number. Only a zip code, so I can tell you she's local."

Sharpe thanked her and returned to his office.

• • •

Judah, Frank James and Rinny Mallach drove onto the campgrounds on the outskirts of town and pulled up to the long red and yellow semi painted with Clowney's likeness. Immediately, a half dozen men in clown makeup emerged from nearby tents and headed for them. From one of the campers, a burly clown with a white, bristly five o'clock shadow and light brown hair strode within a few feet of the car. With him was another clown of similar size and shape, but with a shaved head. Behind them and moving more slowly, lumbered a much larger, hulking clown. At least a dozen more clowns were arrayed behind them.

The brown-haired clown took a step toward Judah as he emerged from the car. As Frank got out of the passenger door, the bald clown leaned against the door, to hold it shut. The hulking clown tried to do the same with Rinny, who pulled his door shut, then rammed it open again, hitting the clown in the gut. The clown's cheeks puffed as the air was forced from his lungs and he dropped to his knees.

The other clowns formed a circle around the Escalade, and the circle began to close as the clowns shuffled closer.

"What do you want?" the first clown demanded.

"Not much of a greeting," Judah said, as he turned from watching the fat clown fall.

"It's not a greeting. It's a question. Do I need to ask it again?"

"I own the arena."

"Yeah?"

"The one where you had your rally."

"So?"

"So, I want to talk to your boss about what happened there last night. We need to be on the same page so it doesn't happen again."

Frank James had pushed his way out of the car and was standing very close to the bald clown.

The clown who was doing the talking took out his phone and spoke into it. Then he listened and nodded. "Follow me."

He led the way, along with the bald clown and the hulking clown, who by now had caught his breath. The others followed at a distance. All wore similar makeup and were dressed in red jeans, white long-sleeved shirts and blue vests. All wore the blue caps with red letters spelling CUT.

Clowney was sitting in a yellow beach chair below a green awning that extended from one of the campers. He was drinking an opaque brown bottle of beer, which he slid into a cupholder attached to one of the chair's arms. He didn't bother to stand as they approached.

"Beers?" he asked.

Judah shook his head. "Do you always wear that makeup and out-fit?" he asked.

Clowney looked at his men, then at Judah. He shook his head and held out a palm. "What makeup and outfit? Next question."

Judah got right to it. "If you're going to have events in my arena, we can't have riots."

Clowney looked confused. "What riots?"

"Come on, man. Don't give me that shit."

The clown with the brown hair took a step toward Judah.

Rinny stepped in front of him until they were nose to nose. "Try it. Please."

The brown-haired clown didn't move. "You're one ugly mother-fucker. Makeup could help."

Rinny said, "Do something. Go ahead."

Clowney's eyes flicked from his clowns to Rinny and back again. "The O'Learys are the heads of my security team. Actually, Larry O'Leary is the head of the team, with Barry and Gary helping out. Larry was a pro boxer, which comes in handy. Barry is a poet and Gary is, well, Gary is Gary."

The hulking clown grinned and his bald brother turned to face Judah, set his legs a few feet apart and squared his shoulders. He began to recite.

"There once was a lovely old town,

that excelled and gathered renown.

The people who lived,

there a shit couldn't give.

And today they are led by a Clown."

There was a short silence and Clowney laughed, which was the signal for his men to laugh along with him.

"Look," Judah said, when they stopped laughing. "I need to know that there won't be any rioting at these rallies. We have a contract, but if you look at it closely, you'll see that it's negated by violence."

Clowney rose from his chair and stepped close to Judah; his men gathered around them. "And what am I supposed to do if elements in the crowd cause trouble? That's what my security guys are for."

"You know damned well," Judah answered, "that the trouble last night was because of your guys assisting the troublemakers."

"I know no such thing."

"I'll tell you what," Judah said. His voice had gone quiet, and Clowney had to step closer to hear. "My A-team will be at the rest of the rallies. And if your guys cause trouble, they're going to find more trouble than they can handle."

Clowney held up both hands and shook his head. "I wouldn't have it any other way."

• • •

Junior was sitting at the kitchen table eating Mama's version of a loose meat sandwich on a burger bun, which was hamburger meat and baked potato mashed up with ketchup and a little bit of spinach—a grisly-looking red and white goulash with a bit of green running through. But Junior and Norman had loved them since they were small.

"Well, now we can plan," Mama was saying.

"Plan," Junior repeated softly, glancing across the table at his brother, who was subtly shaking his head. *Don't argue with her.*

"Now that we know where your former friend Benny's mother lives." Mama's voice rose to a shout. "The bunch of them deserve to be beaten to a pulp!" The jowls of loose skin that hung from both sides of her jaw quivered as her head shook with rage.

"They weren't so bad, Mama," Junior protested. "He was just not the right friend for me at the time."

Mama smiled so hard that her eyes disappeared and her cheeks went red from the effort. It was not a good smile. It was the smile she saved for when he said something so stupid that all she could do was smile for all she was worth and tell him some new truth he needed to learn. "Not the right friend? You had a play date to go bowling! Remember that? And what did Benny tell you about his mother?"

Junior tried to remember. "He told me his mother wanted him to stay home because he had strep throat."

She nodded and the smile persisted. "That's right. So we went bowling with Kenneth, didn't we? And who did we see there?"

Junior knew the answer to that. "We saw Benny and Alfred and Todd, who had been dropped off there by one of their mothers."

The smile was gone now. "The liars," Mama snarled. "The goddamn liars. I lost track of them, but that was his mother we saw today in that car. Now that we know where they live, we can bide our time and scout the property, and plan…"

"Maybe we should just forget it, Mama." Junior looked at Norman, but his brother was staring into space, saying nothing.

"Forget it? That's what they want! They'd like us to do that, wouldn't they?" She patted the side pockets of her jeans. "We have our list and now they're on it. What we're gonna do is keep track of their comings and goings, like with the others. Then, when the time's right, we'll fucking DESTROY them! And you and your brother will cut 'em up and stash them around town."

A corner of Junior's mouth twisted from anxiety. "I'm going to go hang out with Tim, okay?" he asked.

"You do that," Mama said. "I've got some thinking and planning to do."

Once Junior found Tim he felt a bit better. Tim was probably the coolest person Junior knew, and just being around him calmed Junior down. Tim was glad to do whatever Junior suggested. Together, they went out to bars, bought beer and whiskey and went drinking with the others. Tim had convinced them all that Junior was okay. So now he had a place to go and people to be with when Mama was at her worst.

• • •

Cortez watched as Gold ended the call and pocketed his phone. She waited.

"Forensics," Gold said. "The items found in that dumpster were doused in bleach, which destroyed any DNA."

"Shit." Cortez sighed, then shifted back to their earlier conversation. "So, in hindsight," she said, "you've got to admit it would have made sense to have officers on duty at the event—at least nearby."

Gold finished his bagel and wiped his mouth with a napkin. "It's a private facility with its own security. Not only that, but the people renting it out had their own security team. So, no, I don't think it was a bad call not to have officers at the rally."

Cortez sipped her coffee and watched the traffic pass by the window of the bagel shop. "I heard they're having rallies every week or two. So, what about the next one?"

"Not my call."

Cortez grinned. "Copout."

Gold took a pull from his coffee, his second since they'd been at the bagel shop. He waggled the half empty cup in her direction. "Insubordination."

"What about this possible serial killer?"

Gold rolled his eyes, though he knew his partner was baiting him. "I'm more concerned with heroin dealers showing up out of nowhere than I am about a couple of missing hookers."

Cortez replied quietly. "Come on. Two missing girls."

"Maybe," Gold agreed. "But the heroin dealers are real, and they just might kill who knows how many good kids if we don't do something about them." He paused. "And none of this is your call."

Cortez waved what was left of her toasted sesame bagel with butter at her senior partner. "I agree about the drug dealers, Abe, but we can't just ignore two missing women…"

"Not women—escorts—and who says they're missing? And stop calling me Abe, for God's sake."

"Their parents."

"And if they are, so what? They're probably off with paying customers having a bang-up week. Everybody happy all around. We went through the lists, checked the families and last knowns. We did our job. What else should we do? More importantly, how do you propose to address these smack shops?"

Cortez thought about this while finishing her bagel. "Well, we know there's a late model black Dodge Charger possibly involved, and one or more black Harley Fat Boys ridden by guys with red capes. We put BOLOs out on those. We know they use bars after hours. So, we cruise those at closing time and look for the bikes and that car."

Gold looked at her steadily until she shrugged and looked away. "Least you're making some sense."

After receiving coffee refills, they were headed toward the police station when the squad car's radio crackled to life.

"We have a 10-45D at the fishing pier."

Gold and Cortez looked at one another. Before either could speak, a familiar voice came over the radio. "Better get over there, Abe."

They arrived to find four squad cars and an ambulance converged around the entrance to the pier. Once they made their way between the cars, they found a bulky middle-aged man with brown hair streaked with gray and wearing jeans, a flannel shirt, a denim jacket and black sneakers sitting in the back seat of a squad car with his feet on the ground and the door open. On the ground in front of him was a fresh puddle of vomit. An EMT was standing near him with a half full bottle of water.

The police were on the pier and when the detectives approached they found them huddled around a nest of fishing line that lay near a discarded fishing pole, a bucket of water, an open tackle box, and a net capable of landing a striped bass, which was what the man had been fishing for. In the net was a grayish human head, one eye and part of its cheek eaten away by crabs. The long hair and what was left of the facial features clearly indicated that the head belonged to Jennifer Teitlebaum.

Chapter 7

After speaking with the Towson Police Community Information Officer (CIO) Karen Latrelle, a polite round woman with a light brown complexion, Raisa was up much of the night putting together two stories for the *Gazette*, one a straight forward news item about the circumstances surrounding the grisly discovery of the head of Jennifer Teitlebaum, and the other a feature about Jennifer and the prevalence of prostitution in and around Towson.

Raisa wrote that Jennifer had last been seen on video leaving the lounge at the Towson Hotel. Just prior to leaving, she had been speaking with someone the police would only refer to as a "person of interest," someone they had spoken to earlier but wanted to bring in for further questioning.

Uniformed officers had shown Harriet Teitlebaum a photo of the intact side of her daughter's face, one that did not show that her head had been severed from her body, though Harriet had been made aware of the fact. Part of Jennifer's skull had been caved in, but whether the wound had been her cause of death had not yet been determined, a police spokesperson said, and may never be determined unless and until the rest of her was recovered.

Authorities said that the waters around the pier would be dredged in the hopes of finding Jennifer's body, though the movement of the tides and the volatile weather may impede that part of the investigation. Raisa knew that another suspected prostitute had been reported missing by her father, but the police would not discuss that case, saying only that their policy was not to comment on open investigations.

She asked Judah about Jennifer and any other prostitutes who worked for him, but he refused to comment. He would only say that he had been told that the young woman was someone who occasionally frequented the hotel lounge. He had never met her and had no personal knowledge of her. His focus, he said, was on quelling the notion that she had been the victim of a serial killer. He had a business to run and serial murder was never good for business.

• • •

"I see Clowney's wasted no time blaming Stafford for this girl's death," Cortez observed, as they drove.

Gold sucked air in between his teeth and lower lip, making a whistling sound. "What is it Yeats said? 'The best lack all conviction, while the worst are full of passionate intensity.'"

"Oh, so that's who said that," Cortez replied, rolling her eyes.

"He was talking about political asshats like Clowney, who are all about blame."

"Is that what Yeats called them—asshats?" Cortez asked.

Gold turned to stare at her.

"Watch the road, Abe."

"I *am* watching the road, and I told you not to call me Abe."

"Well, calling you detective wouldn't make sense, since we're both detectives."

"Call me Gold, Cortez." He gave her a hard look. "You know you're getting to be a real pain in the ass."

"Okay, Gold Cortez," Cortez said, and smiled to herself, pleased that she was getting under his skin.

They arrived at the brick ivy-covered home to find its driveway and all the parking spaces for several houses in either direction filled with cars. They double parked in front of the house and Gold left his blinkers on as they walked up the steps toward the front door. A small table had been set up outside on which were a pitcher of water and a roll of paper towels, next to which a garbage bag was held down by a brick.

"They're sitting shiva," Gold said, as he poured water over his hands, tore off a few sections of towel and dried himself. He indicated that Cortez should do the same.

"Shouldn't we knock?" she asked, as Gold opened the outer door. He ignored her and went inside; she followed.

The living room smelled of roast chicken and was filled with people, most of them in their forties or fifties, with a few teenagers and young adults sitting quietly to one side.

Harriet Teitlebaum wore a black house dress and was sitting next to a man with similarly colored reddish hair and brown eyes that looked like hers. He was wearing a dark gray trench coat and black fedora and was clutching her palm with both hands. On her other side was an older woman in a long navy-blue dress and black *sheitel* wig holding her other hand.

The woman was talking quickly, without pausing at the ends of her sentences. "Rivka doesn't want to wait. She and Yakov agreed to get married in April, during Pesach, so Yakov doesn't have to miss any more work than he has to. It's his busy season so all five of his brothers will be in town. His sister, Hilde, just had her third child, another boy, and by then she'll back here with her sister-in-law's family and her parents, so we'll all be together for the wedding."

"Excuse me, Mrs. Teitlebaum," Gold interrupted. "Could we have a word, please, in private?"

Harriet looked up and her expression cleared with recognition. "It's the police," she explained, and started to disengage from the people on either side of her.

The woman in the blue dress gave Gold an angry look. "Can't you give her a little peace to mourn her child?"

"It's okay, Charlotte," Harriet said, and patted the woman's hand. "Just give us a minute."

Gold and Cortez stepped to one side and followed Harriet down a short hallway and into an office, where she closed the door behind the detectives, turned and faced them.

"We're sorry to bother you at this difficult time," Detective Gold began. "We'd like to get contact information for the rest of your immediate family and any extended family Jennifer might have been in contact with, as well as her friends."

Harriet looked back at Gold, expressionless. "Maybe you could have tried a little harder to find her when I first came to you."

Gold pressed his lips together but said nothing, as Harriet began going through her phone and reading off numbers, which Cortez logged into a list in her phone.

No one spoke until the detectives were back in the car and on their way to the station.

"Well, that was pretty brutal," Cortez said.

Gold said nothing.

"What now?" the junior detective asked.

"Now we bring in Kofi James and the other escorts from the Towson Hotel."

• • •

Having responded to an ad in the newspaper, the nascent breakfast group sat at a round table in the back room of the Towson Diner. The counter and the booths at the front of the diner were bustling, but the back room was empty, save for the breakfast group. Coffee was delivered and breakfast ordered, and then the gray-haired, bearded man in his early seventies stood. He removed his glasses, held them at an angle in front of his mouth and breathed hotly on them, then wiped them on the hem of his shirt and put them back on. The conversation around the table died down as everyone present turned toward him.

"As many of you probably know, I'm Mason Marx. Have we decided on what we're going to call our little breakfast club?"

"Why not the Towson Breakfast Club?" asked Jerry Levito, who was tall and lean and clean shaven.

Mason asked, "How about we each introduce ourselves with our name and what we do?"

Levito held up a hand. "I'm Jerry Levito, Bright Smiles Dentistry." He raised his eyebrows. "What do you do for a living, Mason?"

Marx looked embarrassed. "I apologize. I assumed everyone knew. I'm the news editor at the *Towson Gazette*." He looked at Levito, who had mumbled something. "Sorry?"

"Oh," Levito said. "I was … talking to myself."

A well-dressed man with dark dyed hair and a fake tan put up his hand. "Taylor Richmond. I'm in real estate. Do we really need a name? We're just a bunch of local guys having breakfast."

Lev half rose from his seat. "Lev Hammer, elementary school science teacher. Why not call it that? Local guys having breakfast?"

A dark brown man with a receding hairline and gold rimmed glasses held up his hand. "Rick Corbain, accountant. How about GAB. Guys at breakfast?"

Levito grinned. "That's good!"

A sturdy bald man in a white shirt and blue vest stood. "If we're called something clever, it will last forever." He nodded. "Barry O'Leary, security."

Next to him, a thin man with small dark eyes and dark blond hair tentatively put his hand up. "Walter Gibson, bike messenger." He turned to O'Leary. "Do you always talk in rhyme?"

O'Leary grinned. "Some of the time." His blue eyes traveled over the faces around the table. "Great Old Dudes Of Towson could be our name. We'd call us GODOT, but the meaning's the same."

Marx appraised O'Leary and looked impressed. "That's not bad. I say we vote on it. All those in favor?" Everyone but Taylor Richmond raised a hand. "Opposed?" No hands went up.

Richmond put up his hand. "Abstain."

A waitress arrived and began doling out glasses of water and mugs of coffee and tea.

"What are we going to talk about?" Richmond asked.

No one answered at first. Then Marx said. "Whatever's going on around town."

"What about this girl who got murdered?" Corbain asked. "I didn't even know we had prostitutes around here."

"There's prostitutes everywhere," Levito commented, as he shook two packets of Splenda, tore the ends off and tapped them into his coffee.

Gibson nodded in agreement.

O'Leary grinned. "Do you know because you know?"

Levito shook his head. "Nah, I'm married thirty-two years."

Lev Hammer said, "I saw in the local paper today that Clowney blames the mayor and Chief Green for what happened to this girl. He says that another girl is missing, so this might be a serial killing." He looked at the faces around the table. "I don't know about you guys but saying something like that seems a little irresponsible." His eyes narrowed. "Stirring up trouble."

"Or stirring up votes," Marx agreed.

"But isn't what he's saying true?" Levito argued. "A girl was murdered. Her head was fished out of the bay. Another girl is missing. Both were apparently prostitutes. So isn't it reasonable to say we have a law-and-order problem?"

As the waitress arrived with everyone's orders, Barry O'Leary added, "I don't know about you, but I say what he says is true."

• • •

Raisa returned from work at the *Gazette* office, her mind still echoing with the arguments she'd had with Mason and Joanne. They rarely argued nowadays; they knew one another's points of view so well. But there was something polarizing about Clowney. Raisa thought he was all performance art. Local politics meant nothing to him, but rather were a target into which to lob grenades. Mason, who as news editor was the decision maker, advocated for taking Clowney at face value. He was on the ballot, so he was a candidate, and he should be afforded the same space and attention as other candidates, which in this case meant the mayor. Joanne, well, Joanne was just Joanne. She enjoyed picking apart other people's arguments and being a general pain in the ass, without taking much of a real position on anything.

Their disagreements had bled into their coverage of the lead stories, the murder and prostitution. Raisa wanted to cover the murder as its own story, with the prostitution relegated to small sidebar, at most. Joanne, who, of course, knew all about Judah's involvement with both prostitution and Raisa, wanted to do full exposés on any and all prostitution in the Towson vicinity. As soon as Raisa called her bluff and suggested Joanne do her own research, reportage and writing, she backed off and was not quite so interested anymore.

The result was that Raisa had written stories about both the murder and Jennifer Teitlebaum, begun a follow-up about Jennifer's family, and set up a meeting with the police about the other missing girl, Rebecca Hamilton. Joanne was looking into prostitution from several angles—escorts connected to venues, street walkers, and online app-related hookers, in addition to her regular beat—the Towson area music scene.

Another local story that was gaining traction was the increasing incidents of men in blue vests hanging around street corners and haranguing or accosting passersby. Some wore clown makeup, others did not. Sometimes they had clipboards, pads or iPads and asked people to commit to voting for Clowney, and verbally hassling or scorning them if they refused. Raisa had begun researching this by calling Clowney's campaign phone number—there was only a single phone number, not a campaign office as far as Raisa knew—and was told by whomever answered the phone that these were private citizens, rather than people working for Clowney. *Hmm. Food for thought.*

Raisa poked her head into the dining room to find Judah and his sister. Dinah was cutting carrots and chard on a wooden cutting board and sliding the cut vegetables into an enormous pot that sat on a low flame on the stove.

"Is Rachel upstairs? Ooh, smells good in here. Stew?"

Dinah smiled without looking away from her work.

Judah put his arms around Raisa, drew her close and kissed her. "I think Rachel's in the den with Josh and Zebby." But as he spoke, Rachel appeared in the doorway, saw her mother, and went to her, arms wide.

She clung to Raisa's pants leg. "Ah wah bah bah."

Raisa stepped away from Judah and took her daughter firmly by the shoulders. "You're too big for a bottle, Rach. And please use your words."

"Bah bah!"

"It's a bottle. Say bottle. You're not a baby anymore!"

Dinah flashed a look at Raisa and quietly said, "You know what this is about."

Raisa frowned as Josh appeared in the doorway, saw Rachel, took her by the hand and began leading her back to the den.

"Come on and watch TV with me and Zebby," he said, and the adults watched as Rachel allowed herself to be led away by her cousin.

Raisa looked quizzically at Dinah.

"It's this girl's murder. It's"—she made a rolling motion with her free hand—"bringing back her trauma from the kidnapping."

Judah winced and nodded. "She's right."

"Be patient with her," Dinah suggested.

"Smells good in here," Lev said, from the doorway. "Stew?" He looked at Dinah, who didn't answer.

"Know what I've been doing? Changing Zebby's diaper." He looked around, but no one spoke. "He's a grown man, and you're welcome." After a moment he added, "He needs to be somewhere with round-the-clock care."

Dinah shook her head. "He *is* somewhere with round-the-clock care."

"And yet I just changed his diaper."

"You're proving my point," Dinah said wryly.

Judah looked from his sister to his brother, shook his head and left the room. Raisa followed him into the great room.

"You know, Jude, Mason gave Joanne the prostitution stories."

Judah sat down at the dinner table, which had been set for seven with a space left for Zeb and his wheelchair, which had a snap-on tray attachment. He poured himself a glass of red wine from a carafe, held the glass up and looked at it.

"Did you hear what I said? I said Joanne's—"

"Yeah, I heard. Joanne's writing stories on prostitution. So?"

"So if I was writing them, I could talk about the story of prostitution here in town the way you want."

"The way I want to tell it, babe, is not to tell it. There's no story. It's simple capitalism. There's a market for sex and some women fill it and get paid for the work. The fact that some of the women work for me, if that's what you're getting at, is neither here nor there. That part's not going to be discussed in any public forum."

"It's not going to be flattering if Joanne tells it," Raisa said.

"So if you tell it, it'll be flattering?" Judah sipped from his wine, sat back and crossed his legs. "Tell me your flattering story about local prostitution. Use your journalistic integrity to tell it in a flattering way. Or, we can have a fight and there'll be no sex for three days."

"Jude! The kids will hear."

"No, they won't. They're in the den."

"Yeah, we will!" Josh's voice called from the den.

"Kid's got fuckin' ears." Judah sighed, got up and went to the den's doorway, from where he saw Josh seated on the couch with Rachel's head against his shoulder. They were watching an episode of Sponge-Bob SquarePants. Zeb was in his wheelchair, staring into a computer that was mounted on a tray. He was bent over his new trackball controller.

Judah peered into his screen. "What are you doing?"

"Playink a gambah."

"Really?"

Zeb didn't answer, and Judah went back to the table in the great room and sat down beside Raisa.

Reuben's voice, Reuben sounding very sure of himself, was audible from the kitchen. "You wait. Between the news and the cops asking if anyone's seen the girl at the lounge, we'll see an influx of people with free floating anxiety—"

Judah called in Reuben's direction, "The cops are asking if anyone's seen someone at the lounge? My lounge?"

Reuben appeared in the doorway to the kitchen. "It's the last place she was seen, so, yeah. They think she was probably killed Thursday night or Friday morning. Can they tell that from a head?"

Lev was behind Reuben and tapped him on the shoulder. Reuben stepped into the great room, allowing Lev to pass. "Jude, you put that girl at risk," Lev said.

Judah looked away and sighed. Then he caught sight of Raisa trying to hide a grin. "Ah, here we go." He looked back at Lev. "How'd I do that?"

"By giving her that job."

Judah gave his brother an impatient look. "Come on. She'd have just worked somewhere else."

Lev nodded. "Yeah, and probably be alive."

"Maybe, maybe not. Either way, I didn't kill her."

"You kinda did."

Judah looked squarely at brother. "So, all the girls who didn't get killed, I'm saving their lives by not giving them jobs?"

"Don't be a dick," Lev accused.

"Says the dick," Judah answered.

"You know," Reuben said to Lev. "If you care so much about people, why don't I see you at homeless shelters or food banks?"

Lev grinned. "Ah, so here he is! Chaplain Reuben, the moral center of everything he sees!"

"How 'bout we have a nice dinner together?" Judah said.

Dinah's voice called from the kitchen. "Could someone get the kids, and could everyone bring their bowls here, so I can ladle out the stew?"

• • •

Sharpe was fighting a losing battle. He lived for cases like these but they quickly turned into tugs of war with the beast, and he soon found himself on street corners or in doctors' offices jonesing for any kind of fix, until he didn't know what to do with himself.

He found Kofi's number and called, but it went to voicemail.

He dialed another number.

"Hello?"

"Is this Victoria Sandford?"

"What is this in reference to?"

"My name is Sam Sharpe. I'm a private investigator."

"Um, yes?"

"I'm trying to find Rebecca Hamilton. I understand you two went to the beauty parlor together?"

Silence.

"Ms. Sandford?"

"Well, um. We weren't really friends."

"Okay. Can you point me in the direction of anyone who—" Click.

He forced himself to go to a Narcotics Anonymous meeting, but the speaker was talking about God, a word that was not in Sharpe's vocabulary. How could he believe in God? *Look around. Look at the world, at what people do to one another. Where's God in all that?*

The speaker talked about trying to find God and explained that he had found God inside his own heart. Sharpe wanted to shout at him, to ask what good that did him. *Well, maybe he didn't get high,* a voice in Sharpe's mind told him.

Fuck that.

He couldn't sit still, so he left the meeting and drove around until he found himself at the pier where Jennifer Teitlebaum's head had been found. He got out of his car and walked out onto the pier, the salt air chilling his nostrils. Only two people were fishing. He approached the first, a bulky young man in a green jacket who was working a weighted rig with live bait.

"Stripers?" Sharpe asked.

The man nodded.

"What are you using for bait?"

"Menhaden," the man said, and continued reeling in his line.

Sharpe didn't know what the word meant, so he waited until the man cast out again before speaking. "Did you happen to see anything in connection with that girl who was found?"

The guy looked at Sharp and kept reeling. "You mean the head?"

Sharpe waited.

"I didn't see anything, no."

Sharpe moved on to the next person, a thin Black woman with wild white hair wearing a blue sweater, jeans and black high-top sneakers. Her rod was leaning against the rail, and she was watching its tip gently bob with the motion of the water. "How's the fishing?"

"The fishing's fine. The catching's not so good." She gave Sharpe a smile.

"Did you happen to see anything connected to the girl whose head was found here?"

The woman's smile disappeared. "You a cop?"

Sharpe took out a card and held it out. She squinted at it but didn't take it. "I heard something about a red pickup someone saw from one of those houses." She nodded toward the row of houses facing the bay that began fifty yards to one side.

"A red pickup—any idea of the make?"

The woman shrugged and shook her head. "Just something I heard."

"Any idea which house?"

The woman looked toward the houses. "Gotta be one of the first few, right?"

It was the first house. A matronly woman named Cora McTeague answered the door and when Sharpe handed her a card, she stepped outside. Behind her an old black lab was barking and wagging its tail.

"I was walking Joey early Friday morning, really early. He's old and kind of incontinent, so if I don't take him out every few hours, I end up having to clean." She gave a rueful smile. "Well, as we were coming down the steps, I saw a guy getting into an old red pickup and drive away."

"Maybe he was fishing," Sharpe suggested.

"Maybe, but I didn't see any fishing gear. And he was at the rail of the parking lot, not on the pier. People do fish from the rail. Not most people, but some do."

"Could you tell the make of the truck? Did you see a plate?"

Cora shook her head. "I'm not good with types of cars or trucks and I was too far to see the plate. I didn't think much of it until the news broke about that poor girl."

"What about the guy? What did he look like?"

"I couldn't see his features."

"Was he tall, short, fat, thin…?"

She paused, thinking. Her dog had started barking again.

"He wasn't fat. I couldn't say for sure, but I don't think he was very tall. I'm only going by his height compared to the truck, and I'm not sure what kind of truck it was, but it wasn't a really big one. It wasn't a Ram or one of the big Fords. Maybe a smaller one. Maybe Japanese."

• • •

Junior knew that Mama had pushed him to do terrible things, and hanging out with Tim, Tyra and the gang didn't assuage the guilt he bathed in. When he drank, Mama blamed him even more, claiming their problems were all his doing.

So he time traveled. In his mind he visited the days when Mama was kind, even gentle. They played patty-cake and she sang to him and his father was still with them. They went to restaurants, all four of them—Mama, Papa, Norman and him. They played board games and watched TV. They went to the zoo.

Mama had liked to cook in those days; she cooked most nights, while Papa, Norman and he played ball on the lawn until Mama called them all in for dinner. Afterward, he and Norman watched TV, often with dishes of butter pecan ice cream and chocolate sauce. During summer, he and Norman went outside after dinner and ran races or played ball with the neighborhood kids until eight o'clock or so, when Mama would call them in to get ready for bed. After brushing their teeth and washing their faces, she would read to him and Norman, then say goodnight and he and Norman would talk for a while until they fell asleep.

He remembered some of his school friends, boys who lived walking distance away and whose houses they would play at.

He remembered sitting at the wide front window with the big oak tree outside, the sun streaming in. Outside it smelled like freshly cut grass and roses. Inside it smelled like broiled chicken and baked brownies.

He could hear Mama moving about. Saying something. Saying his name. Calling to him.

Papa left a few days before his eleventh birthday. That's when Mama began to turn mean.

The bad thoughts were coming now and he could hear Mama calling his name, so he yelled back, "I need to go to the store, Mama. I'll be back in a little while." He started for the door. "Maybe I'll find a girl," he added over his shoulder, as he hurried outside, got into his truck, and drove back toward the old house and the streets where he'd had the happiest days of his childhood.

After a while he decided to drive by one of the bars and see about a girl. He knew this could be dangerous, but he also knew that if he brought one home he might make Mama happy, and wouldn't that be something?

Chapter 8

"So, none of you has seen Scurge at all since Tuesday?" Judah said. Do I have that right?"

"I saw him Tuesday afternoon," Lou said.

"So did I," Frank added. "He was at the Nickleby and said he'd be at the lounge."

"He's been avoiding the lounge," Lou said.

Rinny grunted in agreement.

Judah sighed inwardly. Scurge had been obsessed with Jennifer and he'd had the impression that she liked him too in the strange way that escorts formed relationships, when they did at all. He'd become more and more depressed since she disappeared, and had fallen off the face of the earth when her head had been discovered.

"Stop the car," Judah said suddenly.

Frank pulled to the side of the road and Judah leaped out, leaving the door open. Three men in white shirts and blue vests were standing on the street corner. Two wore clown makeup. One had brownish hair. The other was bald. The clown with the hair was jabbing a finger into a chubby man's chest. The chubby man had both hands up as if saying "what did I do?"

"I heard about you," Judah said to the clown with the hair. "Hassling people on street corners now?"

The clown turned toward Judah. "We're canvassing and we have a permit. What do you care?"

He pushed Judah, who stepped to one side and hit him with two quick rights to the face. The clown went down but got back up again, in a boxing stance. He began circling Judah, jabbing. Judah dove at his legs, lifted him from the knees, flipped him onto his back, and began raining punches and elbows to his face. The bald clown jumped onto Judah's back and snaked a forearm around his neck.

Rinny jumped out of the car and Lou followed, pulling a handgun from a holster. Rinny turned and patted Lou's hand and shook his head. Then Rinny pulled the bald clown off of Judah by the back of his shirt, toppling him backward. He straddled the clown's chest, held his head down with his left hand and slammed his face over and over with his right elbow.

The clown with the hair had managed to struggle to a hip and wrap his opposite arm around Judah's chest and back, keeping his body close to Judah's to keep from being punched, while pivoting on his hip to spin to his feet.

Lou saw that people had begun filming with their phones. "Jude, we need to go!" he yelled.

Judah got to his feet and, as the clown with the hair charged toward him, kicked him in the groin. He grabbed Rinny, who was still on top of the bald clown, pulled him off and toward the car. Rinny jumped into the back and Lou pulled the door closed.

Judah stood beside the passenger side door and pointed a finger at the clowns, who were on their feet and glowering.

"Tell your boss," Judah said. "This shit's got to stop!"

Fifteen minutes later, they had circled a residential block and stopped in front of an old, apparently abandoned bar.

"You're sure?" Judah asked.

Frank looked back at him, anything but sure. "I'm sure of what I was told. How true it is, who the fuck knows?"

"Park close enough so we have a clear path to the car. Stay here and keep the motor running."

Judah, Rinny and Lou got out of the car and went to the front door and knocked. Waited. Knocked again. There was no answer and no sound from inside the bar.

"Let's try the back," Judah said, finally.

They knocked at the back door, which opened a crack. "Yeah?" someone said.

With a two-step running start, Rinny threw himself at the door, which slammed open. Judah, who had pulled a Glock from the small of his back, followed, with Lou behind him, also armed. They swung their guns in wide arcs and squinted into a dark room with a faint orange light glowing from behind the bar.

"Been waiting for ya," a voice said.

The two men inside the door had their hands up, but the three inside the room did not. Two had guns drawn and aimed at Judah and his men. A smaller man with a tight Afro had a gun drawn and aimed at the head of the man whose neck he had in the crook of his elbow.

The man with the gun was Dante; his gun was aimed at Scurge.

"I think you lost this," Dante said.

"We need to talk," Judah said.

"Yes, we do," Dante agreed. "This motherfucker been coming around and startin' shit—jus' askin' for trouble. I mean really asking. As in sayin' to a room full of armed motherfuckers, 'let's go, come on.'"

Judah bit the inside of his lip, looked at the floor and nodded slowly. "What the fuck, Scurge?"

Dante looked at Scurge. "Yeah, what the fuck?"

"You on a suicide mission?" Lou asked his friend.

Scurge didn't answer.

Judah said to Dante, "That girl, whose head they found." He nodded toward Scurge.

Dante sounded more sympathetic. "Sorry to hear." He looked at Lou, Frank, and Rinny. "Maybe put your shit away and sit down. 'Sides, you hit one of my spots."

Judah made a low humming sound. "You had a spot in my territory…but that can be addressed."

"Maybe make us feel welcome and we'll put our shit away," Frank said.

Dante laughed and waggled a finger at Judah and nodded toward Frank. "I heard you had a Black man with you." He waved a hand at his men and they all put their guns away. He let go of Scurge, who stood and rubbed his neck. Everyone sat down at several wooden tables.

"So, here's the thing," Dante said, once everyone was seated and drinks had been handed around. "We got these fuckin' clowns showing up at our pops. This some fucked up shit."

"Okay," was all Judah said.

"So we chase 'em out but outside there's a little car with a fuck load of them, with automatic rifles and a god damn rocket launcher."

Judah said nothing.

"And they everywhere. I don't think they just trying to cause trouble for me. These clowns are all over the fuckin' place, causing shit for everyone."

"They are," Judah agreed.

No one spoke for a long moment.

"Seems to me it's best we work together to get rid of these damn clowns—seein' as how there's so damn many of them." He laughed. "They're like fuckin' cockroaches."

His men laughed with him.

Judah chewed the inside of his lip and nodded.

"I don't got the guys to do it myself," Dante said.

Judah said, "Well, they haven't caused me much grief, so I'm not sure why I would get involved. But we have been seeing them around. Ran into a few on the way here," he admitted.

"Yeah, but look. I know you got product, and if you stop and think about it, we got different product." He waved a hand. "For the most part, anyways. We not really in competition."

"You think?"

"Yes, I do. You got heroin"—he pronounced it hair-ON—"and I got crack and the new blue. You got crank, and I got oxy. And you got muscle. You got more guys. But I bet it's still not enough, all these fuckin' clowns. But together—"

Judah agreed. "I do have more guys. But the heroin and oxy over-lap."

Dante ignored Judah's last comment. "You got enough to defend against like a million fuckin' clowns?" Dante asked.

Judah thought about this. "Maybe not on the street, in the open. But in an enclosed space, I have the strategy and tactics and guys to do that, yeah. I believe I do. Especially with a few of your guys mixed in, if that's what you're thinking."

"It is. So whatchoo you say we team up on these fuckin' clowns?"

Judah said, "Well, they need to be dealt with, so I agree it's a good idea, especially as part of a bigger strategy that decides which of us does what in which territories."

"I hear that," Dante agreed.

As they were driving back to the hotel-casino, Frank had an idea.

"Do you know what WhatsApp is?" he asked.

"I've heard of it," Judah said. "But not really. What is it?"

"It's an app people use to talk to each other. Like a text chain, but everything's encrypted, so no one can get access to the conversations from the outside."

"Okay…"

"So we give the lounge girls WhatsApp, and they have their own little group, and we tell them to keep their eyes open and to talk about whoever's hiring them and whatever's going on. It's not perfect, but they can keep eyes on each other that way. And of course, we have the app too, so we always know what's going on."

"Great idea," Rinny said, emphatically. "Here's how we make it even better. One of us keeps an eye on the app, and when one of the girls has a client, I, personally, put direct eyes on him and do whatever needs to be done to keep the girl safe."

"Hmm," was all Frank said. "Could scare the clients off."

Rinny said, "Keeping our girls safe's got to be the priority."

• • •

Sheri and Ruby shared a suite near the elevator on the second floor of the Towson Hotel, where Judah kept a handful of rooms available for escorts to use with clients. None of the girls lived there permanently, but rooms and suites were available as needed for hourly or overnight stays.

Rinny Mallach emerged from the elevator and knocked lightly on the girls' door. He carried a small bouquet of roses.

"Who is it?" came Sheri's voice from inside the suite.

"Rinny Mallach. Is Ruby here?"

Sheri held open the door. "She's in the shower."

"Should I come back?"

"Let me ask."

She knocked lightly and opened the bathroom door enough to be heard inside. Rinny waited awkwardly by the door to the suite. He could hear the shower and Ruby's startled "Oh!" from inside. Then the shower shut off and Sheri returned.

"She's coming." She walked into the living room and patted a couch cushion. "Why don't you sit down? You're making me nervous standing there."

"Oh, right. Sorry." He followed her to the couch and dutifully sat.

"So … how's it going?" Sheri asked.

"Oh, fine. Fine." Rinny nodded nervously, and his face contorted into an approximation of a smile. Sheri looked away.

Ruby appeared in a bathrobe, her hair wrapped in a towel.

Rinny stood and held out the flowers.

"For me?" She touched a hand to her chest.

Rinny nodded.

"Let me put those in water," Ruby said, and she took the flowers and headed for the kitchen.

Sheri stood. "I'm just gonna…" She pointed to one of the bedrooms and headed in that direction.

"We don't have a vase," Ruby called from the kitchen. "So we'll have to make do." A moment later she returned with the flowers in a quart milk carton, its top torn open. "I put some water in here." She set the flowers on the long, low coffee table in front of the couch.

"Pretty," Rinny said, his eyes on Ruby.

"They are," Ruby said, smiling at Rinny, who looked back at her, concern in his eyes.

"So … how you doin'?" he asked.

Ruby swallowed; her face fell. "You really want to know?"

He looked back at her, sincerity in his eyes, and nodded.

"I'm freakin' terrified. Someone's killing sex workers? I mean, what did we ever do to hurt anyone?"

"Come here." Rinny patted the couch next to him and was surprised when Ruby came and sat next to him. He took her hand gently between his scarred fingers. "You didn't do nothing. There's crazy assholes out there is all."

"I know!" She was starting to cry.

Rinny covered her small brown hand with his other hand.

"Judah wants you girls to start using What's Up."

Ruby squinted, thinking. "What's that?"

"No," he said earnestly. "What's Up?"

Ruby laughed. "I think you mean WhatsApp."

Her laughter broke through Rinny's anxiety, and he laughed with her. "I guess…"

"No, WhatsApp!"

After a pause, Rinny saw the joke and they both laughed again.

"All of you girls will talk about whoever you're seeing and Judah and Frank and me and Lou and the rest of the guys will see to it you're safe."

Ruby put her arms around Rinny and hugged him, her head against his chest. "Thank you, Rin."

Rinny sighed; it was the happiest moment he could remember.

After a little while, Ruby pulled her head away and looked up at his face. "Does anyone know who could be doing this?"

Rinny slowly shook his head. "Not that I know of."

She was thinking hard, her eyes narrowing. "Frank's brother was with Jen just before…"

"I heard."

"It sure did look like that guy was her next client."

"Did it?"

Ruby pulled away from him and looked him solemnly in the eyes. "It really did. He went out the parking lot door, and she went out right after. And then…"

Rinny didn't answer. He was letting her words sink in.

Eventually, Ruby asked, "How's Scurge?"

Rinny said nothing. His mind was on Kofi James.

Ruby tapped his thigh.

"Huh?"

"I asked how Scurge is doing."

"Not well," Rinny said, shaking his head. "Not well at all."

• • •

Rinny found Frank James in the back room at the Nickleby Tavern.

"Where's your brother at?"

Frank didn't look up from his beer. "Bathroom."

Rinny sat down next to him as the bartender brought him a beer.

The bathroom door opened and Kofi emerged.

Rinny got up from his seat and charged him, grabbing him by the front of his shirt and propelling him back against a wall. A framed picture of the boxer Jack Dempsey fell to the floor, its glass shattering.

"Whoa, whoa, whoa!" Kofi yelled.

"You fuckin' killed Jennifer! Come on, motherfucker. Admit it!"

"Get off him, Rinny!" Frank was trying to pull Rinny away, but Rinny spun and hit Frank with two straight rights and a hard left hook, and Frank sank to the floor.

Lubbock and Malik, who had been at the bar in the front room, appeared in the entrance to the back, saw what was happening and each of the big men grabbed one of Rinny's arms. Rinny struggled to free himself and managed to pull away from Malik and lowered his head to tackle Lubbock, but Lubbock wrapped Rinny's head and neck in a guillotine, leaned back and held on. Malik wrapped Rinny in his arms.

Frank had managed to get to his feet, a hand over the side of his face. "Stop it, Rin," he yelled. "Would'ya fuckin' stop?"

Rinny stopped struggling and Frank went to his brother, who was slowly getting to his feet and watching Rinny fearfully.

Lubbock and Malik released Rinny, who stood up and pointed at Kofi.

"He fuckin' killed Jen. He made the date and they left together. He was seen!"

"No, he didn't, Rinny. He fuckin' didn't."

Kofi walked up to Rinny, a couple feet away, and faced him. "I didn't make a date with her, and I damn well didn't kill her. I'm sorry she's gone, but I swear, it wasn't me."

He paused, while Rinny glared back at him.

"It's true I talked to her." He looked at his brother. "Because I was looking for Frank." He turned back to Rinny. "I asked her where Frank was. There was another guy. Rat-faced guy with light-colored hair. He caught her eye and, I don't know how it works. Maybe he made a date. He was by the bathroom when she left, and something went on between them."

Now Rinny looked interested. "Rat-faced guy with light-colored hair?"

• • •

Judah, Frank, Kofi, Rinny and Lou were standing outside the cage in the arena. Inside the cage, Malik and Lubbock were waiting with two new recruits.

Judah was holding his phone so that the others could see.

"You just open the app, invite whoever you want into the group, and now you're talking to each other. Frank and I and maybe Rinny will be in a group with the lounge girls, and every time they make a date, it gets posted to the group and we put eyes on the guy."

"How 'bout we get pictures, too?" Rinny suggested.

"Clients won't go for it."

"Fuck 'em if they don't," Rinny replied. "Besides, they won't know."

"Yeah? How do we pull that off? Look, we want the girls safe, but we don't want to scare away business," Judah pointed out. He put his phone away. "Let's get started. New guys will train with Malik or Lubbock. I'll decide which." He turned to the first man. "Let's start with your names."

"Myron Beckett," said the slim chestnut-colored man in black pants and a white T-shirt over which he wore a black button-down silk shirt. Around his neck was a long, gold chain with a thin, flat, gold letter "M" that was two inches in diameter.

"You okay training in what you're wearing?" Judah asked him.

Myron shrugged. "It's what I'd be wearing anyway, right?"

"What about the chain? Like a loose shirt, that could be a problem for you in a fight."

139

Myron smiled and instantaneously slipped behind Lubbock, whipped the chain off and held the M to the big man's neck.

Judah laughed. "Let me see that." He held out his hand.

The man stepped to the cage door, held out the necklace, and Judah ran a finger over the base of the letter.

"Sharp."

"Slices and sticks real good," Myron explained.

"Come here, Lou," Judah said, and Lou came over and took a look.

"Very cool," Lou said. "Long as no one gets hold of the chain first and chokes you with it. You best be fast."

"I am fast."

"Maybe we have him and Scurge go at it with blades," Lou suggested.

"Interesting idea," Judah said, then looked at Myron. "Since you're so fast, let's switch it up. You're with Malik. Lub, come on out."

Lubbock stepped out of the cage and Malik entered.

"Okay. We've got another rally in a few days, and we are the security. You might have heard that our guys didn't handle the last rally so well. So, we're beefing up, and you guys are the beef. Now, you get to use your hands. Might be you'll be armed, and we'll see about that if you make it through this. You can have a blade but not cut or stab. Just get it in place and we stop right there. Okay? Before any cutting."

"But we can punch for real? Kick for real?" Myron asked.

"Yes, you can. Go ahead and knock Malik out, if you can. But nothing to the eyes, throat or nuts. And try not to break anything. I need my guys for the rally."

"Just say the word," Myron said, with a little smile.

Judah nodded and pointed a finger. "Go."

Myron whipped an uppercut to Malik's gut and Malik grunted and bent forward but didn't fall. Instead, he straightened and used his upward momentum to whip his own uppercut to Myron's jaw. Myron went down on his face.

"Best to stay there," Malik advised.

"Best to shut the fuck up," Myron said, and pushed himself to a standing position. He circled Malik warily, jabbing a few times, but his opponent didn't bite on these or any of his hip fakes.

Then Myron launched a roundhouse kick at Malik's left ear, which Malik moved to block with his right hand. But Myron rerouted his foot and kicked Malik in the gut, folding him forward again. Then he stepped quickly forward and kneed Malik in the face and the latter fell backward, groaning, blood spilling from his nose.

Myron moved to follow up, but Malik went with the momentum of his backward fall and did a backward flip to his feet, then he jumped forward and appeared to throw a left front kick, which Myron moved away from, backward and to his left. Except that the kick was not a left front kick, it was the first half of a scissor kick, where the first kick is not a kick at all but a sham kick that is used for leverage to energize the other leg, which is the real kicking leg. The right kick landed on

Myron's left cheek, but he did not go down. Instead, his body shuddered, and he stepped forward, planted his right foot at an angle and spun in what otherwise would have been a spinning backfist. But mid-spin, Myron whipped the chain from his neck, grabbed the gold "M" as he spun and arrived in front of his opponent, one hand holding the letter-shaped blade to Malik's neck, the other holding his head in place.

"Game over, brother," Myron said.

Judah grinned, applauded and walked to the entrance of the cage, opened its door and extended a hand to Myron. "That, was impressive."

Myron didn't smile. "So, am I in?"

"Well, my sister, Dinah, has some questions for you—about your police record and job history—but if that goes well, it's looking pretty good. Malik, bring him to see Dinah."

"You got it, boss." Malik had picked up a nearby towel and was wiping the blood from his face. He swiped the towel over some blood stains on his pants leg, muttered to himself, and ushered Myron from the arena.

"So, who do we have here?" Judah looked toward the cage, where Lubbock, all six foot seven, three hundred fifty pounds of him, was ushering a slightly smaller white guy with a shaved head and full sleeves of tattoos into the cage. He had tattoos peeking from the neckline of his shirt, and even one tiny tattoo on his ear.

"This is Glenn Collard," Lubbock said.

"You been inside?" Judah asked.

"Yes, sir, I have."

"Okay, well I—whoa, whoa. C'mere."

Lubbock stepped toward Judah.

"What's that on your ear?"

Collard instinctively touched his left earlobe. "It's a tattoo, sir."

"I see that, but what is it?"

The man didn't answer.

"Lubbock, did you see this?"

Lubbock stepped close to Collard and peered at his ear. He shook his head, his lips pressed together. "I'm sorry. I didn't see what it was." He looked at the ground.

Judah spoke to the new man. "You know that I'm Jewish, don't you?"

Collard shook his head. "I did not, sir."

"Do you think that's a bad thing?"

"Doesn't matter to me, sir. Not a'tall."

"Doesn't matter to you. Well, do you know what that thing on your ear symbolized?"

"I think the Germans used them."

"The Germans? The Nazis."

"Yes, sir."

"Do you know what Germans did to the Jews, Glenn?"

"Well, they killed them, I guess."

"You guess? Yeah, they did. They killed them. A lot of them. Millions. Members of my family. So, why, I've got to ask, did you get this tattoo?"

Collard didn't answer.

"I need to understand. Why did you get this tattoo?"

"Symbolizes strength, I guess."

"Huh—more guessing. Well, you know what? Lubbock, come on out of there. I'm going to work this guy myself."

Lubbock exited the cage and Judah took off his shirt, shoes and socks; he set the shoes and socks neatly under his chair, folded his shirt and laid it on top of the chair. Then he entered the cage, set his feet shoulder width apart and tapped the right side of his face. "Take your best shot."

Collard looked confused and unsure. "What do you mean?"

"I mean you can go ahead and hit me and I'm not going to try to hit you until you do. So go ahead. Take your best shot. Come on. Go ahead."

Collard threw a meager right cross and hit Judah in the face. Judah shook his head and looked disappointed.

"You can do better than that. Come on. Take another one."

Collard took a deep breath, looked away, then looked back at Judah and loaded up with a right that started low and connected with Judah's temple.

Judah rolled with the punch, took a step back, touched his palm to his left ear. "Better." He grinned.

"So, you get to hit me now?" Collard asked. He looked nervous.

"Nope. Now we just, go." He stepped forward and slightly to his left and threw a right cross, which Collard partially blocked. Judah continued with his own momentum, and threw a spinning wheel kick, and his left heel connected with Collard's left eye. Collard went down and Judah was on him, in full mount, raining punches with both hands onto Collard's face. Collard was unconscious after three punches, but Judah continued to rain punches down on his face. Finally, winded, Judah got up and started to leave the cage, but turned around and stood over Collard again. He spat down at the man.

"Lubbock, get him the fuck out of here." He stopped suddenly. "Wait." He bent down, grasped Collard's left earlobe in his fist, and, with a roar, tore the bottom half of the ear clean off.

Lubbock, who had been watching, turned away. "Aw, man! Fuckin' hell!"

"Now," Judah ordered. "Get him out of here. Drop him at the emergency ward."

At that moment, one of the double doors that connected the arena aisles with the rotunda around it, and where refreshments were served, opened and Dinah walked in followed by police detectives Abe Gold and Barbara Cortez.

Judah finished putting on his shirt.

"What'd you do to your head?" Gold asked, as he approached, hand extended.

Judah shook Gold's hand and nodded in the direction of Lubbock, who was dragging Collard from the cage by his feet, a trail of blood pouring from the unconscious man's face.

"That's the other guy," Judah said.

Judah asked Gold, "So, what can I do you for?"

Gold pointed toward Kofi James, who was in a front row arena seat. "I'd like to ask that young man some questions."

"Well, there he is," Judah said.

"Downtown."

Frank James came over and stood before Gold and Cortez. "He's my brother. Is he under arrest?"

"No. We just want to talk…for now."

"Does he need a lawyer?" Frank asked.

"Well, that's up to him," Gold said, and he walked to a spot behind Kofi and made an "after you" gesture with an open palm. Cortez led the way and the two detectives and Kofi started from the arena.

"I'm coming with you," Frank announced and followed.

Gold stopped and turned. "No need," the bald detective said.

"You saying I can't?" Frank demanded. "If I'm allowed, I'm coming."

"I guess it's okay," Gold said, as he and Cortez exchanged a glance.

Chapter 9

At the police station, the police led Kofi and Frank into a bare interrogation room in which there were only a table and three chairs, two of which were on one side of the table, one on the other.

"I'll get another chair," Cortez said, and she and Gold left the room.

"Frank," Kofi began, but his brother laid a restraining hand on his forearm.

Frank chinned toward the wide wall opposite the single chair. He shifted his eyes toward a corner of the ceiling on that side of the room, from which a small camera hung. "They can see and hear us," he whispered.

Kofi held out a hand and shook his head, his eyes wide and lips pressed together, indicating he had nothing to hide. His brother patted his arm, telling him to calm down.

The door opened and the detectives reentered the room, with Cortez carrying a chair, which she set down next to the single chair.

"Have a seat, gentlemen," Cortez said, with a polite smile.

The brothers sat, with Gold sitting opposite them. Cortez remained standing behind her partner. Gold cleared his throat.

"Now then. Please state your full name."

"Kofi James."

Gold leaned forward, staring intensely at Kofi. "Didn't I hear somewhere that you're Nigerian. Is James a Nigerian name?"

"Actually," Kofi said, "I'm American, of Nigerian descent. Our parents are Nigerian."

"Is there something wrong with being Nigerian?" Frank asked.

Gold turned and stared at Frank. "Nobody's talking to you. You can be here if you keep your mouth shut."

Frank looked angry but said nothing.

"So?" Gold looked back at Kofi.

"My full name is Kofi Irikefe James Adebayo."

"Why'd you change it?"

"Our father changed it. James was his father's name. Our grandfather. I can't speak to his reasons."

Gold was silent for a full minute, then sat back and tipped his head to one side and then the other, studying Kofi. "Tell us why you killed Jennifer Teitlebaum. She not kinky enough for you?"

Frank jumped to his feet. "Hey! What the fuck, man!"

Kofi calmly held up his hand. "I didn't kill anyone."

"Come on!" Gold countered. "You picked her up. We have you on film arranging it, then leaving the bar at the hotel with her."

"That's not what happened!"

"It's on film!" Gold roared.

"Abe." Cortez put a hand on Gold's shoulder.

"I told you not to call me that!" Gold chastised, over his shoulder. He turned back to Kofi. "We have you on video having a conversation with the victim, a known prostitute. Then, moments later, we have you on video leaving the lounge with her." He glared from Kofi to Frank and back to Kofi.

"That's not what happened," Kofi answered patiently.

"It's on God damn tape," Gold maintained.

"I had just arrived, just got out of an Uber. I spoke to her, assuming we're talking about the same person. I spoke to a young woman and asked where I could find my brother. A little while later, I left the lounge and went outside. It's possible we left at about the same time, but I wasn't paying attention to her. I was looking for Frank. That's all it was."

"That's not all it was! And that's bullshit—transparent bullshit, at that!"

"Gold…" Cortez touched his shoulder again, but he shook her off.

"We brought you in to give you a chance to explain yourself, and you're giving us a line of bullshit."

"I appreciate you giving me the opportunity to explain. Thank you for that. It's what I'm doing—explaining. Everything I've told you is the truth."

Frank stood up again. "If you're not charging my brother with anything, we're going to leave now."

Gold and Cortez looked at one another.

Cortez said, "Okay. You're free to leave. Will you be around, in case we want to talk again?"

Kofi nodded mildly. "Sure. Anytime."

• • •

Mama was yelling at him to find another girl and Junior didn't want to do it. He kept seeing the women's faces as they realized they were about to die, their wounded terror after the first blow failed to kill them. He felt awful now about everything he'd done. He vaguely remembered feeling differently, but that was then.

What was he supposed to do? No one could handle Mama. Certainly, neither of her husbands could, and she still deeply hated them both —at least as much as she had when they were around.

Eventually, he couldn't take it anymore, so he got in the pickup and drove to the casino, hoping to come home and placate Mama with evidence of better luck this time.

He quickly won $80 on the slots. A happy surprise. From there he started toward the blackjack table but navigated instead to the lounge. He'd already won, so why not quit while ahead? Find another way to win.

In the lounge, he saw the same beautiful dark-skinned girl he'd seen the last time when she'd been part of a group. He even managed to catch her eye. She came over and asked his name. He gave a fake name and asked hers. Ruby. Mama would like her.

"Pretty name," he told her, "for a pretty girl."

"Do you have plans for tonight?" she wondered.

He smiled shyly back at her. "I do now."

She touched his hand, and a bolt of electricity ran through him. He felt he was being watched and looked around. At the other end of the bar, the same nightmare of a man he'd seen here before was staring at him—the man with the monster face.

Gotta get out of here.

• • •

When he got home, Mama was madder than a kicked bees nest, as she liked to say. "We're going to the all-night market, so don't even take off your coat!"

"Can Norman come?" He wanted a buffer from Mama's rage, which was on full display, even if the buffer was his own brother. Anything to draw her attention away from him.

"Norman's in the basement, so get in the damned car!"

Once they were driving, she started in again.

"You've had enough practice for today. Now we get to the real deal!"

"Okay, Mama." *What did she mean?*

"We're gonna start on the list."

"Okay, Mama." *What list? Am I supposed to know?*

"And it ain't gonna be so easy, so you'll need to practice more."

At the market, Mama took him directly to the fruit section, where she pointed to different kinds of melons and had him pick three of each. They bought cantaloups, watermelons and musk melons. Mama wanted pumpkins, but the market had none.

He wanted to ask the question, but he didn't know how, so he tried different ways in his mind. Eventually he asked as simply as he could.

"What's the list, Mama?"

But Mama refused to answer. When they got home, they went into the kitchen, where Mama told him to get out the cutting board and put it on the counter.

"Now put one of them watermelons on the cutting board and go get a knife. We start with the watermelons, because they're the easiest. The softest. Make sure the knife has a blade with a point and a sharp cutting edge. The blade should be as long as your hand. We'll order a folding knife later online."

Junior did as he was told.

The kitchen counter was waist high, with a cupboard above it, so Mama had Junior move the cutting board and melons to the kitchen table.

"Get some paper towels and spread them under the cutting board," she ordered. "This is going to get messy."

He did as he was told.

"Now grab the knife in your right hand. No, in your fist ... Yeah, there you go! And grab the melon on the left side with your left hand

and … now, stab it with the knife! No, stab down! Down! Harder! Harder! Yes! Yes! YES!"

He murdered the first three melons, driving the knife down through the soft skin and into the flesh over and over, until the red pulp was all over the table.

He needed a break between melons, as he was out of breath and his arm was getting tired. Each melon had a progressively thicker skin and required harder work.

"I think I need to change arms with the knife, Mama."

"No! You're right-handed, so you'll always use your right hand. Your left will be awkward and inaccurate. Can you throw a ball with your left?"

"No, Mama." He saw her point.

"You're gonna need to start doing pushups to get stronger."

"Okay, Mama. I will."

"Now we have to figure out a way for you to stab someone in the back of the neck…"

Junior waited while Mama looked around.

"Come on over to the living room. Now take all the books off that top bookshelf and the middle shelf. You can put some paper towels on the shelves and on the floor. Put a watermelon on the shelf and hold it forward against the wall with your left hand. Good. Now, STAB THAT FUCKIN' THING!"

He did. He stabbed the melon to death, leaving chunks of its skin and insides all over everything. Murdered melons and a messy murder scene.

"Not bad, Junior. You're learning. Now we do something a little bit different. We put them on the middle shelf, and you'll grip the knife like you're shaking a man's hand. Grip it hard now. And you're going to grab the melon with your left hand and stab forward, like you're stabbing someone in the back. Okay, now. A hand height above the waist. Now let's see you do it. Yeah, that's it. Now harder! HARDER! YES! YES! YES!"

Afterward, he sat, panting. Mama made him wash his hands and clean the mess and take out the garbage. Then they sat down at his computer and went to an online tactical supply store, where they looked at knives.

Together, they ordered two spring loaded folding tactical knives with blades longer than his hand and a serrated edge on the side opposite the slicing side.

They were done for today, Mama said, and she left him alone after that.

Which Junior appreciated. He was exhausted.

But he still wondered about the list.

• • •

The beast was a contradiction. It feasted on the hunt, and yet it was that same hunt that kept the beast at bay by occupying Sharpe's mind with the investigation.

The beast was cunning and baffling, and way smarter than he was. And Sharpe thought he was pretty smart.

He drove around for a while, keeping his eyes open for a smaller model old red pickup. Eventually, he ended up at John's Barroom and drank ginger ale while sitting at one of two tiny tables in the back. The beast was yelling at him to order good scotch or at least a bourbon and beer chaser, but he refused to listen.

Maya and Louise were there. Maya glanced at him now and then; Louise ignored him entirely. He called Victoria Sandford several times, but she didn't pick up.

A thought occurred to him; he went to the bar and directed John to send a drink to Maya. He waited until that had been done and John nodded toward him as her drink arrived. She looked confused. Her eyes flicked toward him, then back to her glass. After she'd taken a few sips, he sidled over to her.

"What can you tell me about Becca's regulars?"

"I *can* tell you whatever I damn please."

He waited a beat. "*Would* you. *Please?*"

She finished her glass and waggled it, so he ordered her another. He wondered how much the drinks affected her honesty. She seemed to drink constantly, whereas Louise barely sipped whatever she was drinking. He suspected the vodka at John's was watered down.

"She saw a tall, skinny guy with a red beard and long hair in a ponytail."

"Hair red too?"

She nodded.

"Name?"

"Red Jack, they call him."

"Who else?"

"Guy named Andy. Kinda short, kinda fat but not real fat. Jus' a little fat."

"Hair color?"

"Black. Always needed a shave."

Five o'clock shadow... "These are white guys?"

"Yeah."

"Any idea how to find 'em?"

She shook her head. "They jus' came in here now an' then."

"Haven't seen them this week?"

She shook her head. "Not yet, an' it's Friday."

"But you don't know if they saw her last Thursday."

She sipped her drink, said nothing.

Outside a car door slammed, and when Sharpe looked in that direction, he saw a pair of eyes at the window, and the top of a truck's red cab. The eyes disappeared and, seconds later, the truck started.

Sharpe rushed to the door in time to see an old red pickup driving away. It disappeared around a turn in the road. He ran to his car, spun through a U-turn and gave chase, but when he passed the bend where he'd seen the red truck, it was gone.

Sharpe slowed and took the first turn he came to, drove a short way, but saw nothing of the truck. He considered his options, made a decision and another U-turn. He sped the short distance to the hotel-casino and drove around the multi-level parking lot.

No red truck.

He went into the lounge, ordered a ginger ale and took a seat at a booth. The handful of working girls, all but two he'd never seen before, were at another booth. After a few minutes, he went over and caught the eye of the only one who looked directly at him. He got the vibe that she was in charge, to the degree anyone was. The girl was dark skinned and very pretty. He'd seen her before.

"Hi. I'm a private investigator. I wonder if you could tell me if Jennifer had any regular customers."

The girl put out her hand, flat and palm down, limp fingers extended. "I'm Ruby. I'm not sure if we've met. You look familiar."

He took her fingers gently between a thumb and forefinger. "Sam Sharpe. Judah knows me." He felt eyes on him, turned toward the bar and saw Rinny Mallach staring at him. He waved at the awful looking man, but the stare continued, unblinking.

Ruby said, "She had regulars, but I don't know what I can tell you."

"Do you mean you won't tell me?"

"I mean there isn't much to say. They mostly came in, met up, went upstairs. We're starting to keep better track, communicate between the girls." She nodded toward Mallach. "And Rinny's keeping tabs."

Sharpe thought about this. "Did any of them take her anywhere else?"

Ruby thought about the question. "A few guys, now and then." She shrugged. "Sorry."

He glanced at the bar, but Rinny had turned back to his drink and the small group of men he was with.

Sharpe approached them. "Excuse me."

Rinny turned and Sharpe beckoned to the door. Together they walked outside into the chilly evening.

"I'd like to spend some time with the ladies."

"Nobody's stoppin' you. But you gotta pay, like everybody."

"I don't mean that. I meant, can I just hang around here? Kind of keep an eye on the girls?"

"Already taken care of."

"It might help catch whoever killed Jennifer."

Rinny looked hard at him, then shrugged. "Sure. Why not."

• • •

Judah was prepared for the second rally. He kept one of his best men on each aisle between the entrance and the stage. These included

Rinny, Malik, Lubbock, Frank James, Myron and himself, all of whom were armed with handguns and automatic rifles. None patrolled alone; each had two additional soldiers along with them. The additional men were off duty cops, ex-military, and local martial arts instructors who could handle themselves. All were armed with batons and pepper spray. Those with carry permits had handguns.

Scurge and Lou remained at the lounge, overseeing business. Dinah was at the office.

This rally saw far more attendees in clown makeup. Many wore blue caps with the clown grin and the CUT logo.

While the lights were on and the stage was still bare, the crowd began a chant of "Towson Rules," which slowly morphed into "Stafford Sucks."

When the lights went down, the chants turned to cheers then to a roar as a spotlight shone on one of the entryways and a line of clowns danced toward the stage. Clowney was not among them.

An amplified bugle blew reveille, and a platform descended from the ceiling on which Clowney stood, waving and grinning—at least Judah thought he was grinning. The paint on his face made any other expression difficult to discern.

"Welcome! Hello and Welcome!" Clowney waved and pointed and waved some more, basking in the adulation. Eventually, he patted the air for the crowd to quiet, and the cheering died down.

"It's so wonderful to be among my people. Citizens of America. Residents of Towson. Descendants of our founding fathers and mothers—and I say mothers because, contrary to what some silly people say, I love women!"

The crowd roared.

"Yes! Don't you love women too! Oh, I love women! And, mind you, I don't say that a woman's place is in the home. A woman's place is wherever she wants to be. Of course, I hope she wants to be in the kitchen. She wants to be in the bedroom…"

The crowd, a majority of whom were male, roared again.

"But if she wants a job, then I say more power to her!"

More cheering.

"Now there's a rumor that I said that a woman's place is probably on her knees. I never said that. Of course, if she chooses that, then who am I to—" The rest of his sentence was drowned out by cheers. "What I actually said, and I was joking, was a woman's place is on top. That's progressive thinking, isn't it? For years it was always the man on top. But I wasn't talking about the bedroom. I was talking about everywhere. Women deserve to run things, and we should let them. They should run businesses. Heck, much of my business is run by women. Look!"

Several clowns around the perimeter of the stage waved. Upon closer inspection, Judah could see that they were women.

"And anyway, men, if the women are running things, you can kick back and relax, have a few beers with the guys. Now, let's get serious. I want to talk about Mayor Stafford."

Boos rained down on the crowd.

"No, no, no!" He waved a finger, chastising the crowd, or pretending to. "I'd like to tell you about our Mayor, my opponent."

The boos continued. Clowney held up a hand and they subsided.

"I've called him boring, because I think he is. But my team has corrected me and unearthed some information that tells me he's not as boring as I thought. So, I'm going to share that with you now." He looked at his teleprompter.

"Did you know that Mayor Stafford has a drinking problem? Yes. Or so I heard. I'm not sure, but it's a rumor that seems to have some validity. It's been a poorly kept secret for years. He had to fix his own DWIs! Several of them. I also heard, now this is just something I heard, so I can't verify it. But I heard that Mayor Stafford killed a kid with his car in a hit and run a few years ago. I don't know if it's true of course. Maybe it isn't, but who knows. I feel sorry for him. But at the very least I can tell you that Mayor Stafford is not nearly as boring as I thought!"

The crowd was boisterous and rowdy, perhaps because alcoholic beverages were sold in the arena, though not in the stands. So many people wore blue vests, the Clowney-branded hats, and makeup, that it was hard for Judah to tell whether the rowdiness was caused by Clowney's employees or event attendees. Perhaps, he realized, this was by design. There was, thankfully, no real physical violence, other than some pushing and shoving by a small band of sign-wielding Stafford supporters who were vastly outnumbered and probably too intimidated to do very much.

· · ·

The brown-haired Clowney employee, who Judah now knew was a bodyguard, approached Judah several minutes after the end of the event. With him was his bald co-worker.

"The big man requests the honor of your presence," the brown-haired clown said.

"Okay." Judah looked around, saw that the crowd had thinned peaceably and nodded for Frank and Rinny to come along.

They found Clowney in a large dressing room, reclining in a lounge chair with a fat cigar and a tall glass of what appeared to be scotch.

"Have a seat," he said, and waved the cigar to a row of nearby chairs along a mirrored wall.

Everyone sat.

Clowney sipped from his scotch, drew on his cigar and looked at Judah with satisfaction. "Judah Hammer." He nodded and looked impressed. "You're quite a guy in this town. You've achieved so much, branched out in ways your father never would."

Judah's expression darkened. "What do you know about my father?"

Clowney smiled. "Everything, more or less. I'd like for us to work more closely together. I like the way you operate, and I'd love to have your support. That way, once I'm mayor, your road will be pre-paved."

Judah said nothing.

"Oh, I know. You're a cautious man. I admire that." He waited, and when Judah didn't answer, he shrugged. "Listen, I've got guys chomping at the bit to do what you do around here, and they're good. But you're already in and vested. So, better that you maintain your place, you know? But you should also know, there's others knocking at the door."

"That sounds like a threat."

"Oh, come on," Clowney protested. "It isn't! I didn't mean that at all! This is just information I'm sharing with you. Please don't take it that way. This is just a friendly conversation."

Judah waved him away, thinking, *I don't even know this guy's real name...* He said, "Why don't we keep things the way they are for now."

The big clown's eyebrows twitched, but his eyes looked hard at Judah. "Fine by me," he said, the threat clear in his tone.

Chapter 10

The GODOT breakfast group sat at a booth toward the rear of the diner. Lev was pleasantly surprised that everyone attended this second meeting. It was good to be out of the house and away from his brothers for a change—particularly Reuben's self-righteousness and Zeb's extreme special needs. For the most part, he was okay with the others. Dinah was tied up with Josh whenever she wasn't working. Izzy was either playing piano somewhere, was high and giggling in the den with Zeb, or was fast asleep. Judah was either working or with his own family at his and Raisa's townhouse.

He looked around the table. Everyone but Mason Marx was looking at their phones—reading the *Gazette* or perhaps the local news on Fox or CNN. Marx caught his eye, smiled politely and nodded.

"Morning," Lev said.

"Morning to you," Marx replied. "Eggs today?"

Lev shook his head. "I think … pancakes. Chocolate *chip* pancakes."

Marx looked impressed. "Special occasion?"

Lev spread his hands and shrugged. "Because I can."

Rick Corbain looked up from his phone toward Marx. "Interesting night at the rally."

Marx's eyebrows went up; his eyes twinkled and glanced around the table.

"Not sure I'd like a mayor who puts down women," the accountant continued.

"Who's putting down women?" Barry O'Leary asked, rolling his broad shoulders. Despite the brisk weather, he was dressed in a white T-shirt, a blue vest and khaki shorts. He wore sandals on his otherwise bare feet. "He's just kidding around, and if you look specifically at what he said, there was nothing offensive there. Really, it was all true." He sat back, crossing his legs and throwing an arm over the booth's backrest. He surveyed the room and his eyes came to rest on Walter.

"You stopped talking in rhyme," Walter observed.

O'Leary didn't answer.

A middle-aged waitress appeared in a blue blouse and skirt and a white apron. "Coffees all around?"

Everyone nodded.

"I'll take your orders if you're ready," she added.

Everyone gave their orders.

When she was gone, Taylor Richmond looked at his phone, then rapped its base twice on the table next to his place settings.

"I've been working with Mayor Stafford his whole career—and his father before him. Knew his grandfather, too." His eyes went around the table and landed on O'Leary. "I'm not inclined to dismiss a family

165

that's done so much for this town for generations based on what some loud clown who puts down women says."

O'Leary started to speak but Richmond raised a hand. "I know. He says he's all *for* women. Look, all of us here are 'all for' women." He looked around the table. "At least I assume we are. But your guy's whole shtick is based on making everything a joke. We're talking about people's livelihoods, their dinner tables, their taxes."

"So are we," O'Leary said quietly. "And we see people muscling in on what our citizens are entitled to. We're all about making sure everyone gets what's coming to them."

Richmond held out both palms. "Well, now you're making threats, Barry."

"Huh? No threat. I'm just tellin' it like it is."

Richmond leaned forward, his expression intense. "There's a hint of violence in everything you people say and do. There's a story in here—" He held up his phone. "—about your people inciting violence, not only last night at the rally, but around town, on street corners, at bars. I mean, what the hell, pal?"

"Well, right there's your problem," O'Leary shot back. "You're referencing a biased source."

"What does that mean?" It was Corbain asking the question.

The conversation paused as the coffees arrived, along with cream, milk and sweeteners.

"So, Barry," Marx asked. "Are you saying my paper's biased in favor of Stafford?"

166

"Isn't it true," O'Leary asked, "that you've always run pieces that represent the city?"

"We do. It's in the public's interest to hear from our government—for them to have their say—and then we write follow-up articles that offer different perspectives that are often critical of the city. We also print letters from residents that represent every reasonable point of view."

"Define reasonable!" O'Leary said harshly. "Never mind. My point is that the paper does give the city a mouthpiece, a bullhorn actually."

"The city. Not Stafford."

"But Stafford *is* the city," O'Leary emphasized.

"We do not give Stafford any editorial space vis a vis the election," Marx said, sounding miffed. "We give the city space, which will continue no matter who wins the coming election."

"It's more than that," O'Leary countered. "You have a particular writer—one of your primary writers. I don't know her title, but she reports, writes, and, I think, has some editorial responsibilities. He jabbed a finger. "She's biased!"

"Raisa Tolleson," Marx said.

"Exactly. She's married to Judah Hammer." O'Leary paused, and continued when no one spoke. "Who is a criminal, and a Stafford ally." O'Leary looked around the table. Eventually his eyes focused on Lev. He shrugged and smiled. "Sorry, man. I know he's your brother."

Lev chuckled. "You're kind of preaching to the choir."

"Really?"

"Yeah, and they're not married, though they are a couple."

"Let me make something clear," O'Leary said. "One of the reasons I'm here is to listen. Clowney wants to take the city's pulse. He'd be stupid not to. But we want the communication to go both ways. We aren't bullying anyone. There's no vigilantes."

"I don't know," Corbain sounded dubious, and Levita nodded in agreement.

"Hear me out," O'Leary went on. "We're helping to keep the peace in what is obviously a town that's out of control. Stafford has relation-ships with some violent people around here." He looked at Lev. "His brother admits it. Yes, we're seeing unrest and maybe even potential violence. But it isn't *us* causing it. It's the population. They're upset by what they're seeing. They want change! They want the Nigerians out of their gas tanks. I mean shouldn't some of our citizens be able to own freakin' gas stations?"

Corbain snorted. "You mean white citizens…"

"Not necessarily," O'Leary disagreed. "You want a gas station, Rick? You should be able to have one. And you're a Black guy—not a thing wrong with that. Wouldn't you agree, Taylor?"

Richmond tipped his head, conceding the point.

O'Leary continued. "Our guys are just regular citizens who are helping to keep the peace. And a lot of folks around town have volun-teered of their own free will to join our ranks. What you see out there are your neighbors being neighborly, doing neighborly deeds to help keep the peace."

• • •

It was windy on Halloween afternoon and the Towson streets were populated by excited, costumed children led by parents, many of whom were also in costumes. Many children and parents were in groups of fours and fives. Preteens trick-or-treated in pairs and clusters without parents, and as day darkened into night, the family groups gave way to larger gangs of teens.

Rinny Mallach loved Halloween, which was perhaps the only day of the year that no one gave his distorted features a second glance. He was with Scurge and Lou, heading into the poor part of Towson, the north side, which was populated by tenements, row houses, dilapidated shacks, and the occasional well-kept home, lawn and property. Scurge was driving with Lou beside him and Rinny in the back seat with the suitcase of product. They parked a dozen yards from a brown brick apartment building.

"We're meeting on the roof," Scurge said, as he opened the door and exited the Escalade. Scurge had arranged the deal.

As they approached the building, Rinny saw the security detail through the glass around the double front doors. "Access?"

Scurge walked past the doors and around to a side entrance. "Combination," he said, and entered numbers into the door's lock and swung the door open, holding it for Rinny and Lou.

"Lou first," Rinny said. "Then me, then you, Scurgie." This was the usual protocol. Guards on either side of product.

They climbed the nine floors and emerged onto the roof, with Lou and Scurge brandishing weapons.

"Stop there!" a voice called.

They did.

"Lower your weapons," the voice said.

Rinny nodded and Lou and Scurge lowered their guns.

Crouching on the far side of a low, stucco wall were two men with pistols leveled at them. An unarmed lean Latino who appeared too young to be involved, rose slowly. He beckoned.

"No need for guns, Carlos," Rinny said, as he approached the young Latino.

The young Latino nodded to his men, who lowered their guns.

"Let's see the product," Carlos said.

Rinny laid the suitcase on the top of the wall and opened it.

"May I?" Carlos extended his hand toward the suitcase and Rinny nodded.

Carlos looked at the bricks inside, but instead of removing one, he undid the cellophane wrapping from its corner, touched a finger to his tongue and then to the brick. Then he licked his finger and closed his eyes.

At that moment, the door to the stairwell banged open and a long line of Black men in dark clothes and red capes emerged, duckwalking low around the roof, surrounding both Rinny's and Carlos's men. All had automatic rifles.

"Drop the hardware," said the last of the men to step onto the roof. He was of average height, heavily muscled, and had a full beard and mustache.

"What the fuck is this?" Rinny demanded, his eyes on Carlos.

"You tell me," Carlos snarled back. "Puta madre!"

"Close the case and hand it over," the Black man said, holding out a hand. "You should know better."

Rinny closed the case and extended it toward him. But as the man reached for it, Rinny grasped the case with both hands and shoved it hard at the man's face. The man started to raise his hands to block it, but Rinny was too fast, and with the case in front of him, he propelled the man backward, slipped a foot behind his leg and tripped him.

Automatic rifle fire erupted, and Rinny, who had already landed one punch, froze before throwing a second.

"Get the fuck off me," the man said.

Rinny did.

"Back up, to the side of the roof," he ordered, and Rinny did.

"Now, jump, motherfucker."

Rinny didn't move, and the man said something to one of his comrades, who leveled an automatic weapon at Rinny's legs.

Another of the man's comrades spoke. "Shit," he said. He'd been looking at his phone. "Jeremiah." He leaned toward the man who had been doing the talking.

Jeremiah seemed to see Rinny for the first time. He looked alarmed and he shook his head and responded to the man who had spoken to him.

"Is this true?" he asked. "You work for Judah Hammer?"

Rinny nodded.

"Hold on." Jeremiah took out a phone and made a call. "I need to hear this for myself." He spoke into his phone, then ended the call. "Open the case," he said.

Rinny opened the case.

Jeremiah looked at the case's contents and took a deep breath and nodded several times. "So, I'm told your man and ours have a deal."

"You work for Dante?" Rinny asked.

"I do."

Scurge spoke up. "It seems your internal lines of communication leave something to be desired."

• • •

As Barbara Cortez sat in the bathroom stall, she was startled by a pounding on the bathroom door and was glad she was already seated.

"Cortez, let's go! It's an emergency!"

"Damn it, Gold. I *am* going, and whatever it is, it'll wait a few seconds."

She heard him muttering and cursing. He pounded the door again as she was fastening her pants. This time she didn't answer. He'd just have to wait. She washed her hands and took a few extra moments to dab at what little makeup she wore around her eyes, wetting the tip of a finger and swiping a smudge from an eyelid.

"Jesus, Cortez. You're taking forever in there!"

She smiled to herself and exited the bathroom to find Gold looking at his watch.

"What is it, Abe? Where's the fire?"

He was already speed walking toward the door. "Lady says she found one of the missing girls in a strip of lawn. Come on!"

She ran to catch up. "Found … in a strip of lawn?"

"That's what she says."

They arrived at the address given in the report, which was in a run-down section of town, to find three uniformed officers, two men and a woman, arrayed around the scene, holding back an eager crowd of on-lookers.

As they approached, Gold said, "I'm not seeing shit."

But Cortez did.

The neighborhood was a seedy section of Towson. Across the street was a fence that bordered train tracks leading from the Towson train station to the next town. The area along the fence was littered with garbage thrown from passing cars and kids who drank and partied along the fence. Because it was set back from the road and the homes across the street, the area was not well traveled, making it a perfect gathering spot for young people at night.

One of the male officers stood on the sidewalk beside a wide-eyed blonde woman in gray sweats, red sneakers and a purple headband. Next to the woman sat a leashed golden retriever. Several feet from the dog, in the center of a patchy strip of grass, were mounds of loose dirt. Beyond the dirt was a hole about eighteen inches long and half that in width. The hole was about a foot deep.

Cortez quickly understood what she was seeing but it was to Gold that the officer spoke.

"This is Adrienne Humphreys," the officer began, as Cortez peered into the hole. "Her dog—"

The woman started talking immediately.

"I was walking Clifton. And he started barking like, I mean, crazy. And there was no one around. It was the weirdest thing. And then he ran in a circle, and then he started digging!"

At first, Cortez didn't see anything. But when she stepped closer, careful to keep her feet on the sidewalk so as not to damage any footprints, she could see a bit of torn plastic tarp. Within the plastic was something small and yellowish—a toe. As she started to bend down for a closer look, she felt her partner's firm hand restraining her.

"Lemme look." He bent to glance into the hole, then stood and took out his phone. "Back everyone away. This is a crime scene."

• • •

Within hours, Cortez had, with Jason Hamilton's permission, retrieved hairs from a brush in Becca's room, and by the following day Linwood Sherman had fast tracked the DNA and confirmed that the pair of legs the forensics team had dug up belonged to Rebecca Hamilton.

Gold and Cortez returned to Jason Hamilton's home to break the terrible news.

Cortez rang the bell.

Hamilton had been smiling when he answered the door, but as soon as he saw the detectives' faces, his smile disappeared.

"I'm sorry, Mr. Hamilton," Gold said. "We have discovered remains that testing has confirmed … are Rebecca's."

His features sagged. "You're sure?"

Cortez nodded. "I'm afraid so, sir."

Hamilton buckled at the knees, as the strength went out of his legs. Gold caught him beneath the arms to keep him from falling.

"What am I going to do?" he asked in a weak voice.

Gold grasped Hamilton with a forearm below the man's arm. Cortez led him by the other arm to a couch, where he sat down heavily.

Gold stood several feet away. He had taken out his phone and was grimacing at whatever he was seeing on it.

Cortez spoke gently as she knelt beside the grieving father. "You're going to reach out to family. Becca has a sister in New Jersey, isn't that so?"

Hamilton looked at Cortez as though seeing her for the first time. "What?"

Cortez glanced at Gold, who mouthed "shock.'"

"I think you should consider calling your daughter in New Jersey. Mary, right?"

Hamilton nodded, his expression blank.

Gold said, "It's going to be a little while before we can have Rebecca returned to you, Mr. Hamilton." He gave a helpless wince. "Procedures."

"I need to know that you have family you can be with," Cortez said. "Mr. Hamilton?"

Hamilton blinked. He was starting to cry. His mouth opened; he was trying to form a word. "How? How? How am I—?"

Cortez looked up at Gold. "Give us a minute, won't you, Gold?"

Gold was only too happy to leave his junior partner with Jason Hamilton. He touched a hand to Hamilton's forearm and gave him as meaningful a look as he could manage. "You're going to get through this, sir. Get with your family, and lean on them, okay? Get through this together." Still holding his phone, he hurried out to the car.

Ten minutes later, the passenger door opened and Cortez slid into the seat next to him.

"Good job in there," he said, as he shifted into gear and drove quickly toward the main road toward the police station.

Cortez's lips were a thin line. Her expression was sad and resigned.

"He'll get through today," Gold assured her. "And know that you helped."

She nodded appreciatively. "And it'll get better from there."

He shot her a knowing glance. "Green's called a press conference."

"I figured he might." She sounded anxious and looked more so.

Wide-eyed and worried, Gold thought.

"Come on," he said, with a facetious grin. "This'll be fun!"

She gave him an alarmed look. "You're freakin' crazy."

Though it was a Sunday, news vans with satellite dishes were already arrayed on the street alongside the police station. There was the *Towson Gazette*, the *Long Island Daily* and even the *New York Times*. There were also camera and sound people from three TV stations, along with the papers' online video crews.

Gold and Cortez parked in the lot behind the police station, walked around to the side of the building, and edged through the crowd until they were near enough to the front to get a good look at the proceedings.

The afternoon was windy and cold for early November and many of the media people were dressed for winter weather. Chief Green, however, was in shirtsleeves, slacks, and a forest green tie. He looked like a football coach before the big game, focused and intense. Mayor Stafford stood to one side in a long, sandy-colored coat, his hands in black leather gloves, his shoulders hunched. Beside the mayor was his newly hired chief-of-staff and campaign manager, a young, Black, well-educated lawyer named Zane Larson.

The police chief scrunched his nose several times, tapped the microphone and began to speak.

"For those who do not know, we have confirmed that Rebecca Hamilton, the young woman who had been reported missing, is confirmed to have been a victim of homicide. We have no further details about the crime at this time. I speak for all of us at the TPD and I can confidently say that I speak for the city and the mayor as well when I say that we are four-square behind the Hamilton and Teitlebaum families at this terrible time."

The chief paused and stepped back.

A reporter from the *Long Island Daily* waved a hand. "Can you confirm that both these women were escorts?"

Green's expression shuttered. "We cannot confirm that, no."

"But do you deny it?"

The chief took an impatient breath. "We cannot confirm nor deny."

Raisa Tolleson, who was several yards from the front of the crowd, shouted a question. "Do these two deaths mean we have a serial killer on the loose?"

Green had to crane his neck to see her. "Now, you ought to know better than that."

"Answer the question, chief!"

"No!" Green answered, emphatically. "It means no such thing. We have two homicides. That's what we have."

"But if you take a step back—"

"No, you take a step back! I know you've got to sell papers, but what we do at the TPD is police work. We do not make assumptions, we do not generalize, and we do not sensationalize!" He glanced at the mayor and his chief of staff. The mayor was looking away and shaking his head with disgust.

Green glared at the crowd. "No more questions! This press conference is over!"

Chapter 11

Sharpe was physically and emotionally exhausted. He'd been progressively less and less able to sleep and last night he'd twisted and spun in his sheet and blanket until they merged with the jeans and T-shirt he'd slept in. He continued this way through the morning and into the afternoon, hoping to drift off for a few minutes here or there that might add up to something that would mitigate his fatigue.

Finally, he'd given up and doom scrolled on his phone until he'd seen the police chief's press conference, which had been the nail in the coffin of his case.

"I hope the coffee's ready," Sharpe said, as he pushed open the door to his office. His eyes were on his feet, to make sure they were working.

That Rebecca Hamilton's remains had been discovered meant both that someone was killing prostitutes, whatever the cops might say, and his case had gone to shit—along with the remnants of his self-esteem and most of the rest of his life.

With some satisfaction he registered the smell of coffee, but when Robin didn't answer, he looked up and saw Jason Hamilton sitting on his office couch. The man looked at least as tired as he was, with dark circles under reddened, haunted eyes. His sport jacket was rumpled and the shirt beneath it was stained.

The frustration on Robin's face told him that she'd hoped he might have been more attentive and prepared for what was awaiting him. Not only was she annoyingly cheerful but she was frustratingly focused on customer service. While he understood this was a business, he was an investigator first and a people pleaser second, if at all. In his view, what pleased clients most was solving cases.

All at once he was acutely aware that this man had just been told that his daughter's remains had been found, and barely more than that.

How 'bout you stop thinking of yourself for a second, Sharpe.

He'd been heading for the coffee machine but now veered toward Hamilton and thrust out a hand while arranging his face into what he hoped was an expression of sympathy. He said the only thing that came to mind; in fact, it didn't come to mind at all but emerged from his mouth of its own accord.

"I'm sorry for your loss, Mr. Hamilton."

"Jason. And thank you. I appreciate that. Your assistant was kind enough to bring me a coffee."

Before he could ask, Sharpe saw out of the corner of his eye that Robin was bringing him one as well.

Hamilton had pulled a checkbook from his inside jacket pocket. He opened it and took out a pen. "My daughter has died and I need to plan her funeral, but I wanted to take care of you first."

Sharpe waved the check away. "Keep your money. I didn't find your daughter."

Hamilton paused, then looked at Robin. "What's the amount?"

Robin was looking at Sharpe, waiting.

Sharpe shook his head. "Please put the checkbook away."

Hamilton reluctantly did as he was asked.

"I didn't find your daughter, but I'm going to find her killer. Nothing to do with money."

He walked Hamilton to the door. Once he'd gone, Sharpe turned and saw that Robin eyes were alive with approbation. She blinked and the look was replaced with concern.

"Can we afford that?"

He sat down heavily behind his desk and fumbled with the papers in front of him with little understanding of what they were. Envelopes, advertisements, bills… "Afford's got nothing to do with it." He looked up at her. "Could you please do something with this shit?"

He badly wanted a drink. The need to find his client's daughter had been pulled like a rug from beneath him and he was falling, with nothing to grab onto, nothing to catch him, and nowhere to land. He didn't want a fix. The beast had gone back to its cave, back to whatever it did when it was dormant.

He was left with little besides the hollow and painful self-pity of having failed to find Rebecca Hamilton. He had said he'd catch her killer, but he hadn't really meant it. It had been the thing to say—what real men said. But doing it?

Without a word to Robin he got up and walked out of the office, determined to find a drink somewhere he could be alone.

• • •

"We don't know enough to say, yet," Gold protested. Sweat stood out on his bald head, reflected in the fluorescent lights of Chief Green's office.

"Well, what the hell *have* you got?" Green demanded, as he sat back in his chair and folded his arms across his chest.

Gold turned to one side, took a few steps, turned back and took a few steps to where he'd been originally. Green's office left very little room for pacing between the desk and the tables bearing lamps and photos of family, several mayors and council members.

Cortez could see that Gold was frustrated and more than a little bit anxious, so she took a deep breath and spoke without knowing quite what she was going to say. "Well, the Teitlebaum and Hamilton girls were clearly both escorts. Hamilton worked out of John's Barroom and Teitlebaum out of the Towson Hotel Lounge. Both were local and loners, and neither had a social media account in their name, though perhaps they had others. Escorts just don't have many real-life connections other than other sex workers and the clients. We've been watching the accounts of former high school classmates and we aren't seeing any tags—just prayers and thoughts and such." Cortez could feel

Gold's eyes on her and sensed grudging gratitude that she was taking the lead. So she plowed on.

"Hamilton had a lot of boyfriends and apparently needed money, which is how she got into the life—via both. Guys were just drawn to her. She was supposedly going to community college in the daytime, only she wasn't. This was apparently just something she told her father."

Green looked frustrated, which, Cortez thought, was better than enraged. "No mother?"

Cortez shook her head. "The father gave us some names of childhood friends, but none have had contact with her in years. These were elementary school and junior high friends. She has a sister, but she lives out of state—Mary, I think. Teitlebaum was friendly with the other escorts at the lounge, but they won't talk and Judah Hammer categorically denies that any of them work for him, though it's clear they do. He says they're just women who hang out at his place and whatever they do, they do on their own."

"Bullshit," Green mused.

"Yeah, well," Cortez agreed.

Green made a rolling motion with his hand, encouraging them to continue. "What about the johns?"

Gold answered quickly and Cortez could tell he wanted to demonstrate some modicum of success for the chief. "Hamilton's was a phone call. She had a few regulars and we have descriptions and we'll be keeping an eye out for them. Teitlebaum's—well, she'd adopted the name Spencer, for business—she looked to be with the guy we brought in."

Green nodded. "The brother of Hammer's lieutenant."

Gold widened his eyes and nodded, then Cortez watched his frustration return. "But there's nothing to hold him on, except he was seen from inside looking to be making…" He rolled his hand again, searching for the word. "…the arrangement, the date, then heading for the exit. What about cameras outside?"

Gold shook his head. "None."

Green's eyes cleared and he appraised them both.

"So, you've really got nothing."

Gold said, "We had an anonymous call from someone who said they saw a red pickup with plates beginning with the letters 'TLT' at the pier the night Teitlebaum went missing."

"What's the DMV say?"

Gold grimaced and sucked air through his teeth. "Not much."

"Have you … tried?"

Gold nodded and said, "You put question marks into the database where you don't have the info. So far, inconclusive."

The chief rapped his knuckles on his desk. "What about by the train tracks, where they found the Hamilton girl's legs? Any ideas about the rest of her?"

Gold said, "Our guys dug up half the street. She ain't there."

"Well, she's fucking somewhere. What about dogs? Can we get some dogs out sniffing for the rest of her?"

Cortez said, "We'd have to walk them all over town."

The chief looked suddenly interested. "You have a dog, don't you, Cortez? Can't you take them, like, up and down different streets over time? A few streets today. A few tomorrow. Like that?"

Gold huffed a laugh. "She don't have a dog. She has a fuckin' horse."

"Well, not with my dog, but we could do that with cadaver dogs," Cortez said. "It could take forever, but it assumes that bodies are buried in Towson."

Gold added, "And it assumes they're buried period. Teitlebaum was in the water."

Cortez said, "I spoke to another escort at John's Barroom. Name of Maya. She says Rebecca had a problem with pain killers. Got smacked around by a john and got herself a prescription, then started buying them on the street. From some little dude named Matty. Works for a Black gang on the north side and a couple of the towns over that way. Rockville and Fremont. Gang run by a guy named Dante."

Green scowled. "Dante Hibbert. Nasty piece of work." He waved a hand. "Probably unrelated to the death, if this is serial."

"Don't we need three for it to be serial though?" Cortez asked.

Green tipped his head in acknowledgement.

"Still could be related," Cortez said, a little defensively.

Gold exhaled a sigh. "The Teitlebaum girl is hard to figure. The family is mostly older—nobody really close to her in age—and very respectable, as was Rebecca, for a while anyway. Mother says she was a good student, popular at school, involved in extracurricular activities."

"Like lots of working girls." Green held out both hands. "And yet she has no old friends who kept up with her."

Cortez added, "Who are willing to talk to us."

Chief Green slapped his desk. "So, let's rebroadcast and post both girls' photos and appeal again to the public. And comb through everything once more."

Gold pointed a finger. "Something else we can do. We can go through ATM photos and see if either one shows up. Might get lucky there."

"Good," Green agreed. "Do it!"

The office phone rang and after a second ring, Green picked it up, then looked at the detectives and mouthed, "The mayor." He spoke into the phone. "I'm with them now, sir. I'm putting you on speaker."

He pushed a button and the mayor's voice crackled through the room. "Whatever happened to that guy we questioned? Coffee?"

"Kofi James, sir," Gold responded.

"That you, Abe?"

"Yes, sir."

"Is the guy cleared?"

"Sir?"

"I mean are you God damned sure he didn't do it?"

"Well, not a hundred percent."

"Then rearrest him, and make sure the papers hear about it. The TV news too. I can't have people thinking there's a serial killer running around and nothing's being done."

"We don't really have anything to hold him on sir," Green protested.

"And I don't care what you have or don't have." As angry as Green had been, the mayor was angrier. "Are you listening?" he raged. "Rearrest him and hold him as long as the law allows! I'm in the fight of my life here!"

The detectives looked at the chief, who raised his eyebrows and both palms in helpless acquiescence.

"Green. You there, Green?"

"Yes, sir."

"Well, grow a fucking pair and get this done. Get some evidence on him. I can't have this fucking clown spreading dangerous bullshit about lawlessness. We need to show the rule of law in action. You hear?"

"I hear, sir."

• • •

As the orange sun set and darkened to violet, Sharpe was heading for a dive bar, just about any dive bar—just not John's Barroom. He didn't want to run into Maya or Louise and be reminded of his own inadequacy, so he headed north and out of town. He was beyond critical mass and he'd decided that he needed a drink. No heroin, no oxy, no meth. A fucking drink.

And yet, he'd gone further than that. He'd made the *decision* to have one. Needing the drink wasn't the problem. Having the drink wasn't even the problem. Making the *decision* to have the drink—that was the challenge, and he'd passed that test or failed that test or … he was *beyond* that test, which had been the hard part. He'd made his choice. He was on his way.

And, after all, what was the downside? This was the easy part. It wasn't like he had no experience. He'd been drinking since he was 12. He was an expert at drinking and at dealing with life while drinking or drunk.

He could certainly drive drunk—piece of cake. Had done it a million times.

So he was heading into familiar territory, willingly, eyes open. He would stay away from the dope. He had also made the decision to step away from the twelve-step program he had begun and all the God stuff he had found so confusing and get back to what he knew best—kicking back and having a few. And forgetting. *Ahh, the forgetting!*

He saw the lights in the distance. Red and white and blue. But not a flag. And they weren't flashing, so not a police car. And it was too early for Christmas lights, though one could never tell. There were always people who had their lights strung up while their pumpkins and skeletons were still out.

As he approached, the lights came into focus. Now he could see. They were lights that ran around the perimeter of a sign on the lawn of a church. The sign faced the road, and the colored lights were part of the sign. The sign itself was backlit in white with black letters that appeared one word at a time with a string of red, white and blue running around their perimeter.

The letters were plain and visible from more than a block away, growing as he drove closer. They appeared, remained for a few seconds, and disappeared—each word giving way to the next. A three-word cadence. One word at a time, speaking to him—*at* him, repeatedly. Rhythmically.

Never.

Give.

Up.

Never.

Give.

Up.

He felt an odd stirring in his chest. A swell of something that was at first undefinable and which grew and blossomed into a faintly familiar emotion.

Hope.

His frozen heart struck back.

"Fuck you," he said to the sign.

Never.

Give.

Up.

"Fuck you!" he said again.

Never.

Give.

Up.

The words hammered at him as he passed the sign and now it was playing in his head. The lights burning in his memory, each one an image that gave way to the next.

Never.

Give.

Up.

As he continued to drive he continued to see that echo and cadence of the words playing in his mind's eye, and it was as if the lights were sunlight that shone on the seedling of hope that was barely alive in his cold, dead heart, that heart that wanted to drown his guilt and failure and make damn sure it stayed drowned.

Despite this impossible environment, the seedling sprouted and grew into a more recognizable sapling with the help of the lights.

Hope.

He had the strange feeling he was supposed to see the sign, that it was speaking to him.

"Listen to the sign," said a small voice from a corner of his mind.

He was startled. The voice had actually spoken to him. Aloud. He'd heard it speak. A whisper, but it was there.

"Listen to the sign. Never give up."

His car turned around of its own accord and headed back toward the Towson Hotel-Casino.

• • •

Sharpe walked into the lounge and saw two things that pulled him in opposite directions.

First, he saw the bar, the light glinting off golden bottles hung on high shelves like an indoor sunset.

Then he saw Kofi James seated at a table with his brother Frank and Rinny Mallach.

Sharpe was undecided for a brief moment, then walked to the table where Kofi rose and pulled him in for a loose, shoulder-slapping hug.

"There's my man," Kofi said, giving him a searching look.

"You got a minute?" Sharpe asked.

"For you, I've got a lot more." Kofi looked around, saw an unoccupied table and nodded in that direction. "C'mon, let's sit." He stopped. "You know what? Let's step into the restaurant area. Less distraction there."

Sharpe knew he meant "less *temptation* there." He followed Kofi into the next room, which was an open area, a conduit between the lounge and casino that was more restaurant and less bar.

"So? How can I help?" Kofi asked as they sat down.

"I think I'm done," Sharpe said.

A waitress appeared and said, "What can I get you gentlemen?"

"Iced coffee for me," Kofi said.

"Coffee. Regular coffee," Sharpe said.

"Coming right up," the waitress said, and left.

"I was all set to go out and have a few drinks," Sharpe began. "Probably more than a few. Wasn't going to be a big deal. No hard stuff. Just a few drinks. And, I don't know what happened. I saw a sign."

Kofi nodded and smiled.

Sharpe continued emphatically, "No! An actual sign, on a church—like an electronic billboard. It said, 'Never give up.'"

"And you took it to heart." Kofi was nodding and smiling, as if this sort of thing was nothing new to him. "But do you really want to stop? I mean, really?"

"I think I do."

"If so, there's work for you to do. Some reading and some writing, and some meetings to attend."

Sharpe sucked in a corner of his lip. "Man, I just know I can't go on the way it's been going. The pain, man. The pain. It's too much."

A disturbance at the door drew their attention. Frank and Rinny Mallach got up from their table and headed in that direction. Moments later, they approached the table where Kofi and Sharpe were sitting, trailed by Detectives Gold and Cortez.

"We need you to come downtown to answer a few questions," Gold said to Kofi.

Sharpe could see he looked uncomfortable. "Is he under arrest?"

"You need to stay out of this, Sam," Cortez said to Sharpe.

"He's not under arrest, yet," Gold said. "But if he doesn't want to come that may change."

Kofi stood. "That's all right. I'll go."

• • •

"I don't understand about this list, Mama."

"Just keep driving, Junior," came her voice from the back seat. "We'll find them. You'll see. Make a left here and then a right two blocks down."

Junior did as he was told.

"But who are the people, Mama? How can I find them if I don't know who they are?"

"I told you about Patrice, didn't I?"

"Yes, Mama. Patrice Gamble. Lives with her husband, Clayton and Marsha, their daughter."

"Good boy, Junior. You remembered!"

"Thank you, Mama." He continued to drive, happy now.

"And the asshole who lived on the corner with his stupid bitch of a wife and those idiot children. The one who didn't know his own garbage can."

"Peck."

"That's right. Clifford Peck."

"And Mary, and their kids were Michele and Will."

"Exactly. Good boy!"

"So, we're gonna kill them too?"

"Darn tootin,' Junior."

"Um, can Norman help?"

"Yes, he can. Norman's always a big help."

"Who else, Mama? Are there more?"

"Okay, turn here and go past the row of stores and then one more block and make a left at the light."

"Okay, Mama."

"There's a few more on the list. The lady at the dress shop."

"Daisy's Dresses. Susan was her name, right?"

"That's right. The cashier. Susan Pierre. She said I was fat."

"You're not fat, Mama."

"You're a good boy, Junior."

"Thank you, Mama."

"And that waitress. What was her name?"

"Lakeisha."

"That's the one. Now if you just make the right up here. You'll see a stretch of road by the lumber yard. And she should be…Yup. There she is, Junior. Right there!"

"I see her, Mama."

"Now just tell her to get into the car. You know what to say. Get her in. Get her in and take her to the house! To the basement! Norman will help!"

Junior pulled the car over and one of the women who had been standing under the streetlight along the fence outside the lumber yard stepped over to the car. She wore a tight red mini dress, fish net stockings, a tight red top with a plunging neckline and a short suede coat.

"Looking for a date?" she asked, when Junior lowered the passenger side window.

When Junior popped the locks, she opened the door, climbed in, and laid a hand on Junior's thigh. As he drove away, Mama whispered into his ear from the back seat. "Bedroom then basement."

• • •

Sharpe was driving again. He wanted to check on any escorts he could find. He saw men in white shirts and blue vests on many street corners around town. Some were speaking with passersby. Some had clipboards. Some wore clown makeup. A few did not. Some approached cars and knocked on drivers' windows.

He saw them all over town except on dead end roads. He saw gangs of them walking the painted line in the middle of the street, which made driving difficult. They neither moved nor turned around when he approached them from behind. When he beeped his horn a few turned and the group parted. One of them approached his window and motioned with his hand for Sharpe to roll it down. When he did not and kept driving, a few clowns slapped the side of his car.

He also saw groups of men in black and wearing red capes on a few street corners, with motorcycles parked nearby. He knew who the clowns were and what they represented. But he didn't know the identities of the men in red capes.

Despite his previous intentions, he drove to John's Barroom and found three men sitting at the bar in clown makeup. The bartender didn't seem bothered.

Louise was at the short end of the bar, ignoring the men in makeup. She didn't even look at Sharpe.

He was surprised that, despite his recent intense cravings, he somehow didn't feel like drinking at all. Something had changed in him. Something had shifted. But how long would it last?

He walked to the end of the bar and asked Louise, "Can I buy you a drink?"

She answered without looking at him. "Already got one."

"I want to make sure that Maya's safe."

Louise drank what remained in her glass, turned and looked at him. "I'll have another."

Sharpe motioned to the bartender to bring her another of whatever she was having. Once the drink was in front of her, Louise grasped it with the hand on the far side of Sharpe, as though he might take it away. Still, she did not look at him.

"Whatchoo care about Maya?"

"I want to make sure she's safe."

"Bullshit. You a private cop, and you doin' cop work."

"I'm no kind of cop," Sharpe insisted.

"Maya's safe," Louise says.

"She's with a client? Did you see the guy?"

"Yeah."

"Who?"

"I ain't sayin' who."

"Someone you know? Just tell me it's someone you know…"

"Yeah, someone she know. I got my drink, now get the fuck outta here. You fuckin' wid my bidness."

He went back out to his car and drove to a desolate street where he saw a small group of women smoking along the side of the lumber yard. They were in silhouette because of the streetlights behind them.

A vehicle was pulled over and a woman was leaning into the driver's side window. He saw her walk around to the passenger side, open the door and get in. As he got closer, he saw that the vehicle was a red pickup.

He followed at a distance.

The pickup suddenly sped up and turned a corner.

Sharpe stepped on the accelerator and sped around the corner in pursuit. He found the pickup backing out of a driveway on the left, having just performed a K-turn. The street was too dark for Sharpe to see the face of the driver, but he had no time to think, as the pickup was heading straight for him. He gripped the steering wheel as his mind tried to quickly choose from among his options.

Hold steady. He's just trying to scare you.

He held onto the wheel and grit his teeth, but the pickup wasn't swerving. It was growing larger, filling his windshield, with no move to either side.

He isn't going to swerve!

At the last instant, Sharpe cut the wheel to the right and his car bumped over the curb and onto a lawn and he had to hit the brakes hard, lest he end up in the living room of a green split-level ranch. His car skidded to one side, away from the home's front steps.

A light came on above the front door and a dog began to bark. Moments later the door opened and he heard a man's voice calling back toward the inside of the house.

"Probably a drunk! I don't see any damage, except skid marks on the lawn. Go ahead and call the cops. I don't think the guy's hurt, but who the hell knows—he could be dangerous."

• • •

Junior didn't bother with sex. While it was true that sex was easier after they were dead, the acts no longer interested him. His job in life, in everything, was to do exactly as Mama told him. He was her son, after all, and he was a good son. Junior was proud of that.

He brought the girl to his room as a pretense, since she would expect this. She was suspicious, this one was. She was Mexican or Puerto Rican and said her name was Selena. She was also very young, sixteen or seventeen at most. She hadn't said anything besides her name on the way to the house. She'd laid a hand on his thigh, looked at him once, then turned to look out the window as they drove.

She said nothing as they went inside and just nodded when Junior had said, "Shhh. Mama's here."

She'd smiled then, as though they shared a secret. She apparently understood about being quiet in houses at night because Mama might hear. Maybe that's the way her house was.

But he didn't want to think about that. He didn't want to think about anything except doing what Mama wanted and getting Norman to help with the work in the basement. He hoped Norman was around and awake.

He wished he was faster with his hands. Like one of the others, she saw him when he came at her with the weight. She'd been removing her skirt and was briefly turned away, and he'd leaned to one side and taken one of the five pound weights he kept on the floor on his side of the bed, in easy reach. Then he'd scooted down to the foot of the bed, taken a single step and brought the weight up.

And she'd turned. And screamed.

The scream frightened him because the neighbors might hear.

He realized that putting on some loud music would have covered the screams.

Stupid. Stupid! Stupid, not to have put on music.

But there was Mama, egging him on, saying nothing about the scream or the forgotten music. Maybe she knew he'd take care of that next time.

So he'd hit her again and somehow she'd screamed again. But then he'd hit her in the mouth and the scream disappeared into a gurgling sound, as he smashed in her teeth, and then her nose, and finally her eyes and forehead.

He hoped Norman would be willing to come upstairs and help clean this mess.

But Mama didn't mention the mess, which was a relief.

"Just get her downstairs. Norman's waiting. He'll help. Just take her by the feet, and under your arms. That's right. Good boy. That-away!"

He bumped her down the stairs and just like Mama said, there was Norman, who agreed to come up and help clean the mess, going over everything carefully so they didn't leave a trace, before heading back down for the saw, the bags, the tarps, and the refrigerators.

He would take this one out over a few days, and he'd take her a town or two away. There were several parking lots with piers. Those were probably best.

Once they were done and the basement and upstairs mess were cleaned, he made himself a nice, hot peppermint and chamomile tea. He lay back on the sofa with his head on a cushion and listened to his loop of "Boulevard of Broken Dreams."

He lay there for a while, thinking about what to do with the sheets and blanket and the clothes he'd been wearing. Dumpsters concerned him. Their contents were so out in the open.

An idea came to him. He went to the laundry room and took two black plastic garbage bags from the box, went down to the basement and stuffed the sheets, blanket, and clothing into one of the bags, then stuffed that bag into the other. He brought this out to the car and put it in the trunk. He came back to the garage, found an iron shovel and put that in the trunk too. Then he drove to the beach and parked on one of the side streets, where the street ended and the beach began. He carried the bag and shovel to a section of fence he had cut away and reattached with small segments of coat hangers. The area was infrequently traveled because it was not a beach entrance, but simply a bit of irregular fence that was not so different from the rest of the miles of fence that kept people and animals from wandering onto the beach.

The area was unlit, so he did everything with only the light of the crescent moon to guide him. Once through the fence, he walked a dozen yards to an area between homes and began to dig. He dug deep enough to bury the bag with more than a foot to spare. He laid the bag in the hole, filled it with sand, and used the shovel to even out the top layer of sand so that the spot looked like the surrounding area.

As he drove home he thought about burying the body parts in similar holes on the beach. As he considered this, the girl's face appeared in his mind. He remembered how young she'd looked. She had worn very little makeup, unlike the others, who were older and more heavily made up. This one was little more than a child, with a child's simple innocence.

"Mama," he whimpered, as he tried to push the thoughts away.

Fighting back tears, he drove home, got out of the car and went directly upstairs. He sat down on his bed with his arms crossed over his stomach.

He didn't feel well at all. His breath was fast and shallow, and his skin was taut around his face.

"Mama? This time was different, Mama. It wasn't good." He could feel himself starting to cry.

"Junior…" Her voice had a threatening edge.

"Mama. I don't like this."

"Junior. It's fine. You did good. You did what I—"

"Mama!" he screamed. "She was a fucking child!"

"Don't you ever, ever, EVER use that language with me!"

But this time had been different, and Junior knew he had to do something about it.

Chapter 12

Reuben was looking through his list of clients at Insights. His job at the counseling center required him to wear several hats. He was an ordained minister and chaplain; he performed weddings, presided at funerals, and occasionally spoke to the public when circumstances warranted. He counseled individuals and couples and helped them cope with relationship challenges, financial hardship, addiction, depression, and loss. He visited the sick at several hospitals in the vicinity. He ran support groups, primarily for those with addiction-related issues or who were dually diagnosed. He had been in line to be the next Insights director, but after taking actions that the current director, Melvin, had deemed unethical, he had lost his place in line.

Reuben knew that he was not what many expected of a chaplain. He was a deeply ethical and moral man who believed in doing what was right, whatever anyone else might think. He and his brother, Judah, were cut from the same cloth, and would do whatever was necessary to help and protect the greatest number of people. Reuben was at peace with his values and his choices.

His office phone rang. He picked it up. "Insights."

At first he heard nothing, then breathing, then a man's hesitant voice.

"I need to speak with someone."

"Would you like to see a counselor?"

"Right. A counselor."

"I'd be happy to get that set up. Let's start with your name."

Silence.

"Sir? Are you there, sir?"

"My name."

"Yes, sir."

"My name…is John."

"Okay, John. Your last name?"

"Paper … went."

"Paperwent?" He spelled it back and waited.

"Um, yes. John Paperwent."

"Okay, Mr. Paperwent. Is the number you're calling from the best number for you?"

"The number I'm calling—um, yes. Fine."

"Great. Could you tell me a little bit about why you want to speak with a counselor? Oh, and would you prefer a man or a woman?"

"A woman, please. I—I just need someone to talk to. Someone besides … Mama."

"I understand. I see we have an opening with Arlene Dunn. She's been with us for many years, and I think you'll like her. Would tomorrow at 2 p.m. work for you?"

"So fast?"

"Would you prefer something next week?"

"Um, no. Tomorrow at 2 would be fine. Thank you."

"Thank you, Mr. Paperwent. Is it okay if I call you John?"

But the man had ended the call.

• • •

Reuben arrived home to find the big white house fragrant with sautéed garlic and simmering meat sauce.

He checked the den and found Rachel and Josh watching TV not far from Zeb, who was bent over his computer, its trackball clutched against his chest on the platform desk that was attached to his wheelchair, his arm stationary, fingers flying over the controls.

Reuben went into the kitchen and glanced at Dinah and Raisa, who were on the other side of the room. He took one of the sauce-covered spoons from atop the stove, dipped it into the pan of meatballs and marinara and softly slurped from it.

"Oh, wow," he exclaimed.

Dinah and Raisa were deep in conversation. "Look," Dinah was saying. "I'll read it. But who do they think they are sending such a thing home when they don't know us? They don't know our family." She glanced away from her sister-in-law, took a quick step toward Reuben and ripped the spoon from his hand and slapped his shoulder with her other hand.

"No tasting the sauce!" she admonished him and brandished the spoon. "It's not ready!"

Reuben pretended to cringe away.

The front door opened and Lev appeared in the kitchen doorway, along with a breeze of chilly air. "I found a place for Zeb!" he announced. "Just came from there. It's perfect! And, they have an opening for him."

Dinah's mouth fell open and her hands fell to her sides. "What the fuck, Lev. What the actual…"

Raisa interrupted. "We need to finish—"

"Right," Dinah agreed. She turned back to Lev. "We'll talk about this later. You had no right."

"Aw, c'mon!" he cheerfully countered. "Zeb'll love it, and he'll get great care." When no one responded, he left the room and headed toward the den.

Reuben and his sister exchanged a look of shared impatience.

"I know," Dinah said. "Excuse us, Reub," she added.

"I'll get washed and get the kids," Reuben said.

"Why don't we set up an appointment with the principal and go in together," Raisa suggested, once Reuben had gone.

Dinah's expression showed she agreed. "You'd think someone in the school administration might have a vague idea of what being a parent involves."

Raisa gave two quick nods. "And about childhood trauma."

Dinah speared a meatball with the tines of a long metal fork and used a knife to spread the meat apart. "This is ready. Rai, can you give out the ziti? I'll follow you in with the meat sauce."

"Just a sec." Raisa donned two oven mitts and carried the steaming pot of simmering ziti to the sink and dumped it in a colander. She set the pot back on the stove, turned the burner down, went to the sink and shook the water from the ziti. Then she poured the pasta into a deep dish, helping it along with a large wooden fork. She leaned a spoon into the dish beside the fork and carried it into the great room, where everyone was seated but Izzy, who was upstairs, and Zeb, who was in the den.

"Zebby!" she called. "C'mon, Zeb. Meatballs and spaghetti!"

"Ziti!" Josh corrected at the top of his lungs. The boy often expressed himself at the top of his lungs.

Reuben was at the head of the table, with Lev beside him.

As Raisa began dishing out ziti, Dinah came in with a deep dish filled with meatballs and sauce. She paused and looked at the three empty seats. "Well, I know Jude's working, but come on." She turned toward the den. "Zebby!"

"Okaaay!" came his answer.

Dinah turned toward the stairs and took a single step in that direction. "Israel!" She paused listening. "Izzy!" Then she shook her head, returned to the table, and began ladling out meatballs and sauce. "What do you have to do around here to get people to come to dinner?"

Rachel gave her aunt a solemn look. "Make bwownies."

Raisa smiled.

"Butter!" Josh yelled.

"Butter…?" Dinah prompted.

"Butter, please!" the boy yelled, even louder. Dinah dropped a few slides of butter onto his noodles.

Once everyone's portions were handed out, Raisa and Dinah set the serving dishes on a nearby tray and were seated.

Dinah remembered something and clapped her hands. "Vegetables!" she exclaimed.

"Shit," Josh said, under his breath.

Dinah glared at him, said nothing, got up and went to the kitchen. She returned with a dish of breaded, broiled Brussels sprouts.

"Uh, bitter," Josh said.

"Eat one," Dinah suggested.

"I like them," Rachel announced.

"She can eat mine!" Josh yelled.

"Eat one," Dinah reminded him.

"So, I visited a place that would be great for Zeb today," Lev began, his eyes cautiously roving the faces of the adults at the table.

No one answered.

Dinah said, "Well," and then fell silent and stared at her plate. She speared a meatball, hard, with her fork. It made a scraping sound.

"This is terrific, as always," Reuben remarked.

Raisa cleared her throat. "Something happened with the kids today at school." She glanced at Dinah and something unspoken passed between them.

Lev leaned forward on his forearms. "What happened?"

Raisa said, "Rach, why don't you tell everyone what happened today at school with you and Josh."

"Nope!" Rachel said, emphatically shaking her head. Her frown was so deep her eyes nearly disappeared.

Raisa continued. "What did Mommy tell you when you asked what you were made of?"

Rachel grinned. "Love and light!"

"That's right."

Dinah beamed, surprised and delighted. "That's what our mommy told us many years ago."

"Rachel mentioned this to someone in the schoolyard this morning—someone she thought was her friend."

"Darlene!" Rachel said, her lips pooched in a pout.

"And what did Darlene do then?" Raisa prodded.

Rachel shook her head very fast.

"What did she do?" Raisa asked again.

She shook her head again, her brown braids whirling.

"Rach?"

Rachel answered in one long stream of words. "She made fun of me and told all the girls and they made fun of me too and then the boys made fun of me and then Joshy came and punched a boy and then the bell rang and everyone went in the building and Joshy got in trouble."

Everyone stopped and looked at Rachel—everyone except Dinah, who was looking sadly at Josh.

"Oh, Rach," Reuben said, and covered her little hand with his. "You know we all love you, right?"

She was frozen in place now, and had begun to cry silently, tears running down her cheeks.

"Was anything done about this girl and her friends?" Lev wanted to know.

Raisa shook her head.

Lev looked at Dinah, who said, "They sent Josh home with a pamphlet on 'How Best to Regulate Challenging Children.'"

"Lovely," Reuben said, with an arched eyebrow.

"Isn't it?" Raisa said.

"Violence is never the answer in these situations," Dinah admonished Josh.

"I love ziti with Mary Nary sauce," Rachel yelled suddenly.

"Me too," Josh agreed. "Long as the ziti doesn't have lines."

"That's wight!" his cousin agreed. "Me and Joshy hate ziti with lines!"

"Joshy and I," Lev said.

"You don't like them too, Uncle Lev?" Rachel wondered.

Everyone laughed as Zeb rolled in. "Sahghetti an meatah bolls!" he yelled, as his chair came to a halt at the open space in front of his plate.

Dinah sat down next to him and tied a napkin around his neck.

"Takah offah mah shewt!" he ordered.

"Really?" Dinah asked.

"Yesah!" Zeb confirmed.

"Okay." Dinah removed the napkin from around Zeb's neck and pulled his polo shirt up and over his head.

"Put ih on da bahk," he said.

His sister laid his shirt over the back of his chair.

"Dis mah sahghetti shewt!"

Dinah giggled. "Your spaghetti shirt?"

"It's lovely," Raisa said, smiling.

"You shewd wearah it!"

Raisa gave him a disapproving frown. "You are not getting me to take off my shirt, Zebby," she chided.

"Whyah naht?" Zeb asked, his eyebrows raised and his head shaking innocently.

Dinah fit the fork, complete with speared meatball, into Zeb's fist and helped him guide it into his mouth.

Zeb focused on chewing his food. Then he said, "I'm not going to live in any newsig homah!" He was glaring at Lev.

"It's not a nursing home," Lev said, as he lifted an empty glass. "It's a regular home, just like ours, but it's specially designed for people in your…situation."

"Booshit!"

"It's not bullshit, Zeb. It's the best situation for everyone."

"Yaw mah famblee!" Zeb cried, his voice cracking.

Dinah had filled a fork with ziti and was holding it, poised and ready for Zeb. She laid a gentle hand on his shoulder, but he jerked his head away and turned in the other direction.

"Sure smells good down here." Izzy was standing at the bottom of the stairs, absently scratching his belly through a purple T-shirt.

"Got time to eat or you goin' to work?" Dinah asked; she had laid down Zebby's fork.

"For your meatballs and sauce, I'll make time." Izzy sat down at his place and pulled his chair beneath him. He passed his plate to Raisa, who spooned ziti on and passed the plate to Dinah, who added meatballs and sauce. "Cheese?" Izzy requested.

Josh passed him the parmesan. "Are you playing at the lounge tonight?" he asked.

"I am," Izzy confirmed.

"Can I come and listen?"

Dinah glanced at Reuben, who shrugged.

No one spoke.

"You were in some trouble today, weren't you, Josh?" Lev asked.

Dinah glared at him and he said nothing more. Finally, she said, "Well, the pamphlet does mention music as a good behavior regulator for young people when…"

Raisa finished her thought. "…school wraps them too tight."

• • •

Izzy arrived at the lounge with Josh minutes before he was due to go on. He knew this was frowned upon by Scott Mason, who, as the casino and lounge manager was technically his boss. But what was Scotty going to do? His brother was the owner. Izzy was resigned to the fact that he was habitually late. Anyone he worked with would just have to deal with it.

In another sense, he was grateful that Scotty was the lounge manager. Scotty had accepted him as an opening act when Katy and the previous manager, Connor MacDougal, had been unhappy with his singing. Having Katy, who was herself a singer, and Connor disrespect his singing was more than he could bear, and Izzy had stayed home and watched TV with Zebby for a month before trying to find another gig. Since then, he had played and sung at several nursing homes, and the folks there had loved him. Seniors were terrific audiences. He suspected this was because they were so unhappy so much of the time that any music really sparkled for them. When your body and mind are falling apart, a little music—any music—is likely to brighten your day.

But Katy was gone and Connor had been found murdered in a closet in the hotel's basement, and now he had Scotty to deal with, and Scotty agreed to allow him to play from 7 to 9:30. p.m. now and then as a warmup act—which suited him just fine. He suspected that Scotty had been prodded into this by Judah—also fine by him.

He was delighted that Josh had wanted to come along. The kid was so much like he'd been at that age—open hearted but a magnet for trouble. Izzy was pretty sure that Josh had been labeled ADD by the school. Back in the day, when Izzy's mouth had gotten him in trouble at school, he'd been suspended and given a beating or two and was grounded for a few days. Which was tolerable. He stayed in his room, smoked weed out the window, played video games or watched porn to pass his sentence.

He also practiced piano and worked on his singing. When he played downstairs his parents had yelled at him, "Stop banging on that damn piano!" So he'd played upstairs, and now he was paid to play. Sometimes life did give you lemonade.

He set Josh up at a table in the front to one side of the stage, making sure to leave the center tables free for patrons. He didn't want Josh to attract Scotty's attention, though he knew Scotty would be just fine with Judah's nephew being in attendance.

The audience included a small crowd of regulars, several of whom were in their sixties or seventies, a few more in their fifties and one or two in their forties. The early dinner crowd was a staple at the lounge. They were the oldest of the lounge's patrons, in their eighties, if not older. Judah called them the "broiled fish crowd" because they were health conscious, light drinkers and often ordered broiled fish with vegetables for dinner. This crowd might outlive him, Izzy thought.

He played the music they loved—Sinatra era tunes like "Fly Me to the Moon," "I've Got You Under My Skin," and "You're Nobody 'Til Somebody Loves You." He added Beatles, Stones, Pearl Jam and Dead for the sixties and seventies folks and tunes from later eras for the younger crowd.

Izzy was glad Josh had wanted to come. He'd encouraged Josh's interest in poetry and the boy had written a moving poem for his mother. Now, perhaps he was interested in music. The boy reminded Izzy of the way he'd been at ten or eleven—the trouble was already starting. Creativity had helped him and maybe it would help Josh. Izzy was determined to try to be a positive influence.

As he played the finishing flourishes of "Strangers in the Night," he glanced toward his nephew and saw that a man had sat down beside him and was engaging him in conversation. The man looked familiar. Izzy thought he'd seen him around the lounge before.

When he finished the first of his two sets and took his ten-minute break, he pulled a chair up to the table where the man was sitting with his nephew and put out a hand.

"Izzy Hammer."

The man, who was slight, with small black eyes and dark blond hair that fell in bangs and over his ears and collar, took his hand in a limp handshake. "Walter Gibson."

• • •

"Look at this. He's got his own cable channel."

Judah had just walked into the bedroom in the townhouse he and Raisa shared. Raisa was on the bed, fully dressed with her shoes off, leaning back against a pillow that was behind her head, the TV remote in her hand.

Judah turned toward the TV and saw Clowney's head and chest. He wore his usual white shirt and blue vest and was talking into the camera, punctuating his words with jabs of his index finger.

"That whole portion of the county has been overrun by murderous, thieving, corrupt, rapist Nigerians. And not only that. Not only that! These crafty Africans—you know, Nigeria is in Africa—have convinced, hypnotized is a better word, many of our good citizens to tolerate them, even work with them! We must take back our cities! We must take back our towns! We must take back our gas stations, and we must fight, fight, fight!"

Judah gave an easy laugh. "Do you think anyone besides us is watching this?"

He walked to the side of the bed and turned Raisa's face toward his. They kissed.

"Yeah, I do. He's running Facebook ads that link to this thing. The feed is coming from his website, but he's got a cable channel running from the same feed. People are watching, and, believe it or not, people are supporting what he's saying. People agree with him."

"Probably just bots. Ignore him. He's a politician—well, sort of."

"I can't ignore him. He's crazy and dangerous...but, I've gotta say, I can't stop watching him."

Judah sat down in front of her, blocking her view of the TV. He gently took the remote from her hands and laid it on the night table. Then he lifted her chin and kissed her gently, loving her lips' soft, wet touch. She pressed forward, deepening the kiss and he pulled away, grinning. She looked surprised, so he leaned forward, kissed her, then pulled back. Then did it again.

She reached behind his head and pulled him to her and they kissed, long and deep. She sank back on the bed, and her hand slid to the back of his neck, holding him against her.

"Forgetting him now?" he asked.

"Working on it," she said, as she pulled his shirt from his jeans and slid her hand beneath it and up his back, then down over the back of his jeans.

He sat up and unbuttoned his pants.

"Mommy?"

They both looked toward the door, where Rachel was standing in her pink, lavender and turquoise sunset pajamas, with the big purple "R" on the left chest. She gripped a tiny fistful of the material at the top of her right thigh, and she looked miserable, with tears in her eyes and her lips pouted. "I wet my bed again."

Judah and Raisa exchanged a glance. Raisa sighed as Judah surreptitiously buttoned his pants.

"It's okay, Rach," Judah said. "Wait here. I'll get some dry PJs and we'll put them on."

Raisa said, "No worries, honey. I'll just change your sheets and you'll be dry and comfy before you know it."

"But I already knowd it!" Rachel moaned.

Judah hid his grin, sat on the edge of the bed, and held out his arms for his daughter, who ran to her father, pressed her face to his chest and sobbed.

After a moment, Judah held Rachel at arm's length and ran both hands down the sides of her head, over her ears and shoulders. "Wait here, Rach."

He returned moments later with new underwear and pajamas to find Rachel running her fingers through her hair, which fell over her shoulders, and wrapping a few strands around her index and middle fingers. She grimaced and yanked savagely, pulling the hair out. She rubbed her fingers lightly together, and the hairs fell to the floor. She then twirled a few more strands around her fingers, and yanked them out as well. To Judah, she appeared to be in a trance.

Raisa came in and Judah held a hand up, stopping her. He wanted her to watch.

Eventually, Raisa said, "Rach, honey. Why are you doing that?"

Rachel, who had been staring vacantly, said nothing.

"Rachel?" Raisa's tone grew more severe. "Why are you pulling your hair out?"

Rachel looked blankly back at Raisa. "I'm not," she said.

"Yes," Raisa said. "You are."

She went to Rachel, took her by the shoulders, and turned her around. She examined the top of their daughter's head, using her fingers to move her hair out of the way. "You have a bald spot. You've pulled all your hair out from this area of your head. Why would you do that, Rachel?"

Rachel's face contorted into an angry pout. "I'm not!" she yelled. "I'm not doing that! And why are you so mean, Mommy?"

She ran from the room as Raisa looked helplessly at Judah and said, "She needs her daddy."

Once Rachel was back in her fresh PJs, on her fresh sheets and lying on her side under the covers, Judah went in, sat on the edge of the bed and rubbed her back.

"Do you know who's sleeping now?" he asked. It was a game they played.

Rachel shook her head. "No, Daddy, tell me."

"Well." He began naming her friends. "Judy's sleeping, and Sharon's sleeping, and Latrice is sleeping…"

"Is Joshy sleeping?"

"Well, Josh is with Izzy, listening to his music. But he'll be sleeping soon. But you know who's sleeping? Latrice's dog—what's her dog's name?"

"Vector."

"Vector's sleeping…"

"Jude." Raisa was in the doorway, holding his phone. She whispered, "Rinny Mallach for you."

· · ·

Rinny stood in the doorway to the lounge, watching Izzy, who was on his break. Izzy was sitting at a corner table with his nephew, Joshua, and a little guy with dark blond hair.

"I'm at the lounge," Rinny said, into his phone. "And your brother just finished his first set and he's at a table with your nephew and this little guy. I've seen this guy before. He's been here a bunch of times, and it just clicked in my mind—I think he's the guy who took Jen the night she disappeared."

"I thought Kofi—"

"Yeah, was there at the time, standing by the bathroom, and something happened between him and Jen. Barely noticeable, which is why I didn't think of it or remember it before and I'm sure no one else did. It was a subtle thing, but it was him asking for a date and her saying 'yes.' It was all done with glances and eye contact."

"You think? Really?"

"Yeah. Really. I do."

"And you're looking at him now?"

"He's sitting right in front of me, talking to your brother and your nephew. I'm fucking tell you, man."

"Where's Frank? I want Frank on this. Fuckin' now."

Rinny hesitated. "He's here somewhere. Not sure, exactly."

"I want you to grab my nephew, right away. I don't want Josh anywhere near this guy. While you're talking to me, stay on the phone —grab Josh and tell him Uncle Jude wants to talk to him. Then bring Josh with you and go get Frank. Put Frank on the guy but be subtle. We need eyes on the guy. Get his vehicle and his plate. In fact, tell Frank to follow him home. I want to know where he lives."

"Got it."

"Don't hang up. I want to talk to Frank."

"Okay." Rinny walked to the table where Izzy was sitting with Josh and the little blond guy. "Joshy, your Uncle Jude wants to talk to you." He took the boy by the arm. Josh looked suddenly frightened— not by Rinny's appearance. He knew and liked his "uncle" Rinny. But Rinny, who didn't know his own strength and was often a stranger to nuance, had grabbed him roughly. Josh was also a little bit afraid of his Uncle Jude, though he knew Judah loved him very much. The boy, who was so often in trouble, was afraid he had done something wrong.

Rinny saw his expression and said, "It's okay, Joshy. You're not in trouble." He looked at Izzy and the blond guy. "Excuse us a minute."

He walked Josh through the crowd toward the back of the room in search of Frank James. When he didn't see him immediately, he and Josh continued into the casino.

• • •

Junior had not expected to pick up another girl at the Towson Hotel Lounge, not with that monster watching him. He knew they were on the lookout for him, especially the monster.

But Mama was on the lookout for *them!* He saw the boy sitting by himself, so without giving it another thought, he sat down beside the boy. Maybe he could talk to the boy; he liked children, though Mama usually did not. He had heard this performer, Izzy Hammer, before, and he liked the man's piano playing and singing.

He wanted to hear some music other than "Boulevard of Broken Dreams." He loved the song, but it was his killing song and right now he couldn't bear to think about the things he'd done. Even though he'd taken one of the girls from this place, he thought of it as a safe place. He'd won money here. There were people here. Lots of people, and he could lose himself within them.

He had also come because he had to get away from Coach Taylor. He enjoyed hanging out with Tim, Tyra and Landry and even Smash. But while Coach was a nice guy, he was a little bit scary—too much like the principal of his school had been, and even a bit like his father.

So, Junior decided to leave the house and drive somewhere, and he hadn't known where else to go. He didn't go to the bar because it was too small and they knew him well there. He would stand out. While people had seen him here at the lounge, he didn't think anyone knew what he'd done. He was just a guy, and there were lots of guys here.

As long as he didn't take a girl, he thought he'd be okay. As long as he stayed away from the girls, the monster would leave him alone.

But then the monster came right up to him, which scared the hell out of him. He'd wanted to run, but there had been no time, and nowhere to run to. He thought he'd shit his pants. He really did.

But he hadn't, and the monster had come for the boy.

He wondered why. What did the monster want with the boy?

He said he had the boy's uncle on the phone.

None of this made any sense, but Junior decided he was going to get the hell out of here the very second he could.

And at that moment, for some reason, the last girl appeared in his mind. Selena. In his mind she was alive and she was talking to him, telling him how much he had hurt her. She wasn't the pretty girl she'd been when he first picked her up on the side of the road. Her face was a bloody mess, exactly as he had left her—like the mashed melons from his practice with Mama. Only her mouth was working, saying these horrible things. Telling him how Mama hadn't wanted this. He didn't want to hear any more. He wanted to do something, break something, hurt someone. Anything to stop seeing and hearing Selena.

Make her stop, make her stop, make her shut up!

• • •

Frank James speed walked into the room with Rinny and Joshua not far behind. Izzy was back onstage, wearing his fedora and sitting down behind his keyboard, adjusting the mic.

The table where he, Josh, and the little blond guy had been sitting was empty.

Frank turned back toward Rinny and spread his arms.

Rinny shrugged.

Frank approached Izzy and leaned close to him. "Where'd the little blond dude go?"

Izzy's eyes wandered, then he nodded toward a nearby stage door. "Out there," he said.

Frank opened the door and stepped into the night. The door was a rarely used exit that led to an alley along the side of the building. One end of the alley led to the front entrance and a parking lot beyond. The other led to the rear of the building, the garbage bins and a small employee-only lot.

Frank listened carefully but heard no footsteps. He heard the faint hubbub of people from the direction of the building's entrance. He heard a plane pass overhead. He put his hands on his hips, and, after a few seconds more, returned to the lounge, where Izzy had begun to play and sing "The Wanderer."

Chapter 13

When Sharpe arrived at the Towson Hotel, he found Frank James in the lounge.

"I need to see your brother," Sharpe said, trying to keep the panic out of his voice.

"Join the crowd," Frank said. "He's being held by the police."

Sharpe was surprised. "I thought they'd already interviewed him and he was cleared."

"That's what we all thought," Frank replied.

"What's the charge?" Sharpe asked.

"No charge, as far as I know, but Judah sent a lawyer over there."

"Why would they bring him in again?"

"I guess they think they have something on him," Frank answered. "But they don't. Kofi's the most honest man I know."

"That might not keep him from being arrested. Anyway, I wouldn't think they can hold him long," Sharpe said. "A day, tops."

"That's what we've been led to believe, but who the hell knows?"

Sharpe could see the fear in Frank's eyes, not what one typically saw in the eyes of Judah's men. The fear stemmed, Sharpe thought, from Kofi's being detained by the police, but just as much from something else. Something more nefarious—a creeping climate of fear, like the feeling one had during a horror movie. But this was no movie.

Sharpe got into his car and began to drive. He was willing to ask for help, but the help he sought was in jail at the moment. He drove aimlessly, thinking that there had to be some other source of hope. He thought about all Kofi had explained to him. Words like "surrender" and "powerlessness" and "God" roiled in his skittish mind. Then he had an idea. He pulled over and performed a search on his phone, looking for an online meeting of Narcotics Anonymous. What he found was a list of virtual meetings on a free online platform. He clicked, downloaded an app, and logged in.

Then he began to drive.

He heard a speaker named Richie share his "experience, strength, and hope."

Sharpe could see Richie and some of the other people at the meeting on his phone, which was mounted to an air vent on the dashboard of his car, a two-year-old leased Hyundai Tucson. Richie appeared to be in his sixties, with a brush mustache, gray eyes, and chiseled features. He talked about using drugs against his will and that once he started, he couldn't stop. The drugs took over his brain and took over his life.

Sharpe understood perfectly. He'd been hoping to talk to Kofi again, to reiterate that he was ready to do whatever was necessary to stop the pain, to stop spending so much of his time and energy finding heroin, pills, or some kind of speed to counteract those drugs and bring him up again while maintaining the effect of the opiates. It was all so exhausting.

He'd been stunned to learn that Kofi had been detained by the police and told himself he feared for the man's future.

But he realized suddenly that he wasn't really worried about Kofi. He cared only about himself, about finding a way back up this icy slope of a mountain he was sliding down.

I'm one selfish motherfucker.

As he listened to Richie's story, Sharpe was drawn in. He heard all about the shame and degradation, the self-hatred and remorse, the regret for some of the things the man had done.

Man, you don't know the half of it. Ever kill an innocent man, Richie?

He heard about the solution. He heard about coming to believe in something greater than himself. He heard about God.

And his heart sank.

God? Gimmee a break. God? Look around the fuckin' world, Richie. Tell me, where's God?

And Richie answered as though he was answering Sharpe directly. "You ask where God is with all the wars, the killing, the hatred, the lying, the stealing, the hurt in the world?" Richie asked.

"Exactly," Sharpe said aloud.

"God's right here," Richie answered rhetorically. "God's right fucking here. And guess what else? All that shit. All the killing and the wars, and the murders, and the raping—God's got nothing to do with any of it. Even wars that are fought in God's name. Nothing to do with God. That's people. We've got free will, man. I want to kill my neighbor and I can get away with it, God's not going to step in."

Hmmm.

Sharpe drove up and down the streets of Towson, not sure what he was doing, except listening to Richie talk as though he were right next to Sharpe in the car, speaking to him from his heart.

"The bad shit in the world—much of it anyway," Richie said, "that's us. I'm a dad. I've got sons. They're grown now, but when they were little and they did something wrong…there were consequences, man. And they had to live with those consequences. That's life. And that's the deal with God. Now you don't have to call whatever you believe in God. You can call it a Group of Drug addicts—see, G.O.D. You can call it Good Orderly Direction. You can call it the Gift Of Desperation, because that's what led me to believe in something. I get that we don't just wake up one day believing in some woo-woo thing. Nope. We got to be beat down. We got to be whupped. We got to have the drugs teach us how powerless we are to stop using them before we're willing to believe in something."

I get that, for sure.

"So, you ask. How do I, who never believed in nothing, who have no religion, get to believe. Get to come to believe?"

Tell me.

"I'm gonna tell you. You got to ask. So, what does that mean? It means, literally, ask. Start talking to this power as though it, he, she, whatever, as though it was right there in the room with you. Embarrassed? Okay, do it in the shower, on the bowl, in the car. But do it. Then watch what happens. Pay attention."

Huh.

Sharpe kept driving. Up and down the streets of Towson. He had to remind himself not to drive to those particular, dangerous street corners where he knew drugs were being sold and where his car might be recognized as a buyer. Or, if he did pass one, he had to keep on driving and not stop and roll down his window.

"I'll leave you with this," Richie said. He was apparently wrapping up his share. "Using drugs the way we use drugs, the way addicts use drugs, is like having sex with a gorilla. You're done when the gorilla says so."

And a strange sound came out of Sharpe. He laughed. And laughed. It was the most refreshing laugh he'd had in a long time. He suddenly saw how funny he was. He laughed long and hard, his shoulders shaking, belly quaking. He laughed until he groaned from the pain in his side. His stomach muscles had clenched from the laughter.

So I've got to act like I have a God in my life by talking to him.

"Hello, God," Sharpe said, feeling strange. But no one else was there, so, so what?

"So, God. What am I doing here?"

He continued to drive, and a thought came to him. He was looking for an old, small red pickup—possibly Japanese.

The truck, he realized, could be anywhere. Or nowhere. It could be in another town, or in a garage…

Well, at least I'm not buying drugs…

He had another thought, an epiphany.

A test.

He said, "God, if you're there, if you're really there, you know I'm looking for this red pickup that might belong to a guy who's killing prostitutes. I'm asking two things. Please help me to not use drugs, at least for today. That's the way they say it, right? Just for today? And please help me find the pickup."

He continued to drive. Up one road, down an avenue, into a cul-de-sac, U-turn, back the way he came, along a straight away, up and down the connecting roads.

He was getting sleepy; he thought about getting a coffee, so he pulled into a 24-hour deli. He went in, got a large coffee, came back out. A truck had pulled into the lot. A red pickup. It was big, shiny and new.

He started driving again. Onto streets that were set back—no through streets.

He saw another red pickup. Also new and probably too large.

And another—also not the right one.

The universe was apparently now sending him red pickups.

So God has a sense of humor…

He drove past an elementary school, continued around a residential road and into a nice part of town.

Damn, another one. Wrong, though.

His vision blurred. He drank more coffee. He was in more of a blue-collar neighborhood now. There were stores, shops, fast food joints. Apartments above the stores.

He drove past city hall and the police and fire houses.

Onto crowded residential streets.

He saw the back of a truck that might be right, but it was parked deep into the driveway, and was partially blocked by the house it belonged to.

He drove around the block and approached the house more slowly.

He noted the number.

He drove around the block once more and parked a half block away. He got out of his car and walked to the house with the might-be old red truck.

It looked right.

He stepped closer and noted the truck's plate number.

It was indeed an old red pickup. A Nissan Frontier.

"Hey! Something I can do for you?" A man in a white T-shirt was leaning out of the second-floor window of the house next-door.

"Maybe," Sharpe said. "I'm looking to buy a truck like this one." He tried to sound embarrassed. "I can't afford a new truck, but this is just what I'm looking for. Small, and not new, and looks to be in decent condition. Any chance you could tell me how to get in touch with these folks so's I could ask?"

"Best to ring the bell, but I'd do it around dinner time, and not today. Probably too late now, and the fella who lives here might not be around during the day."

"Oh, so he works?" Sharpe paused. "What's his name?"

The man was suddenly suspicious. "How do I know you on the up and up?"

Sharpe held up a hand. "I understand, man. No worries. I'll come back and ring the bell. Sorry to worry you, sir. Thank you." He turned to go.

"I'll tell you his first name. Walter."

Sharpe opened the door to his car and the dome light came in. He slid in behind the wheel and looked up at the light. "Well," he said, in the direction of the light. "Thank you, I guess."

• • •

Raisa's phone rang with the ringtone she'd assigned to Mason Marx, the *Gazette*'s news editor, and her immediate superior.

"What's up, Mason?"

"I need to you go over to the campgrounds and interview Clowney."

"Why?"

"He's making a statement and he doesn't want to hold a press conference."

"Oh, really. Do you think he expects a friendly interview?"

"I'm not in the mind-reading business, Raisa. Just get over there and interview him. Unless you'd rather I send Joanne."

Raisa gave a derisive huff. "I'd rather Joanne stay on her side of the street and cover the music scene."

"Well, then. Get going."

She drove the ten minutes to the campgrounds, parked, and was met by a handful of clowns led by the security leader, the brown-haired clown in a denim jacket, khaki shorts and sandals.

"You the reporter?"

"Raisa Tolleson."

"Come on, then."

Raisa followed the clown to the green awning that was affixed to one of the campers, beneath which Clowney was relaxing in his yellow beach chair, drinking a beer.

"Ah, the press is here," he said, waving Raisa to another beach chair. "Can I offer you a beer?"

"You can offer, but I can't accept."

"Suit yourself."

"What did you want to talk about?" Raisa took out her phone. "Mind if I record?"

Clowney extended a hand, palm outward. "Please do. Better to get my wording right, so we don't have to fight about it later."

Raisa sat down and started the voice recorder on her phone. "Go ahead. We're rolling."

"The election's coming, and we've got work to do. A lot of work. Big work. We are having another rally, this one tomorrow night, and this rally's going to be different. We're going to have a rally against murder: R.A.G."

"Rally against murder," Raisa repeated. "What exactly is that? What does it mean?"

Clowney sat forward in his chair so suddenly that Raisa flinched. "It means, dear reporter, that we've had murders in this town. Several of them. Possibly a serial killer."

Raisa groaned inwardly. Marx would not appreciate that phrase being used, and both Chief Green and the mayor would be incensed. In any case, the phrase did not technically apply until there was a third victim of the same M.O.

Clowney's voice rose in anger and volume. "It means that we have lawless elements running rampant over Towson and our county. It means that people are living in fear because they are unprotected. It means that people like your husband, young lady, are preying on our citizens, our residents, our voters! And it's got to stop!"

Raisa was so taken aback that, for a moment, she didn't know what to say. Finally, she said, "I'm not married."

Clowney's response was simply a knowing grin and raised eyebrows.

As she drove back home, she made a decision and began dictating into her phone.

"This is an editorial sidebar to be posted alongside the Clowney interview. Both articles are to be posted after they're proofread and Mason has approved them. In his interview today, candidate Clowney references lawlessness. But it is Clowney himself who is the source of much lawlessness locally. Yes, there have been these horrific murders, and the police have not yet identified the perpetrator or perpetrators. This writer hopes and expects that they will soon do so. This is a police matter, not a matter for the public to take into their own hands, nor one that invites grandstanding from would-be public servants. Clowney has incited lawless action against some of our citizens who happen to be of Nigerian ancestry. *This* is lawlessness. His thugs are accosting people on street corners, bullying them into signing petitions where they give their personal information and promise to vote for Clowney. Now if people were to give such information voluntarily, and I suspect that Clowney will say that is, in fact, what is occurring, that might be acceptable. But that is not what is going on. Clowney's thugs are accosting, bullying, abusing and confronting people and essentially forcing them to guarantee him their votes. We are seeing gangs of blue vests roaming our streets at all hours of the day and night, and it is these blue vests, it is Clowney's own people who are making our city unsafe. So this writer is here to say that Clowney's Rally Against Murder is a sham, a showboating, grandstanding play for your votes, and a blatant power grab!"

. . .

Arlene Dunn had been a practicing psychotherapist with Insights for nineteen years. Previously, she'd been with the now defunct Regis Counseling Center for twelve years. She was a small, tightly contained woman of 65, with hair she would continue to dye black until the day she died. When she looked in the mirror, she could still see the spritely adorable girl hiding beneath the wrinkles that had begun to dominate her features. She never left her apartment without being certain she was fashionably dressed, subtly made up, carrying the right pocketbook and wearing the right shoes for her outfit. She was a model professional.

She liked working at Insights because she liked working with Melvin and Reuben. Both were counselors and yet both were men of God. Melvin was an interfaith minister and Reuben a chaplain. While she had no official religious title, she was a practicing Christian and proud of it, though she would never think of saying so to any of her clients.

Arlene based her judgments of clients on multiple criteria, including their intake information, medical histories, self-provided information and her reaction to their presentation and affect. She also had developed finely tuned antennae she had learned to trust.

John Paperwent was not a big man. He was, to her eye, perhaps five feet six inches tall, if that. He couldn't weigh more than one hundred fifty pounds. He was not overbearing, loud or threatening in manner. Quite the contrary. He was soft-spoken and diffident. So why, she asked herself, was she a little bit afraid of him?

He wore casual black slacks and a light blue dress shirt. His shoes, she noticed, seemed out of place. One would have expected dress shoes of some kind, loafers or oxfords, but he wore hiking boots— rather dirty hiking boots. *Odd.*

She relegated the question to a back corner of her mind as she had him sign the required disclosure statement that explained the limits of confidentiality. John signed the document without reading it, and they began their first session.

She sat back in her chair and put on her work smile, which was polite and blank, ready to morph into an encouraging expression of sympathy, depending on her client's emotional state.

"Tell me a little bit about your life."

"What would you like to know?" John looked steadily back at her.

He had a rather disturbingly direct way of looking, not exactly at her, but into her. She took a breath. "Do you live in a house or an apartment?"

"A house." His eyes remained on hers. He hadn't blinked yet. Not once.

"Do you live with anyone?"

"I live with my mother and my brother Norman."

"I see." She folded her arms over her stomach. "Do you mind if I ask if your father passed away?"

He didn't answer.

"John?"

No answer.

"John?" she prodded.

He was looking toward the window, which was open several inches at the bottom. "Oh, right. My father passed away."

"I'm sorry to hear that." She added a hint of sympathy to her tone, but not too much. A good therapist is careful to avoid emotional entanglement or transference.

"Thank you."

"Would you like to tell me about your mother?"

He frowned and looked taken aback. He blinked. Several times. His eyes filled with tears, and he wiped his sleeve across his eyes.

"What would you like to know?"

"Does she work?"

He shook his head.

"Do you get along?"

He didn't answer.

"John?"

No answer.

"John?"

"Um, yes, as long as I do what she says. She sometimes yells." He frowned again. Something was going on in there. Then he smiled. "I'm a good son."

She smiled back. "I'm glad to hear that. And you're happy?"

He nodded.

"What about your brother?"

"Norman."

"Do you get along with him?"

He nodded.

"Does he work?"

Another nod. "He's a mailman."

"Okay. John, you've reached out to us for a reason. Would you like to talk about that?"

He frowned, paused, and shook his head.

"Was something upsetting you? Is that why you wanted to talk with us?"

He didn't react. Finally, he nodded.

"Would you like to tell me what it is? Or was?"

"Maybe." He bit his lower lip. "Not yet. There are some things."

"Some things?"

"Some…not good things."

"Okay. That's quite all right, John. You're safe here. We can discuss whatever it is at whatever rate you're comfortable with."

"Is everything we talk about here—private?"

"It is." She sat forward, her elbows on her knees. "It's okay to talk to me about anything. Really. It's private. No one will know."

A small smile crept onto his face. "Really? No one will know? Really?"

"That's right."

"But they could make you tell, right?"

She could feel he needed encouragement, and confidence in her. "No, John. They couldn't make me tell."

"So, everything I say will be our secret?"

She nodded, holding his eyes with hers. "That's right, John. Our secret."

Chapter 14

Detectives Gold and Cortez were standing and waiting uncomfortably, while Chief Green stepped from the office to ask someone to bring in a few more chairs.

When he returned and went around to stand behind his desk, the chief smiled and said, "We're expecting quite a party."

"A party?" Gold asked.

Green's smile disappeared. "It'll be anything but." His eyes flicked back and forth between the two detectives. "You're still holding that suspect, James, right?"

The detectives glanced at one another. Gold shook his head. "Kofi James? No. We let him go."

Chief Green looked alarmed. "Why the hell did you let him go?"

Gold looked mildly back at him. "Nothing to hold him on."

Green's lips disappeared as he pressed them together. "Holding him was important, damn it!"

"Yeah," Gold said sardonically. "For PR purposes." He shook his head. "Sorry, Chief."

Cortez gave her partner an appreciative glance.

Green looked unhappy, but only briefly, as the chairs arrived and the detectives sat. Green remained standing as the door opened and a broad smile broke across his face. The expression was so unlike him that Cortez had to stifle a giggle.

An intense young woman with short, dark hair, and wearing a black business suit and a single strand of small pearls swept into the room followed by a middle-aged man who radiated movie star good looks. He was a man who instantly captured the attention of everyone in any room as soon as he entered. He was the county executive, Blake Berkowitz, and he'd been preceded by his chief of staff, Marcia Linklatter. Behind them, occupying the same jet stream, were Mayor Stafford and his assistant, Zane Larson.

Stafford was every bit the political animal Berkowitz was, but of a lower, less subtle order. His naked ambition and self-perceived superiority were more apparent than those of Berkowitz, who hid such attributes behind a genteel businessman's façade. Stafford's features were more prominent, his nose wider and thrust farther forward, his teeth enormous white gates that led to an all-consuming mouth that spouted platitudes of whatever he thought would move him forward and closer to his goals—to campaign funds, committee support, votes, and the approval of whomever was in his vicinity.

Cortez couldn't help but be buffeted by what felt like waves of competitive, aging testosterone, and all of it clamoring for attention. A political pissing contest. All she needed, she thought wryly, was popcorn.

Everyone sat except Berkowitz, who stood with his back to the door, at once commanding everyone's attention and blocking their escape.

"This is an emergency ad hoc save-the city-committee—unofficial, of course, since none of you can acknowledge that this meeting took place." He was the picture of the focused statesman, and his assistant glared at everyone in turn, her head thrusting slightly forward in little bursts, like a blackbird pecking at its prey. She was making sure everyone was paying her boss rapt attention.

"First order of business—get something on Clowney. You were all apprised of today's agenda. Does anyone have anything we can work with?"

Chief Green raised a hand and Berkowitz widened his eyes in his direction while Marcia Linklatter zeroed in on him.

Green said, "As soon as I saw the email, I put my research investigatory team right on it. I'd like to bring in my team leader, if that's okay."

"Please do," Berkowitz said.

Cortez smiled to herself. She knew that there was no research investigatory team—only a few desk jockeys with a rudimentary understanding of databases. Still, even basic skills could be of formidable use.

Green picked up the receiver of his office phone and spoke quietly into it. Moments later a slender, coffee-colored man with black circles around his eyes entered the room.

"May I sit behind your desk?" he politely asked Green.

Green stood aside and said, "This is Zahir Tiwari, one of our information research experts."

The man smiled and took a seat behind Green's desk and began typing and clicking. Soon he looked up.

"Clowney's name is Tagill—easy enough to get via the election commission. He used to live here in Towson with a wife, whom he left years ago, when he got involved in politics. But that's not all he did. He's in the National Crime Information Center database. Eleven years ago, he was arrested for killing a girl, a prostitute. He hired her and allegedly got violent with her. But during the attack, the girl called 911, and when EMS got there, she was dead. He said she fell and hit her head, but the medical examiner argued that, given the call, it was probably a homicide—that he hit her with a blunt instrument, a lamp maybe. The murder case was weak, and yet, the jury didn't buy that it was accidental, and he pled to involuntary manslaughter."

"So, Clowney's a felon." Berkowitz looked thoughtful; his assistant, Linklatter, looked beatific. She inclined her head toward her boss and spoke softly.

"I agree," Berkowitz said, turning to the others. "We need to get the press this information. Let them put it out there and hammer home to the public the truth about this crooked clown. Green, I'm trusting that you and your colorful force—" he smiled at his pun referencing Green and Gold "—can convince the local papers and maybe the county-wide news folks to run with the ball. My team will hand it off to the big guns, state- and maybe nationwide, and we'll blast this grinning asshole out of the water. You with me?"

• • •

Raisa was up late, working on a comprehensive article with the headline "Convict Clowney!" Along with the article, she wrote another editorial sidebar explaining what that meant for the election and the future of Towson. Judah had agreed to take the children to the bus. To Raisa, he seemed unusually tense, but Judah never discussed his business; better if she didn't know the details, given the illegal, often violent nature of his work.

She awoke at 8 a.m., after four hours of sleep. After a few minutes in the bathroom, she padded to the kitchen, her iPad under her arm, to make herself a cup of coffee.

She opened her *Gazette* app and read her article and editorial with satisfaction. The negative and inflammatory comments from the public, if that's really where they originated, irked her, and she wished Mason would shut off the comments feature of the *Gazette*'s website. She suspected the comments' authors were bots, bought and paid for by Clowney.

She put down the iPad and thought about Rachel. The bedwetting and hair pulling were signs of trauma connected to the kidnapping of the previous year. For a little girl who had only just discovered her daddy to be ripped away from both parents, not to mention a house full of uncles, an aunt and a cousin, had to be utterly devastating. The question was, what could she do about it?

An answer appeared in her mind.

Leave Judah.

It had been her go-to solution for years, the one that regularly bubbled up for her—but it wasn't anymore. They had committed to one another as a couple—and with Rachel, as a family.

She pushed the thought away as the phone app on her iPad rang. She saw who it was, realized her phone was still on her night table, and took the call with her iPad.

"Hey, Dinah," she said.

"Great article! So, Clowney's a crook! Who'd have thought?"

"Guilty of manslaughter. Skated on the murder."

"But, come on! People will see what a sleaze he is and they won't vote for him."

"Hope you're right."

"How's Rach?"

"I'm worried about her."

"Did she wet last night?"

"Not last night. But the night before. And two out of three nights before that. I need to buy more sheets."

"She's going to grow out of this. She's not going to go to college wetting her bed."

Raisa took a breath. "Ye-ahh. How's Joshy?" She could hear papers rustling on the other end of the line.

"Let me read you part of something," Dinah said. "It's from the pamphlet the school sent home with him."

"Is that how you think of him? As a difficult kid?"

"It's how the school thinks of him, and I do find him difficult—though I also adore him. Listen—actually, no. I don't want to read it to you. I'll just start crying, but I can tell you. They're saying he's suspended because of persistent 'oppositional defiant'—their words—behavior, and will only readmit him with a note from a psychotherapist, and they're saying I have to take him to their therapist, and bring a note as proof."

"You going to do it?"

"What are my options? The kid is taking over my life."

"He's his father's son, I guess."

Dinah's tone suddenly darkened. "Do not ever bring that man up! *Ever!*"

Raisa realized her mistake.

"I'm sorry," Raisa said. "I'm sorry."

"Do you know the kid watches porn? Doesn't even hide it! And he hasn't even hit puberty! What the hell is he doing with porn?"

"Maybe he has hit puberty. Early."

"I don't know which way to turn. I feel like sending him away somewhere—boarding school or something."

"Don't do that, Dinah. He's your son, my nephew, Jude's nephew. He's got his uncles as influences…"

"They're part of the problem. Reuben's a chaplain, but he also killed a guy and thinks he's right for doing it. Lev is, well, Lev, and Izzy's hammered half the time…"

"Izzy's also been a good influence."

"Hmm. Yeah, I kinda see what you mean. Got Josh into poetry, and that poem he wrote me—uh, makes me cry. And Josh went to one of his gigs. Did you know that?"

"Really? Hey, what do you think about Lev wanting to put Zeb in a home?"

"Zeb'll never go. Or it'll be kicking and screaming," Dinah said. "Well, his version of it."

"How's our Zebby doing?"

Dinah laughed. "Really into his computer. More than the TV now. He still stays in front of the TV, but he's bent over the computer and his trackball, whaling away at something, like all the time!"

"But Lev's still intent on sending him someplace," Raisa said.

"I think so, and I can see why. Zeb's a project. Fills diapers as fast as we can change them, eats, doesn't eat, has emotional issues, lower intestine issues, occasional breathing issues. Sometimes needs a feeding tube or a catheter, none of which is fun. And he's not getting the stimulation he should have—no physical therapy, occupational therapy, maybe even education or, hell, job training that might be available."

Raisa asked, "You think Zebby could work?"

"He's smart as a fucking whip."

"But he'll be mad as fuck if we try to send him anywhere."

"Yeah," Dinah agreed. "He'd have to be restrained."

• • •

An alert on his computer screen drew Gold's attention. He stared for a moment and barked an order to Cortez. "We need to get to Sherman's office, now. We have a third victim."

"Shit," Cortez said. She was thinking of the chief, the mayor and the county exec, and the heat all three would bring down on her and Gold. She could see the sweat already shining on his bald head as he rose, slung his blue blazer over his shoulder, and waited for her.

Linwood Sherman was a small, gaunt ghoul of a man with thinning gray-brown hair, watery eyes above black bags, and a yellowish complexion. He walked with a stoop and spoke with a high, cracking voice. He looked to Cortez like a mad scientist in a horror movie, which was, in a sense, what he was.

He smiled as though harboring a secret. "Come, look at this," he said, in an asthmatic wheeze.

He led them to a long table, which often held a body. Today it held a small, brown foot, connected to the bottom part of a leg, severed below the calf. "A woman," he said. "I would say young, twenties, perhaps." He pointed to something shining on the arch. "Ankle bracelet. I'd venture to say it remained with the foot because someone wanted it there."

Cortez gazed at the tendons and muscles that had been sliced through at the top of the foot and folded her arms across her chest; she was suddenly nauseous.

Gold frowned. "You'd venture to say?"

Sherman said, "I know. That's your job. I was speaking off the record, of course."

"The shit's gonna hit the fan," Cortez said.

"Got that right," Gold agreed.

Cortez thought of something. "Whatever happened with the ATM pics?"

Gold looked at her, disappointment on his face. "There are a ton of pics, but nothing with any of the deceased women in them."

They returned their attention to the foot. Gold said, "Let's find out if any more young women have been reported missing."

Cortez asked, "Does the chief know about this?"

Sherman nodded. "I'd stay away from him, if I were you. He's not a happy camper."

• • •

Judah was in the master bath of the townhouse, trimming his beard. He leaned closer to the mirror. *Was that gray?* Using his finger-tips, he moved some hairs around to get a better look. It was not only gray, but more than the individual hair or two he had seen previously.

"Unbelievable!" Raisa exclaimed. She was on the bed, laptop on her thighs.

Judah went to the door, scissors in hand, eyebrows raised.

"I know it hasn't been a day, but you'd think there'd be an outcry about Clowney being a convicted felon."

"And there isn't? Where are you looking?"

Raisa looked up from the screen, her expression one of grim dismay. "Towson-related Facebook pages, Mom groups, local news groups. Freakin' nothing."

"What about the *Gazette* page where the article appears, or the paper's Facebook page?"

"The *Gazette* doesn't have a Facebook page where you can comment. You can only comment on the web pages where the articles appear, and there the comments support him, saying his conviction isn't a big deal and is a distraction from what's really important."

"Which is what?"

"The Nigerians who own gas stations and others who are stealing jobs from real citizens. Listen to this... 'You are a filthy woke rag that enables foreign ownership of goods and services that are ours by right. Towson businesses should be owned and patronized by Towsonians, not immigrants. Look at all the stores, shops, and businesses we have that are run by immigrants. That's the problem, not some past issue this patriotic candidate had to deal with. Hey, he got rid of another whore—not a bad thing, is it?'"

"That's crazy." Judah gestured with the scissors. "Whatever their heritage, the people who run those businesses are citizens of Towson, as far as I know. Unless they come from one of the surrounding towns."

"And there are people arguing with each other on the page. Some are saying just what you said. Some are saying everyone's an immigrant, if you're not Native American. Then others are saying, 'Yeah, but our families were legal immigrants, not illegals.' Then still others are saying 'They can make laws anytime to make anyone illegal. Immigrants come here, then make laws to keep others out.'" She shook her head. "I've gotta stop reading this shit."

Judah grinned. "Except it's your job to read it." His phone, which was on the night table, buzzed. "Can you get that?" he asked. "I need to finish in here." He returned to the vanity and resumed his hunt for gray. He could hear Raisa speaking.

"What? Oh, my God!"

Judah turned from the mirror to find Raisa rushing toward him, holding the phone out to him.

"The casino's on fire!"

Judah grabbed the phone. "Tell me," he said.

He heard Frank James, who sounded breathless. "I'm out front. Some kind of explosive device went off near the front entrance, which started a fire there, that spread to the hallway. And there was also an explosion on the top level of the parking lot, by the boosted cars."

"Was anyone—?"

"We evacuated after the first one, but I can't say for sure that everyone got out. The firefighters handled that, so I don't know for sure."

"I'm on my way." Judah ended the call as Raisa wrapped her arms around his middle. He turned and folded her in his arms and held her.

"Jude," she whispered. "I'm scared."

He was scared too, but held Raisa and said, "It's gonna be okay. We'll be fine. We'll all be fine."

When Judah arrived at the hotel, he found police and three fire engines in front of the main entrance and another at the far side of the parking lot. The near side of the lot was clear, so he drove in and parked in his designated spot. He emerged from his car and began walking toward the street exit.

"Hey asshole," someone yelled from behind him. He turned just in time to see the crowbar whipping through the air toward his face. A flash of light and a bolt of pain and then…nothing.

He knew he'd been unconscious but was pretty sure he couldn't have been out for more than a second or two, because he found himself looking up at two guys in clown makeup, wearing white shirts and blue vests. He couldn't tell if he'd seen them before; the makeup made identification difficult, except something was familiar about the clown who was speaking to him, and it was a moment before he figured out what it was.

"How d'ya like your medicine, ass bag?" the clown was saying, as he launched the first of two brutal hammer fists down on the bridge of Judah's nose.

Before everything went black again, he was aware of what was so familiar about this clown. The bottom of the man's left ear, the lobe, was missing. The last time Judah had seen that ear, it had been whole and sported a tiny swastika tattoo on the lobe.

• • •

"Junior," Mama said. "I don't want you talking to that woman."

Junior looked at the floor, and didn't answer.

"That's a bad thing you did, telling her about us."

"I didn't tell, Mama. I didn't—really!"

"Junior, I'm warning you. We may have to pay her a visit."

"I understand. I won't talk to her, Mama. We don't need to—"

Mama interrupted, changing the subject. "I found just the thing for us," she said, sounding excited. "This is going to make the next part of the list so much easier and it will bring us closer to the ultimate goal."

"What did you find, Mama?"

"We're going on a trip, Junior," Mama announced.

"A trip? What kind of a trip? In a plane?"

"We're going to a place right here in Towson."

Junior heard a noise from outside and glanced toward the window. "I don't understand, Mama. Why do we need to go on a trip if we're already here?"

"You'll see, Junior. I found something that's going to help us with the list, and you're going to help me set it up. Oh, it's just so perfect, and we're so lucky that I found it!"

"I can't wait to hear, Mama! Can Norman come? Can he? Please?"

"Oh yes, he can. We're going to need his help cleaning up the mess."

Following Mama's instructions, Junior used a fake name and photo to create a profile in the RentUrPlace app, and booked the room Mama told him to book. The profile was not required to be confirmed if the guests paid in advance, which they did. Mama explained that they booked two days because they would need a little time to figure out the lay of the land, as she called it, and decide on a plan of action. They wouldn't have to pack much: a spray bottle of bleach, some rags, some large garbage bags, the saw, a pair of scissors, a folded section of tarp, one or two good kitchen knives, and a ten-pound weight.

A little vacation! This was going to be so much fun!

• • •

The red truck was in the driveway, so Sharpe did his best to remain entirely silent as he sat outside the window, listening to the conversation inside. He heard two voices but couldn't see who was talking. He couldn't hear very well, so he shifted his position to get closer to the window—and stepped on a twig, which snapped.

The conversation inside stopped and Sharpe froze. He forced himself to breathe slowly and quietly through his nose, while remaining perfectly immobile.

The conversation began again. They were planning something, but Sharpe couldn't tell what it was. It sounded like they were planning a trip.

Robin had looked up the owners and residents of the home via a combination of property records, voter rolls, and DMV data, and found that it had belonged to a Charles M. Gibson, who had been deceased for more than twenty years. The house and land had been inherited by his wife, Mildred. Also listed on the property was a Norman and a Walter, but whether they lived there now, Sharpe had no way of knowing.

He did know that he needed to get inside to take a look around and investigate further. This trip they were planning might provide exactly the opportunity he required.

Without moving his feet, he silently rose, then gently lifted his left foot and, glancing to that side, carefully stepped to a spot of open grass that was free of dry leaves. He took another careful step, then jogged to his car and returned to the office, letting the new information about the Gibsons and their local vacation percolate in his mind.

• • •

"I know this is a challenging subject for you, John, but what can you tell me about your family history?" Arlene Dunn clasped her hands together in her lap and watched his face.

"I-I'm not sure I should be here." John looked frightened.

The therapist used her most soothing voice. "You're safe here, John. I promise you."

"Well," he said. "We used to go on trips." His face had relaxed into peaceful pleasure at the memory. "We went to lakes and me and Norman went swimming. We went to zoos. We went to parks." He smiled.

"So you went with Norman and who else?"

John frowned. "With Mama and Papa." He smiled again. "We had picnics at picnic tables, with sandwiches and brownies and soda."

"That sounds really nice. What happened when you got a little older?"

John's expression darkened. "Mama got sick and Papa left and then we got another daddy."

Arlene nodded and asked. "So your first father was Papa and your second was Daddy?"

John frowned and his lower lip trembled and curled above his upper lip. He slowly shook his head.

"I'll tell you what," Arlene said. "I have another idea. Tell me how you're feeling today."

John's features were clenched and his breath came noisily from his nose. "Can't. Scared," he mumbled.

"Okay," Arlene said, encouragingly. "That's okay. You're scared. We all get scared sometimes. Life can be scary for us all. But look at me, John. Come on. Look at me."

He wasn't looking at her. He was looking out the window.

She let it go. "That's okay, John. Take a minute. Just breathe. You're safe here. You're safe. It's okay. Be here. Right here. Right now. And breathe, and know you're safe."

His features unclenched a little. He looked at her, blinking a few times. Then a half dozen times, rapidly.

"It's okay if you need to cry, John. You can, you know."

"No crying!"

Arlene Dunn was jolted by the voice that had barked from John's mouth. It hadn't sounded like John. His face had changed from that of a frightened, cowed man, to an angry...something else. Some*one* else.

"John? Are you okay?"

He nodded, blinking, frightened again. "I'm...scared," he said; he was calmer now.

"What are you scared of?" the therapist asked.

"Of what we're going to do," he said. "It's bad," he said, blinking back tears again. "Really bad."

Arlene took a deep breath, not sure she wanted to hear more. But she had to ask. "Tell me."

• • •

259

A sea of people stood in the chilly November air in front of City Hall, spilling onto the side streets and the main avenue beyond. Vendors sold hot dogs, coffee and hot chocolate.

Clowney had been venting for twenty minutes, a litany of grievances, aimed at the system, and, more specifically, at Mayor Stafford and his supporters.

"He's a crook. It's as simple as that. And he's in bed with a gangster. It's been that way for years. First Slimy Stafford's father, Slimy Senior, was in bed with the crooked banker, Hateful Harmful Horrendous Horrible Hammer. And now Sleazy Stafford's in with Jaded Judah Hammer, a known racketeering crooked criminal."

The crowd booed. Some yelled angry epithets.

"And it gets worse! Now Sneaky Shady Scandalous Stafford is allowing a serial killer—a serial killer!—to run loose! Something must be done. Something! Must! Be! Done!"

The crowd cheered and screamed.

"And Clowney's the answer!" he cried. "Clowney's the answer!"

The crowd chanted along with him, "Clowney's the answer! Clowney's the answer!"

Groups of young men in the crowd were screaming something unintelligible and pumping the air with their fists. Some saluted with open hands, palms down, spearing the air as they yelled.

"How many more murders must there be before something is done?" Clowney bellowed. "How many? We don't have to stand for it.

We won't stand for it! And the Hammer criminal empire has got to go! Stafford out! Hammer out! Clowns in! Clowney in!

Two long school buses pulled up on the avenue beyond the crowd and big men in jeans, white shirts and blue vests began pouring from their doors. They carried wooden bats, metal saps, and telescoping batons. They poured into the crowd, which swelled and roiled.

"I have two special guests with me," Clowney continued. He held up a hand, quieting the crowd.

"This is Jason Hamilton, the father of Rebecca, one of the murder victims."

The crowd roared and cheered.

"And this is Harriet Teitlebaum, whose daughter, Jennifer, was also a victim. Let's show these folks some love!"

The crowd went wild. They cheered for five whole minutes before Clowney could continue. "Now Harriet is too shy to speak, but Jason would like to say a few words. Jason?"

Jason stepped to the microphone, glanced at Clowney who urged him on.

"Somewhere out there," he said. "My daughter's killer is still running free. That's evidence that the police aren't doing enough." His voice cracked, then grew stronger, as his words were driven by emotion. "We have a serial killer, people, and the police simply aren't doing what it takes to bring this murderous scumbag to justice!"

Clowney grabbed the microphone. "Thank you, Jason. Jason Hamilton, everybody!" He waited until the cheering died down. "Did you know," he said, quietly. "That there's a third girl? That's right. A third victim. And where are the suspects, I ask you? Where? I don't see them. No one's been arrested. And meanwhile, we have outsiders running our economy. We have Nigerians owning our gas stations. Have you seen what the price of gas is? Have you been to our shops? Do you see who's behind the counters. And all the while, we have a murderer, a serial killer running loose! I ask you, what is happening to our city?"

The crowd was in a frenzy. Shouting, screaming.

"We need to take back our city! We need to fight, fight, fight!"

The crowd erupted, bursting from its seams, as residents ran in all directions. Led by young men and the blue vests, they rushed in every direction—up and down streets, toward the retail establishments and gas stations, and up the steps of City Hall.

They picked out retail shops chosen beforehand. They stormed through the entrance of City Hall, pushing past security and the two uniformed officers, who pleaded with them to calm down and wait outside. They rushed up the stairs and into the hallway leading to the mayor's office. They poured into his outer office.

The office was empty; the mayor and his staff were not there.

The owners of the retail shops targeted by the mob were not so lucky. Stores were ransacked and pillaged; the owners were dragged from beyond counters, beaten and kicked and left on the floors of their shops, terrified and bewildered.

Much the same fate befell the employees of three of Towson's gas stations. While the owners were not present, the onsite employees were attacked and beaten, and left bruised and bloodied.

• • •

"You wouldn't believe what's going on downtown!" Dinah yelled into the phone.

Judah, who was flat on his back in bed with an icepack on his forehead, didn't have his sister on speaker, but he could have heard her even if he'd put the phone down. She was agitated and frightened, and when she was like that, she got even more intense than usual.

"It's, it's, it's a riot. They're looting and beating the living shit out of people in the street, dragging store owners from their shops. It's like some Armageddon flick!"

"Who is? Who's doing this?"

"Who?" Dinah shouted. "People. I don't know. Just…people who attended this Rally Against Murder thing. And a lot of these blue vest guys. Jude, I'm telling you—the cops are overwhelmed. There's hardly any of them here, and I think some might even be part of the riot. Is there any way you can get some guys over there?"

"Fuck," was all he could think to say. "I don't see how."

"And listen to this: a bunch of them broke into City Hall. Just went in the front door, which was open since they hadn't closed for the day, blew past the guy at the desk, ran up the stairs or took the elevator—"

"Which?"

"Which what?"

"Did they take the stairs or the—never mind. Go on."

"Both. Stairs and elevator, and guy at the desk rang the cops on the fourth through sixth floors, where the clerk is and the mayor's office is and the court—and they have the metal detectors and all—and the cops were waiting with guns."

"So, what happened?"

"They went back down, but they took over the lobby. The desk guy bolted, and I don't blame him."

"Lucky he didn't have a heart attack." Judah ran a hand down his face, trying to focus, but finding it difficult. "So, about getting some guys over there."

Raisa was glaring at him, hands on her hips, from the bathroom door. She was bug-eyed and mouthing, "No!"

He mouthed back an emphatic, "Okay!" He spoke into the phone. "No, looks like I can't get some guys over there," Judah said. "Raisa's sure I have a concussion, and my guys are dealing with shit at the casino. You do know about that, don't you?"

Dinah calmed down. "'Course, I do, and—he did that as a fucking diversion from his rally and this riot. That scumbag clown!"

"Yeah, the bombs, the fire. He did. I know. And not just a diversion for us. The shit at the casino was a diversion for the cops and all the first responders—ambulances too. Caught the whole damn city off guard, while he planned this riot."

"If you have a concussion, you should be in the hospital."

Raisa was nodding emphatically, which made Judah smile through his pain.

"Yeah, Raisa's with you there, but I'm not going. Fuck the hospital."

"So, get some rest." Her voice was suddenly frantic, "But don't sleep! You can't sleep with a concussion."

"I couldn't sleep anyway. I've gotta figure out what to do about that fucking clown."

The doorbell rang.

"I'll get it," Raisa said, and headed to the door.

"I gotta go, Di."

"Kk. Love you."

"Love you." Judah ended the call as Raisa returned looking chagrined.

"It's Chinara, looking for somewhere safe to hide."

"Somewhere…?" Judah realized what she meant, thought about their Nigerian friends, and sat up. But Raisa walked quickly to him and pressed him down again with a hand to his chest. "No, Jude. You're staying here. I'll let her in and bring her to you."

Moments later she reappeared followed by Chinara Chukwu, who wore a brown corduroy jacket over a flowing blue dress, and was wiping her eyes and trying not to let Judah see her tears.

"I'm sorry. I didn't know you were hurt or I wouldn't have come!" Chinara pressed her hand to her chest and hesitated at the doorway, but Raisa led her into the room.

Judah patted the side of the bed, suggesting she sit, but the woman refused to come any closer.

"What happened?" Judah asked, the concern showing in his voice.

"Two of our employees were dragged from our station by a gang of men and beaten in the street. Their faces and bellies and backs were kicked. They are running us out of town," she said, her voice dropping to a whisper.

"Where's Uzoma?" Judah asked.

"He took our employees to a hotel. I don't know where, but nothing local."

Judah relaxed a little. "So Uzoma's safe."

"For now." She nodded but the alarm still showed in her eyes. "But I fear our business is finished."

Judah disagreed. "It's not. Once the police get this under control and the dust settles, you'll have your place again. It'll pass."

"Even if that's true," Chinara said. "I'm not sure I want to stay here. I know some of these people. Having them come into the station, and…" She shook her head. "I just don't know."

Raisa asked, "What about Amadi, Chika and the others?"

Chinara slowly shook her head, her eyes grave. "I don't know. I only know that my Uzoma is safe for now, and away from Towson."

Judah's phone rang and he reached for it, but Raisa was faster. She saw who it was and answered.

"Dinah, it's Raisa." Her eyes flicked to Judah. "Sure." She handed him the phone. "Your sister again."

Judah took the phone. "What?" He listened then looked at Raisa and Chinara. "Would you excuse me for a minute?"

"Come on into the kitchen," Raisa said to Chinara. "I'll make some fresh coffee."

Once they were gone, Judah said, "Go ahead."

"We've got another problem, Jude."

"I'm listening."

"There are a couple of lawyers here with a guy from the New York State Gaming Commission. They're saying our gambling license isn't valid."

Judah squinted against the pain in his head. "I don't understand. Is this because of the fire?"

"They're not saying. They're just shutting us down."

Chapter 15

The Gamble family's home was a modest raised ranch with walnut-colored cedar shake siding and a neatly trimmed lawn. Their RentUrPlace guests were offered a one bedroom, one bath apartment with a small kitchen that featured a stove, refrigerator, and a microwave.

The key was left in a lock box on the porch next to the front door; the combination had been sent via the app's messaging feature.

Once the contents of the suitcase were laid out on the bed, Mama explained the plan.

"We need to make sure that only one of them comes down at a time. If two come down, then we've gotta try again later. I think it's best if we do it early in the morning, while one is sleeping or in the bathroom. Actually, I know. Let's do it when we hear the shower."

"Great idea, Mama," Junior said.

Norman said nothing.

After several hours of waiting, Mama said, "Let's do it now. Late at night is just as good as early in the morning. They'll be in bed, so just one of them will come down. Do it now, Junior. Do it, now!"

"Okay, Mama."

"Put the weight on that little table outside the bathroom, where you can get to it easily, and make sure you have your folding knife ready in your pocket.

Junior did as he was asked, then went into the bathroom and began wadding up handfuls of toilet paper and dropping them in the toilet.

"That should do it," Mama said. "Now, flush."

Junior flushed the toilet, which promptly backed up, spilling water on the bathroom floor.

"Good, now go on upstairs and tell them the toilet backed up."

"Okay, Mama." Junior glanced in the direction of the ten-pound weight, turned and walked up the stairs. He banged on the locked door. "Mrs. Gamble? Mr. Gamble?" He waited, but there was no answer. He banged again. "Mr. Gamble? Your toilet's backed up down here." No answer.

"Use the app," Mama suggested.

"Good idea," Junior said, and he took out his phone, opened the RentUrPlace app, and saw the text from the Gambles.

"Is there a problem?"

"Sorry to bother you," Junior wrote. "The toilet's backed up." He added a sad emoji—Norman's idea.

"Be right down," came the answer.

It was Mr. Gamble. Junior could tell by the heft of the footfalls. He was a dark, balding man with a toothy grin and black framed glasses, wearing an untucked blue shirt, gray sweatpants and red slippers.

"Yeah, the toilet down here can be a little uncooperative," he said, as he stepped into the bathroom.

Junior grabbed the weight in his right hand and the knife in his left.

"Well, here's your problem. This little toilet can't handle—"

Junior lifted the weight high above his head and brought it down on the back of Clayton Gamble's head. The man fell forward and hit his forehead on the porcelain toilet tank cover. His body sagged, but Junior couldn't tell if he was unconscious, so he hit him twice more— once on the back of the head and, as the man sank to the floor, again on the top of the head. Then he drove the knife into his neck.

Gamble's left hand reached out and opened and closed several times against the shower door. He made a grunting noise as blood poured from the wound on the back of his neck. Seconds later, he lay still.

"Hit him again, to make sure," Mama ordered.

Junior did as he was told. He was a good son.

A few minutes later, a voice called from the top of the stairs.

"Clay? Everything okay down there?"

"Shh," Mama advised. "Don't answer. Let her come. Junior, close the bathroom door most of the way so she can't see 'til she gets there, and stand back a little ways so she can walk by you and you can come up behind. And quick, put the weight back where it was and put the knife in your pocket."

Junior did as he was told.

Patrice Gamble came down to the bottom of the steps, looking suspicious and tentative, which worried Junior.

He didn't say anything at first, and she didn't move. She just looked from him to the bathroom door and back again.

"Clay?" She still didn't move.

"Clayton?"

Junior couldn't wait any more. "You should have a look," he said.

She frowned, uncomprehending, and took a few steps toward the bathroom.

Junior gave a couple of quick nods, encouraging her.

She approached the door and began to push it open.

Junior grabbed the weight and hit her twice, fast, on the head. The first blow hit her on the top and slightly toward the left side, the second on the left temple, as she started to turn toward Junior. She staggered back, but didn't fall, so Junior charged her as Mama screamed.

"Kill her, Junior. Kill that fuckin' big mouth bitch!"

He hit her high on her forehead and she went down, the light already fading from her eyes.

"Keep hitting her! Keep hitting her! That's what you get! That's what you get for your fuckin' shit in the street!"

Junior hit her and hit her, caving in her skull. Blood poured from the top of her head, her ears and eyes and from several areas of torn flesh on her temple and ear.

"Good boy. Good boy!" Mama said, cooing with delight.

"Rest up, Junior. You deserve to rest. Norman's going to clean up. Make sure you wipe everything real good. We don't want to leave any fingerprints."

"What about the daughter?" Norman asked.

"Good thought," Mama said. "Junior, go on upstairs. Bring the weight and the knife. See if the daughter's up there. If she is, kill her. If not, well, this is her lucky day."

• • •

Sharpe waited in his car, a short way down the street from the Gibson house, deciding what to do. Eventually, he watched the young man in the khaki windbreaker emerge from the house with a dark brown suitcase, get into the red truck and drive away.

He waited a half hour and decided to risk breaking in while leaving himself an escape route, should anyone else prove to be inside or should the young man return.

He drove around the block and parked two houses beyond the non-driveway side of the house and approached from that side. The area was overgrown with bushes and he didn't want the same nosey neighbor to spot him again.

The windows were bolted and or painted shut and the doors were locked, but Sharpe had come prepared. He unsnapped a leather case on his belt and removed his glass cutter and pressed the suction cup to a ground floor window about four inches from its locking mechanism.

Then he rotated the blade at the end of the arm attached to the cup in a circle, while pressing the blade against the glass. After five rotations, he detached the cup from the glass. He took a small hammer and another suction cup from his belt, pressed the cup to the glass and lightly tapped the glass with the hammer three times. He then pulled the cup and the circle of glass neatly away from the rest of the window, reached in, unlocked the window, and swung it open. Once through the window, he reached outside, grabbed the circle of glass, and closed the window. Then he gently and carefully fit the glass back into place and stepped back. As long as it wasn't touched, the glass would stay where it was. The tiny circular line of the cut would be visible, but only if one was looking closely, a risk Sharpe had to take.

He stepped down into an empty white basement room that smelled faintly of bleach and something metallic. Next to it was a bedroom, the bed neatly made, the shelves bearing stacks of CDs, and souvenir coffee mugs from national parks. Everything was covered with a layer of dust.

Walking quietly, and listening for the occupants' return, Sharpe went upstairs and found the house a mess. Newspapers, clothing, and empty food containers were everywhere; the place smelled of stale food, old socks and sweat. A TV was on, playing an episode of *Friday Night Lights.*

He went into the bathroom and the two bedrooms and found similar detritus everywhere. He looked in the closets, found clothing on the floor and on hangers.

He returned to the basement, intent on leaving the house, but stopped and opened a closet in the empty white room. Inside were multiple packets of unused tarps, a half dozen bottles of bleach, towels, and a chain saw.

· · ·

Reuben was in his office when Arlene Dunn knocked on his open door.

"Come in."

She looked worried, her mouth tight and fists clenched at her sides.

"What's wrong?" he asked.

She covered her eyes with a palm and briefly bowed her head. She took a breath and said, "I think my new client might have killed those two prostitutes."

Reuben didn't speak right away. "Three prostitutes," he said, then added. "Why do you think so?"

She explained her thinking.

Reuben sat back, his head tipped to the left then to the right. He pursed his lips. "Well, I guess I see why you might think so, but that's far from conclusive."

"I—I don't know what to do. He scares me. Seeing him scares me. Listening to him scares me."

Reuben nodded. "Is it possible you're projecting? You're seeing what you expect him to be?"

She was taken aback. "You think I'm imagining—?"

"I didn't say that."

"Shouldn't you be concerned for my safety?"

"Of course. I am concerned with your safety. I'm also concerned with our clients' privacy and wellbeing." He paused. "Of course, the law is that if he's a danger to himself or anyone else…do you want me to go to the police?"

She spread her hands, palms out. "I don't know. I came to you for guidance."

"I think, perhaps, we should be prudent, for now."

"What if I'm right and he kills more people?"

"Obviously, we don't want that. But we're not bound by law to report him, no matter what he's done."

She winced, her mouth twisted into a grimace. "I'm supposed to see him this afternoon."

"Would you like me to have him see someone else? Would you like to cancel today's session?"

She shook her head. "I'll see him."

But John did not show up for his session that afternoon.

• • •

Once the police and fire departments had gone, Judah walked to the top of the parking garage stairs and looked out over the rubble, which included a $600,000 Ferrari Spider, a Maserati Ghibli and a handful of Mercedes and BMWs. None were salvageable.

The firefighters had roped off the front entrance of the casino and Judah's janitorial staff had hung enormous blue tarps from the lobby ceiling, blocking the damaged entranceway from view. Signs were posted around the inside and outside of the facility, directing casino guests to a side exit. The hotel had a second set of doors that was separate from the casino, and which led to several conference and banquet areas. These were now designated as the temporary entrance and exit.

He sat at the long table in his library office, looking out at the fall foliage. He was trying to decide what to do next, but the wound on his forehead throbbed and his thinking was fuzzy and muddled. *The gaming license. What the hell could be done about the damned gaming license?*

His phone rang. He answered. "What's up?"

"I need to talk to you about something. Can I come by?"

"Sure, Reuben. Of course."

"Be there in a few."

He poured himself a glass of water from a pitcher on the table and began to drink it down, but the water was too cold and a stab of pain exploded behind his forehead. He braced himself, leaning forward, his hands on the table. He took a breath, turned to his right and walked to the glass cubicle at the far end of the room. He knocked on the glass.

Dinah looked up, her expression asking what he wanted.

He stepped into her office and sat down, elbows on his knees, his face in his hands.

"Well, you look like shit."

He let his hands slide down his face to his cheeks. "How do we fix the license?'

Dinah cocked an eyebrow. "He did this with pull. We need bigger pull."

"I don't have bigger pull, though I guess I could see what Stafford's got."

"You should do that."

Dinah sighed. "It's not the time to talk about it, but your nephew is making me crazy."

"Shit, what'd he do now?"

"It's not what he did. It's the disrespect. You have no idea how that kid talks to me. He's a fun, mischievous kid with his uncles, but not with me. He's a mouthy little shit with me."

"Do what Abba did with us. Consequences."

"I do, but he doesn't listen. If I say no TV, he watches TV anyway. If I say no gaming, he games anyway. If I say he's grounded, he goes out anyway."

"That's unacceptable, Di. You need to draw a line in the sand."

"But that's the problem. It's fuckin' sand. Do you know he's smoking cigarettes?"

"He's ten!"

"Tell me about it!"

"Di, you need to be like steel with him."

She sighed again. "You don't know what he's like. I'm sort of afraid he's turning into you!"

He heard the knock on the library door, turned and saw his eldest brother standing in the doorway. "Dinah, Reuben's here. I gotta go."

"Kk."

He left his sister's office, went to his brother and hugged him, then squinted against the pain.

"I heard," Reuben said.

"I'm fine." Judah shook his head. "So, what's up?"

"Arlene, one of my therapists, has a client she suspects might be the guy who's killing the escorts."

Judah blinked, digesting this. "Why does she think that? Did he tell her? Did he confess?"

Reuben shook his head. "He's a really jittery guy who said he's done some really bad things. Kind of dances around the details, but it's kind of in there. She's a smart woman."

Judah indicated one of the chairs at the long wooden table. Reuben sat and Judah sat a few feet away, on the same side of the table.

"It's more of a vibe she's getting from him, she says. Something really bad is going on with this guy, and she's pretty adamant about it." Reuben ran his hand back through his thin hair and sat back, a finger to his lips. "Arlene is not the jump-to-conclusions type. She's got her head on straight." He waved his hand. "Of course, it's possible she's completely wrong, given she's talking about a vibe rather than something he's confessed to."

"So you don't think maybe he stole from his job or something. What does he do?"

"He's on disability—for mental illness. Works part-time as a bicycle messenger, I think."

"What's his name?"

Reuben raised an eyebrow. "Pretty sure it's a fake name and he refused to give a license or insurance card. Pays the fee by cash. Calls himself John Paperwent."

Judah leaned back, pressing his chair back on its rear legs and rocking gently forward and back as he thought. "Your office has cameras, doesn't it?"

Reuben nodded. "It does."

"Can we take a look at this guy?"

"I've already done that. But sure. Doesn't look like much. Little guy, from what I can see when he arrives and leaves. Barely taller than Arlene, who's maybe five two or three. Doesn't look like much."

Judah grunted. "You know what? Would it be okay if I reach out to Sam Sharpe about this?"

Reuben looked dubious, shaking his head. "Everything said to a psychotherapist is confidential unless there is immediate danger to the therapist, the client or others…" He raked his fingers back through his hair again, then gave a grudging nod. "Yeah, you can tell Sharpe."

"Good." Judah took his phone out and began scrolling. A Facebook post caught his eye, and with it a link to an article on *Long Island Daily's* website. A couple who ran a RentUrPlace apartment in their home had been discovered, murdered in their home—found by their daughter. No signs of a struggle nor of a break-in were apparent.

Clayton Gamble was found in the bathroom of the basement apartment, and his wife was found just outside the bathroom door in the living room. A spokesperson for the RentUrPlace app told police that the apartment had been rented to a man named John Paperwent, who had paid cash. The spokesperson expressed the company's outrage at the crime, sadness for the family's loss, and sent prayers and thoughts to the surviving daughter.

The police could offer nothing further except to say that the investigation was ongoing, and they were following several leads. When asked if the murders were connected to the recent murders of prostitutes, Towson Police Chief Mark Green stated that they were considered to be separate crimes, since, despite some similarities, the Gamble murders had not involved prostitutes.

Chapter 16

It was nearly midnight when Gold and Cortez finished booking and processing the twenty-seven men and five women they had arrested during the four and a half hours of rioting that had taken place throughout Towson and on the roads and highway leading to and from town.

The charges included simple assault, harassment, aggravated assault, terroristic threats, rioting, criminal trespass, failure to disperse, and reckless endangerment.

Much of the Towson police force had worked overtime, patrolling, answering 911 calls, checking leads, protecting residents and businesses, making arrests, and booking alleged perpetrators. Everyone, including Detectives Gold and Cortez, was tired and tense and those who were finally getting off duty were looking forward to going home and getting some much needed rest.

"See you bright and early, Cortez," Gold said, as he began shutting his computer down.

Cortez was about to answer when Zahir Tiwari approached, waving a hand at Gold.

"Wait. Don't shut down yet. You need to see this!"

Gold closed his eyes, winced, and said wearily, "Can't it wait 'til the morning?"

"I found the pickup with that plate we've been looking for."

Cortez studied the tech, her brow furrowed. "The small red pick-up?"

Tiwari pointed at the computer Gold was about to shut down. "Check it out—red 2014 Nissan Frontier, wanted in connection with the Hamilton and Teitlebaum murders."

"And the ankle bracelet girl," Cortez added.

"Show me," Gold said, and the detectives waited as Tiwari sat down and brought up a computer file.

He began to read aloud from the screen. "Plate number TLT3279. Registered to a Mildred Gibson at 638 Walnut Drive."

"Outstanding," Gold said.

"However, Mildred Gibson doesn't live there," Tiwari added.

"Okay..." Gold said, twirling a finger for him to continue.

"She's in a mental ward that's part of the prison system upstate, the Coxsackie Correctional Facility. She's been there for twenty-one years for beating her husband, Charles Gibson, to death with a frying pan after he refused to give her money for a new car. She was judged 'adjudicated as a mental defective.'"

Gold turned to Cortez. "Not guilty by reason of insanity."

"I knew that," Cortez said, defensively.

"So, do we know who lives there—who's been using the car?" Gold continued.

Tiwari nodded proudly. "I know more than that. The Gibsons have two sons. Norman and Walter. But Norman lives upstate, where he's a postman."

"So, Walter..." Cortez said.

"Yes, Walter," Tiwari agreed. "That's who lives there, as far as we know."

"Good job, Zahir," Gold said, then, to Cortez, added, "We need to have a talk with Walter Gibson."

Cortez blew out a breath. "Can it wait 'til tomorrow, Gold?"

Gold gave her a crocodile smile. "Bright and early."

• • •

Sharpe arrived at Insights and told the woman at the front desk that he had an appointment to see Reuben Hammer. Minutes later, Sharpe was seated beside Reuben's desk while they both watched a video that played silently on Reuben's computer. Reuben watched Sharpe's expression as Sharpe watched the video. Recognition quickly sparked in the investigator's eyes.

"That's the guy I've been surveilling," Sharpe said. "His real name is Walter Gibson, and I think your therapist may be right about him."

"The question is, what do we do?" Reuben said. "Should we cancel his next appointment? I don't want my therapist in there with a possible serial killer, but I don't want to cancel and tip him off that we're onto him, and I really don't want him mad at us. What would be the least dangerous to Arlene?"

"When's his next appointment?"

"Six days," Reuben said. "He missed his appointment yesterday."

"Don't do anything yet. I'm going to call the cops and tell them everything I know. I'm also going to dig some more, see what else I can learn."

"Okay, but please get back to me. I'm sure Arlene will be anxious." He hesitated. "Is there any chance she might be in danger? If this guy's a psychopathic murderer, well, isn't it possible he might look at the one person he's been confiding in as being a threat to him?"

"That's one of the reasons I'm going to the police. Look, if he's feeling guilty and he's confiding in your therapist, she's probably okay. If she sees him, she should make sure not to antagonize him, but I don't think it will come to that. His appointment is six days away. For now, the safest thing for all concerned is for me to talk to the police."

"Well…okay," Reuben said, but he sounded far from convinced.

• • •

Judah, Frank James, Rinny, Kofi, Lou, and Scurge were in the hotel lounge; all but Kofi were drinking beers. Kofi drank a Diet Coke.

"How's the healing coming?" Kofi nodded toward Judah's face.

"I'll never be James Dean, but it's coming along," Judah said. "The pain's gone, anyway."

"Who's James Dean?" Scurge asked.

"So how are we going to hit back?" Rinny wanted to know.

Judah said, "They hit us when they knew we'd be distracted with their rally, right?"

Everyone nodded.

"Smart assholes," Lou said.

"Right," Judah agreed. "I'd like to hear what you guys think about retaliation."

Rinny spoke up. "I'll tell you exactly what we should do and when we should do it." He went on to outline his plan and watched Judah's expression shift from rapt attention to appreciation.

"I like it, especially since it turns the tables on what they did to us, and takes them out."

They continued discussing the plan's details, listing supplies and deciding who would do what.

When they were finished, Rinny and Scurge brought their drinks to the corner table, where the escorts were sitting. Sheri, who was next to Ruby, stood, took a few steps toward Scurge, and gave him a hug. Several of the other girls reached out to touch his arm or shoulder. They knew how much he had cared for Jen, and that she had begun to like him too.

Rinny slid in next to Ruby and she turned to him with an open smile, untroubled by his scarred face.

Frank James and Kofi remained seated with Judah.

"My brother has an idea about getting our gaming license back," Frank said.

Judah turned expectantly to Kofi.

"I went to college with Stafford's chief of staff, Zane Larson," Kofi said. "We were in the same fraternity and we both went to law school at Emory University."

"Kofi's connected with some of the most high-powered Black lawyers and judges in the country," Frank added.

"Correction," Kofi said. "The most high-powered lawyers and judges in the country, period."

"I stand corrected," Frank said.

Judah brightened. "Interesting."

"Frank and I also have an uncle down there who's well connected and might be of help. I'll make a few calls and see what I can find out," Kofi offered.

"I've been thinking that's what we need," Judah said. "More pull than Clowney."

• • •

"This one's going to be a little bit different, Junior. Now that you're ready and have had a chance to practice, we're going after our ultimate target."

"Okay, Mama. I think I'm ready. Is it okay that we're home now?"

"For the moment, yes. And I know you're ready, Junior. In fact, I'm sure you're ready. There will be some special challenges with the ultimate target. There's the choice of weapon."

"Can't I use the weight, Mama? The weight's been good."

"Yes, the weight's been good, and our new knife's good. But you won't have the weight because we'll be going to him. He won't be coming to us. You can bring the knife, but you might have to look around and use something you find there."

"I can do it, Mama. You'll see."

"I believe you can, Junior. Once you get there, you'll have to explain who you are. Do you understand what I'm talking about?"

"So he'll let me in, right?"

"Exactly. So he lets you in. Then you look around for something that's like the weight. Something heavy like that. Something you can take in your hand and bash his God damn FUCKING SKULL in!"

"I understand, Mama. I can do this."

"I know you can, Junior."

"Thank you, Mama."

"You'll have the element of surprise. Once he knows who you are, he'll let you in and listen to what you have to say. He'll want to listen to you. Do you understand what I'm talking about?"

"I do, Mama. He'll be…interested."

"And you just wait for your opportunity. This is the ultimate target, Junior, so we have to get it right. This has been what we've been working for all this time. Everything was practice for *this*."

"I know, Mama. I can do it. You'll see. I'm a good son."

"You are, Junior."

"How will we find him, Mama?"

"I'll show you, when the time is right. Don't worry. Just give it time and we'll know the time and place. Don't you worry."

Mama was saying something softly—muttering, chanting. "The whippet's coming. The whippet's coming. The whippet's coming. Coming for his revenge, his revenge, his revenge. Our revenge."

• • •

Gold rang the doorbell and glanced at Cortez.

"I'll do the talking," he said.

"Of course," Cortez agreed.

"Don't just jump in if you think something's pertinent. We went over everything and we agreed, am I right?"

"I said, okay."

"No, you said 'of course,' not the same thing."

"It's the same thing, Gold."

"No, it isn't really. What you said was a little patronizing."

"Fuck's sake, Gold. It wasn't. It was me agreeing to handle this your way. Stop being paranoid."

He rang the bell again. "I'm not being paranoid. See, that's what I mean. The way you say 'your way' makes it sound like I'm being manipulative."

"Jesus, Gold. Give it a rest. And hey, we need to go public with this. Three murders is clearly a serial killer."

Gold winced and nodded. "It is, but Green won't do it. Too much bad publicity with everything else going on."

Cortez shook her head. "Publicity…Jesus. Priorities, Gold."

Gold was about to ring the bell again when the door opened and a small man with dirty blond hair was looking back at the detectives.

Gold held up his badge. "Walter Gibson?"

The man hesitated, his eyes wandering as though he was thinking or listening to something behind him. "No. Walter Gibson is my brother. I'm Norman Gibson."

Now it was Gold who was hesitating. "Is your brother here?"

The man shook his head.

"Do you know where he is?"

The man knitted his brows, and said, "I think he's at the supermarket."

"Would you mind if we came in and asked you a few questions? Maybe while we're here, your brother will come home and we could speak to him too."

Norman stepped back and waited as the detectives stepped inside. He led them into a messy living room, where a TV was playing an episode of *Friday Night Lights*. He lifted a remote from a coffee table, pointed it at the TV and lowered the volume. He smiled at the TV, but when he looked at the detectives, his smile faded.

"Okay if we sit down?" Gold asked.

Norman blinked and stepped from where he'd been standing, between a dark wooden coffee table and a light gray polyester couch. He sat down in an armchair that matched the couch, waiting.

Several small black remote controls and two red gaming controls were on the couch.

"Okay if I move these?" Gold asked.

Norman didn't answer.

The detectives looked at one another and Gold gently moved the controllers to the coffee table. "I'm just going to put these right here," he said.

Cortez did the same with the remotes, as Norman watched.

The detectives sat and Gold kept his eyes on Norman, who kept glancing at the TV, a small smile playing on his lips.

The senior detective stood and pointed toward the table in the dining area, which sat below a hanging lamp. "Would it be okay if we sat down over there, at the dining room table? The light's better and I think we'll be able to focus more as we talk. Is that okay with you?"

Norman shrugged, got up, and went into the dining area and sat down. The detectives took seats opposite him.

Gold asked, "Could you tell us where you were on the night of Wednesday, September 15th?"

Norman looked off to his right. His lips tightened and he said, "I was here."

"With your brother?"

After a pause, Norman nodded. "And Mama."

Cortez looked at Gold, startled. But Gold looked unperturbed.

"And, Mama," he said. "Okay. What about the next day, Thursday, September 16ᵗʰ?"

Norman frowned again, looked to his right and said, "Here."

"Same as the night before? With Walter…and your mother?"

Norman nodded.

Cortez asked. "Do you remember what you did? Did you watch TV?"

Norman nodded.

Gold rolled his eyes, took a deep breath, and sighed.

"Do you remember what you watched?"

Norman's eyes drifted toward the TV. He smiled dreamily. "I think Tami got hired as the volleyball coach, and Tim kind of told Lyla that he really liked her."

Cortez nodded. "I see. And the second night?"

Norman looked around for a moment, then said, "Smash got in trouble with his parents. Matt was worried about his grandmother and her nurse, I think."

Cortez was about to speak, but Norman interrupted her.

"I might've got the days backwards, but I think that's what happened."

"Thank you, Norman. That's helpful. Oh, does Walter watch with you?"

This time, Norman didn't hesitate. "Yeah, me and Walter, but Mama not so much. Love those guys."

Cortez glanced at Gold, who was eyeing her reprovingly. She asked, "Do you tape the shows?"

Norman nodded.

Gold was staring at Norman. "A vehicle matching your truck's description was seen at the pier late on the night of September 16th, or very early the following morning, September 17th."

Norman said nothing.

"Do you know anything about that?"

After a long pause, Norman said, "Sometimes Walter goes to the pier, when he can't sleep. He likes being near the water. He watches the people fish. It's peaceful there."

"That was the night one of the girls, an escort, was murdered."

Norman said nothing.

"Do you know anything about that?" Gold asked.

Norman said nothing.

"Norman?" Gold prodded.

"I don't know anything about…an escort."

"So you don't know if you or your brother was at the pier very early on the morning of Friday September 17th?"

Norman shook his head. "I wasn't there," he said.

"What about your brother?"

"I don't know about him. I was sleeping. I think he was sleeping too."

"What do you do for a living?" Gold asked.

"I'm on disability."

"And your brother?"

"He's on disability too, and also works part time as a messenger for the city."

"Why are you on disability?"

Norman said nothing.

"Norman?"

"I don't want to talk about that."

Cortez asked, "So your mother lives with you?"

Norman didn't answer.

"Norman?"

Norman began to chew the inside of his lower lip.

"Cortez," Gold said, a warning in his voice. He then quickly asked, "Do you remember if you made any calls on those nights?"

Norman's eyes narrowed and he shook his head.

"No you don't remember or no you made no calls?"

"No calls."

Gold gave a tight nod and said, "Please tell your brother we'd like to speak with him as soon as possible." He took out a card and laid it on the table as Norman watched but said nothing.

Gold stood and said, "Thank you for your time." He looked at Cortez, who rose and followed him out.

Once they were in the car, Gold said. "Didn't I ask you not to go rogue?"

Cortez looked surprised. "Go rogue? What are you talking about? Someone had to ask for some kind of verification of where he was and when."

Inside the house, Walter said. "Thank you, Norman."

Norman answered. "You're welcome."

"You did good, Norman," Mama said. "Now let's get back to work on you know who."

Chapter 17

Election Day in Towson began with thunder rumbling in the distance, and when the rain began to fall, it began with a few heavy drops. Soon, it was cascading out of the west in near horizontal sheets, drumming on roofs and raising a thick mist in the streets. The sewers were overwhelmed as the water ran ankle deep and sometimes deeper, carrying trash from overturned garbage cans and discarded litter and detritus from lawns, yards and driveways.

Lightning flashed and was quickly followed by the crash of thunder, sending small children to their parents' sides and dogs to safe shelter beneath tables and beds.

The GODOT breakfast group was soaked but present, their raincoats and hats hanging on hooks beside their booth or on the backs of chairs.

"Crazy out there," said Corbain, who was already reading the day's news on his phone.

"Ye-ah, almost black as night," Levito agreed, as he glanced around for a waitress.

Corbain looked up from his phone. "I didn't mean the weather."

A waitress appeared. "Everyone here?"

The group looked at one another; everyone nodded.

"Except for Walter Gibson," Lev said.

"Let's order," O'Leary said. "I'm hungry as hell. He can order if and when he gets here."

"Okay by me," the waitress said. "Everyone having the usual?"

There were nods around the table.

"Could we get some waters?" Levito asked.

"Waters? Sure. Sorry about that," the waitress said. "Lorenzo will bring some over right away."

Richmond held up a hand. "Would you make sure my home fries are well done?"

"Will do," the waitress said, and hurried away.

"People are understandably on edge, given the level of violence we've seen," Mason Marx began.

Barry O'Leary leaned forward on his elbows. "People want an end to it," he said, emphatically. "And so they should."

Lev said nothing.

A young man appeared with a tray of waters and began handing them out.

"Could I have a glass of ice?" Richmond asked.

The young man nodded.

Lev took a few sips of his water but said nothing.

"I was curious," Corbain said. "So I went to the rally for a little while. I left when the shouting started, and I walked home, and on the way home, I saw two guys get pulled out of their cars through the windows. One was beat up pretty badly." He looked at O'Leary. "By a couple of guys in blue vests."

O'Leary looked back at Corbain, his expression interested. "I'm betting you misinterpreted what was going on, if that was even what you saw."

Corbain looked hard at O'Leary. "You saying I'm lying?"

"See, that's your problem. Always looking for aggression when it isn't there," O'Leary said matter-of-factly. "What I'm saying is that what you probably saw was some good citizens, likely none of our people, trying to stop some probably violent guy in a car from hurting anyone. Maybe the driver was drunk. Maybe he was trying to run someone down."

Corbain looked doubtful, but unsure. "I, I don't think that's what I saw."

"It was," O'Leary insisted. "Our guys are out there trying to keep order." His expression darkened. "There are violent people around. Some are real criminals." He looked at Lev and patted the air with a hand. "No offense, man, but your brother—" He shrugged.

"None taken," Lev said. "I know it. I get it."

O'Leary continued. "Some are just people who mean well, but are swept up in the moment and think they're doing the right thing. They misunderstand this election and think they need to make a statement by breaking things and picking fights…"

The *Gazette* editor, who was sitting at the short end of the table, was looking at O'Leary with disbelief. "You're saying the people who were rioting weren't Clowney people? Are you kidding me?"

"Of course they weren't! They were Stafford loyalists, sent out to undermine a good and fair election. Those people—Stafford and his crooks—are trying to steal this election, and if they can't—and they won't—they'll disrupt the running of the city and make it impossible for a real administration to take the reigns. Come on, they ransacked through City Hall! Those are Stafford people. That's who has access!"

"That's not what happened at all," Marx said. "Look at the police reports, which are readily available to the public. Those who were arrested were Clowney supporters, most wearing blue vests just like the one you're wearing right here, right now!"

O'Leary looked steadily back at Marx. "Police reports doctored by Stafford's cronies at the police force. You think Mark Green is an honest man? Are you out of your mind?"

Marx was shaking his head. "Come on, man."

"Come on is right," O'Leary said.

"Look at this," Levito said, looking at his phone. "Clowney wants to ship the Nigerian gas station owners to New Jersey."

Marx and Corbain laughed.

"Hey," O'Leary said. "It's not a joke. It's a real thing. Clowney arranged with a mayor from central Jersey for the Nigerians to be welcomed to that city, where they can have their gas stations and they'll fit right in. He's even arranged a fair market buyout of each of their stations here. They can take themselves, their families and others of their kind to New Jersey, to be with, you know, people like them."

"People like them?" Corbain echoed, bewildered. "You mean Black folks, people of color?"

"That's insane," Marx said.

"Come on. That's funny," Lev said, laughing.

Corbain was looking at his phone, "Mayor Stafford says he has the names, photos, and driver's licenses of all of Clowney's personnel, who were the instigators of the riots. He goes on to talk about Clowney's manslaughter charge."

"That's not only old news," O'Leary retorted. "It's fake news, and it's twisted all out of proportion. He was trying to help a young woman —a kid really—and there was a tragic accident. That's the truth of it, if you really want to know." O'Leary looked around the table. "The fact is, Clowney will be great for Towson. He'll support businesses, he'll bring in entertainment, which will draw people from all over and make Towson a destination, which will be good for restaurants, ice cream shops, bars, stores—you name it. It will be good for everyone."

"You know," Richmond said, thoughtfully, as the food arrived. "I think change might be good for everyone, especially if it's aimed at reducing taxes, bringing in business, lowering prices, and all the other things Clowney's for. I'll tell you what. I might vote for him."

"See?" O'Leary fist-bumped Richmond.

"You know what?" Levito said. "I might just be with you."

"I'm considering it," Lev said, as he picked up his fork and speared a sausage link.

Corbain looked at the faces around the table. "I don't know," he said. "The whole thing worries me. Things are a little bit too crazy for my taste."

"I've never seen this town so divided—people this angry," Marx said sadly. "Frankly, it's scary."

• • •

After the violence following the Rally Against Murder, and as the election approached, a mood of strained anxiety descended on the citizens of Towson. People who were normally cheerful and quick to greet neighbors and strangers alike while out and about looked away and avoided eye contact. Many simply stayed indoors.

Social media was filled with insults and epithets—name-calling aimed at both candidates and their supporters. A meme of Mayor Stafford hung in effigy made the rounds. It appeared, hanging from mailboxes and stop signs. Clowney claimed to have had nothing to do with the meme but refused to reject it or castigate those who spread the image. Expressions of exhaustion were common, as was a longing for an end to the conflict, and for the election to be over and for life and friendships to go back to what they had been before.

• • •

Lev waited in the waiting room while the doctor examined Zeb at his annual physical. After forty minutes, the door to the examination opened and the doctor said, "Please, come in."

Lev followed the doctor to his office, where Zeb was in his wheelchair, facing the doctor's desk. Lev sat down, glanced at his brother and listened.

"I understand that Zeb is using a computer now."

"That's right," Lev said. "He plays games, surfs the net and loves it."

"That's rightah," Zeb agreed.

"Any stimulation he can get is a good thing," the doctor said, encouragingly.

"He watches TV and listens to music, too," Lev added.

"And readah books, and playah chess," Zeb added.

Lev looked at him, surprised. "Really?"

"Yes, ah do."

"Well, that's great. All good things." The doctor shuffled some papers on his desk. "Given his condition, I'd say your brother is in pretty good shape. His weight is normal for his size and circumstance, and his blood work and vitals aren't bad." The doctor spun the papers around so they were facing Lev. "You can see that information here." He pointed to a spot on the paper and Lev had to rise to his feet to see.

The doctor was pointing to a handwritten comment on the page that read, "Your brother is likely to live only a few more years at most.

I strongly suggest moving him to a nursing home or skilled nursing facility to extend his life span."

Lev looked up and saw that the doctor was looking earnestly back at him. Lev pressed his lips together and mouthed, "I know," but said only, "Thank you, doctor," out loud.

He drove Zeb home and wheeled him up the ramp beside the steps to the front door, and into the house.

"I waht mah compahutahh," Zeb said, as Lev wheeled him into the den and turned on the TV.

Lev set his brother up with his computer and trackball, then called the skilled nursing facility.

"Hi, this is Lev Hammer," he explained to the person who answered the phone. "I visited recently on behalf of my brother, Zeb, and I think I'd like to pull the trigger on having him live there."

"Just a moment, sir. I'll connect you with sales."

After a short wait, a woman came on the line.

"This is Tara."

"Hi, Tara," Lev said. "This is Lev Hammer. I visited recently. I'd like to get my brother, Zeb, set up with a room there."

"I remember! That's wonderful! We're ready for him as soon as we get his deposit squared away."

"Right. I'll get back to you ASAP on that." Lev ended the call and thought when to break the news to his siblings.

• • •

Sharpe had cleared a little area outside the window of Walter Gibson's house. Once Walter was inside, Sharpe sat on the grass, leaning to one side, watching, listening, and recording the conversations inside with his phone.

A TV was playing, which Sharpe knew would undermine the quality of the recording, but nothing could be done about that.

Apart from the TV, he heard two distinct voices having a conversation. One of them was clearly Walter, and Sharpe gathered from the conversation that the other was Walter's mother, whom he referred to as "Mama."

Sharpe peered through the window but saw no one but Walter in the room.

They were planning another murder, of "the ultimate target," whoever that might be—apparently a revenge killing. The two referenced prior murders, and having used a weight as the murder weapon, and Sharpe wondered if that meant a weight from a set of barbells. A knife was also mentioned.

And then he heard the chanting, and didn't know what to make of that or what it meant. Something about a "whippet."

The doorbell rang, and Sharpe could make out Walter going to the door, having a brief conversation and letting two police detectives inside. They sat first in the living room and then moved to the dining room table.

Sharpe adjusted his angle to improve his line of sight but could not see anyone else in the room besides Walter and the two police detectives. Walter sat with his back to the window, with the detectives facing him. He heard Walter claim to be his brother, Norman, and didn't know what to make of that.

The detectives asked him about his and his brother's whereabouts on the nights of the first two murders, Wednesday, September 15th and Thursday, September 16th. Walter, still claiming to be Norman, claimed to have been home on both nights, watching TV. When the detectives said that the Red Nissan truck had been seen early on September 17th, "Norman" said that Walter sometimes went to the pier at night when he couldn't sleep.

To Sharpe, the conversation with the police detectives added up to two things: Walter was crazy, and Walter had no alibi.

• • •

Dinah opened the oven door and pulled the top rack toward her with one of the black oven mitts. She bent over the long metal loaf pan and examined the meatloaf, which was the dish she traditionally prepared on election night for the family. She had brushed the top of the meatloaf with a marinade made from soy sauce, ketchup and barbecue sauce, and was pleased to see that the top of the meatloaf was browning nicely. Another ten or fifteen minutes, and it would be ready to serve.

She went to the doorway that led to the great room and wiped her hands on her apron, then placed them on her hips and surveyed the scene before her.

Reuben sat at the head of the table, wearing a pressed blue shirt and dark slacks; his thinning light brown hair was neatly combed.

Izzy sat to his left, a tumbler of scotch and ice and a taller glass of beer in front of him. He sipped from the scotch, which he chased with a swallow of beer. He was talking to Josh, who sat opposite him.

She didn't expect Judah, who she knew had work to do, but she did expect Lev and Raisa, who would bring Rachel.

"I love Election Day," Izzy said giddily. "It's a party—a trip. You get to celebrate the new team. Or you can make sure you don't have to *think* about the new team. I'm prepared either way." He raised his glass of scotch, as if making a toast, and drank without waiting for a response.

"Don't try to kid us," Dinah said. "Election Day is just another day for you to get wasted."

Izzy raised his glass again. "To Election Day. To *every* day!"

Dinah turned to look at Josh and saw the admiration in his eyes for Izzy. She sighed and said, "I took Joshy to the therapist today."

Everyone looked at her.

Reuben said, "Therapist?"

"To see about getting him back into school…ending his suspension. I got the form filled out to prove we'd been to the therapist, but I don't think Josh liked him very much."

"He was an asshole!" Josh yelled the last word.

"Joshua Hammer!" Dinah admonished sternly.

Josh glared back at her. "He asked me why I was such a bad kid."

Reuben and Izzy looked at Dinah, whose expression was a mixture of love and sadness.

Izzy laughed.

Dinah said, "He wasn't very nice. That's for sure."

Reuben looked at his nephew, compassion in his eyes. "Nobody thinks you're a bad kid, Josh."

"The therapist did," Josh muttered.

"Speaking of therapists, I'm a little worried about one of mine," Reuben said.

Before anyone could respond, the door flew open and Lev burst in, his face lit with triumph. "Zebby's new place is good to go!"

No one spoke for several seconds.

"I just enrolled him and left a deposit." He looked around and waited. "Come on, he'll probably live longer! I just added years to his life."

"It wasn't your place to do that," Reuben said quietly.

Dinah nodded. "And it wasn't your choice to make."

"Bullshit! Someone's gotta have the balls to do the right thing—what's best for Zebby!"

"We do that as a family," Reuben reminded him.

Lev glared at his brother. "And because you're the oldest, you get to be the one to choose!"

"You know that's not the way it works."

"Hey! I get to decideh what's best for me-ah!" Everyone turned to see Zeb in the doorway to the den, his computer and trackball on the tray attached to his wheelchair.

"Zeb," Lev began.

"Hey, where are Raisa and Rachel?" Dinah asked suddenly.

"I'd have thought they'd be here by now," Reuben said.

"I'll call." Dinah had taken out her phone, pressed the number and was waiting for an answer. "Rachel? Hold on. I'm putting you on speaker." She took the phone from her ear, touched the screen and said, "Where's Mommy, Rach?"

The little girl's voice responded from the phone. "Mommy said she was going out to the car for something, but she didn't come back."

Dinah's eyes wandered over the faces of those present. "When was that, honey?"

"A long time. After she went, I watched two whole TV shows!"

Reuben was up and striding toward the door. "I'll get Rachel. Dinah, you call Judah!"

"Yeah, but Reub." Reuben turned to find Izzy looking at him. He waited.

"Get Rachel, by all means, but there's somewhere you and I need to be."

Reuben thought about this and nodded. "I know," he said, and headed outside.

• • •

Junior was confused. "How are we going to find him, Mama?"

"That fucker can't hide from me," Mama snarled. "I can smell him out. Trust me, Junior. We'll find him and we'll kill him. I promise! We're so close. So fucking close!"

"But *how* will we find him, Mama? How?"

Mama didn't answer right away, and when she did, she spoke slowly and clearly. "We pay attention. We know where he is. What we have to do is figure out how to *get* to him—how to get *close* to him. Real close! Close enough to do it! Oh, this is what we've been waiting for Junior. That piece of shit's going to finally get what's coming to him. Fucking finally!"

Junior was confused. "But *how*, Mama? How can we get close to him? How can I get—?"

"You're not listening, Junior! Just listen! You go on your rounds and you listen. We look, listen, and pay attention. We read and watch —everywhere. Everywhere! We keep our eyes open. He'll come to us. The information *will* come to us. I know that fucker like no one else does. Believe me, he'll tell *us* how to get to him!"

"He will?"

"He will. You watch for the opportunity. And you...*take* it! Take it, Junior! We watch, and we strike! We've already learned so much."

"It's true, Mama. We have. We really have!"

"We go where we *know* he goes. We do what we *know* he does. And we'll see. The opportunity's going to come right to us. You'll see. It's coming. We've just got to pay attention, Junior. You just watch, and wait, and see."

And Junior did just that. He went on his messenger rounds. He paid attention, and he heard things.

And soon he knew where to go and what to do. Mama was happy and proud.

Junior was a good son.

• • •

Later that night, Judah was seated at a round table in a private party room off of the hotel lounge with Frank James, Rinny Mallach, Scurge, and Lou—his inner circle, and what he sometimes referred to as "street team 1."

"What'd you find out?" Judah asked.

Frank answered, "They're holding a victory party at the fancy hotel by the beach."

"The Jupiter Suites," Judah said.

"And, it's open to the public," Frank added.

"Perfect time to hit 'em," Rinny said, his scars coming together to approximate a leer. "We'll know where he is, and he'll be distracted."

"True, but there'll be a ton of security." Judah paused, and looked into his drink, then shook his head. "No, can't do it. It just won't work."

"Okay," said Lou. "But we can attack their home base, the trucks, their infrastructure. That stuff will be unguarded."

Judah winced. "It won't be unguarded. He's not stupid. But it will be less guarded than usual. It'll have to be. The main guys, much as I'd like to take those assholes out, will be with Clowney—at the party. Whatever force they leave at the campgrounds will be less than usual."

A corner of Scurge's mouth twitched. "Their guys will let them know what's going on and they'll come running. We should keep some guys out of sight to outflank their reinforcements."

Judah pointed a finger at Scurge. "That's good. We'll do that." He drank the rest of his drink and slapped the table. "You all know what to do. But first—supplies." He grinned. "Frank's got some surprises for us. Frank?"

Frank got up and went to a stack of boxes against a wall, opened the box on top and held up a white shirt.

"You each get one of these."

Frank opened another box and held up a blue vest.

"And one of these to wear on top."

Frank opened a third box and took out a plastic bag that held a small box. Stapled to the top of the bag was a colorful header card that read, "DIY Red, White, and Blue Clown Makeup Kit."

Judah held his arms out wide. "It's Halloween, boys!" He looked at Frank. "Call Ruby and Sheri and whoever else will be doing the makeup. Tell them we're ready for them."

An hour later, they were made up, dressed up, loaded up and on their way to the empty beach that lay along a corner of the campgrounds and trailer park that held the Clowney encampment. They had brought along several jugs of gasoline and five homemade pipe bombs. Judah and the six vehicles in his convoy parked along a curved stretch of street behind the campgrounds.

"Wait for it," Judah said into the conference call he'd arranged with the men riding shotgun in the other five vehicles. "Listen for the music and follow my lead," he said.

He clicked off and turned to Frank James. "Izzy and Reuben are in Izzy's car, pretending to be drinking—well, Izzy probably is drinking—and they're blasting their music, which for Izzy is easy, since his favorite feature of his car, a Honda Prologue Elite, is the stereo—the best, loudest, and with the baddest bass on the market."

A short while later, they heard the head banging rock and roll from the front of the campgrounds.

Judah exited his car and briefly huddled with his men beside his car.

"We have no way of knowing how many guys they left here or how many the diversion drew, so we're going to keep it simple. We mow through the camp. We shoot on sight. We torch the tents, blow up the trucks, and get the fuck out of there. You see someone, shoot them. Got it?"

Everyone nodded.

"How long are these timers set for?" Judah asked.

"Fifteen seconds," Lou answered. "They're aluminized ammonium nitrate in steel casings, so—"

"We don't need a fucking chemistry lesson, Lou. Let's just fuckin' go!"

Judah climbed over the fence that surrounded the campgrounds, followed by Scurge, Lou and Myron.

Frank, Rinny, Lubbock and Malik passed the jugs of gasoline and the pipe bombs over to them.

Everyone drew their handguns, and Judah's armed posse of clowns spread out and duckwalked toward the encampment.

When they were within ten yards of the first tent, a clown wandered outside and lit a cigarette. He turned, saw the infiltrators and looked surprised and confused. "Hey, what are you guys—"

Rinny shot him in the chest.

At the sound of the shot, two more clowns appeared, and were promptly shot.

Judah's line of clowns advanced to the outer rim of tents, from which more clowns emerged and were promptly shot. Judah's men also approached the entrances to the tents and shot their occupants.

Each tent was doused with gasoline and set on fire.

Before Judah's men could reach the tents farthest from their approach, armed clowns began spilling from them, firing automatic rifles.

Judah's men had only handguns, which were no match for them, and he ordered his men to fall back behind the trucks and tents between them and the clown defenders.

The firefight continued, with Clowney's men hiding behind trucks, stepping out to fire bursts and slipping back behind the trucks.

Judah's men were into their second magazines of ammunition.

"Can you reach the trucks with the bombs?" Judah yelled.

"I think so," Frank answered.

"Malik's got the arm," Lubbock called back.

"I got it," Malik agreed.

"Aim for under the trucks," Judah instructed.

Malik and Frank James sent pipe bombs toward the trucks. Two rolled under trucks and one fell short. A quarter minute later all exploded and two of the trucks burst into flames as the bombs ignited their gas tanks. The third bomb sent a wall of fire into the air but did little damage.

More clowns began to appear from the far side of the encampment.

"They've called in reinforcements," Scurge yelled. "Set our guys on them."

Judah gave the order and watched as the clown reinforcements turned to fight Judah's clowns, who had appeared behind them.

And yet, it wasn't enough. Judah saw hordes of men, some armed, some wielding shovels and rakes, flowing into the field of battle from the direction of the parking lot. There seemed to be no end to the sudden influx of men. Some of these were Clowney's men, others appeared to be locals who were not in clown makeup.

"Fuckin' civilians." Judah glanced around. They were being overrun.

Frank James was yelling into his phone.

"What are you doing?" Judah called to him, but he had no time to talk, as the sheer numbers of men running at them or hiding behind the trucks that were still standing, demanded the immediate attention of all their resources.

Myron and Scurge circled around the far left and right of the attackers, in new flank attacks that were effective but limited by their weapons and lack of support. Still, they continued to hold off the defenders, as the firefight slowed and devolved into a stalemate—but it was temporary at best, due to the sheer numbers of Clowney supporters.

The shooting briefly died down to occasional single shots, when someone on one side or the other stepped into the open to fire a shot and drew return fire.

Men on both sides were wounded—Lubbock in the thigh and Myron in the shoulder. Both remained able to return fire, despite their injuries…for the moment.

Lou suddenly sprinted into the open and threw two bombs in the direction of the big semi. Both skittered beneath it and holes blew open the truck's floor in several spots, and the truck's bed sagged and collapsed.

Shots burst from beyond the truck and Lou staggered and dropped to the ground.

"We need to get to him and drag him out of here," Judah said to Frank James, who was a half dozen yards to his left. "They've got too many guys. The numbers, man."

Frank was about to answer when a rumble came from the other side of the encampment. The rumble grew to a roar, and a sea of red appeared from the direction of the parking lot.

It took Judah a moment to realize what he was seeing.

Red capes. Dante had arrived with a horde of his Inferno. That was who Frank had called. And they had automatic weapons.

The Clowney men soon surrendered, and within ten minutes, the entire Clowney headquarters was destroyed or burning and all its occupants had been killed, were incapacitated or had surrendered.

Judah approached Dante, who was grinning, a smoking AR-15 by his side.

"That was fun, man," Dante said.

"I owe you," Judah said.

"Yes, you do," Dante agreed. "But we best get outta here before the cops arrive. I'm surprised they're not here already."

Judah shrugged with a knowing smile. "I'm not. Most of the cops around here are not fans of Clowney, so they're not rushing to his aid."

"Speaking of Clowney," Dante said. "Where is that fuck?"

"He's with his main bodyguards at what they're calling their victory party at the Jupiter Suites."

"How 'bout we crash that party?" Dante suggested.

"I don't know. That's where the cops will be." Judah took out his phone and saw that he had a message from his sister. He held his phone to his ear as Dante began rounding up his men. As Judah listened he beckoned to his men to follow him back the way they had come.

"Jude," Dinah said breathlessly, her voice edged with panic. "You've gotta come. Now! Clowney's got Raisa!"

Chapter 18

Judah arrived home to find his family in front of Zebby's computer, where they were watching Clowney hold court in a room high up in the Jupiter Suites. On his lap, looking dazed and bewildered, was Raisa.

"They drugged her," Reuben said.

"I know that room," Dinah said. "It's one of the party rooms off the main ballroom. The main party, which is open to the public, is in the ballroom."

Judah put his hands to his hips. "Fuckin' hell." He threw up his hands. "Well, I'll get the guys and we'll go get her."

"Wait, Judah," Dinah said. "You'll be walking into the lion's den."

"With a whip and a chair," Judah said.

"It's what they want you to do," Reuben said. "They'll be waiting for you. Armed and ready."

Judah fixed his brother with a cold stare. "Well, they're gonna get me. And a whole lotta shit they're not gonna want." He turned and walked out the door and onto the porch, calling Frank James as he went.

"Grab the guys and meet me at the strip mall south of the Jupiter Suites. Clowney's got Raisa and we've gotta get her back." He ended the call, got into his car and sped down the dirt drive and into the street.

• • •

The parking lot was full, so Junior was forced to park in the lot of the supermarket half a block from the Jupiter Suites. He closed the car door and tapped his right-side pocket, feeling for the folding knife. It was there.

As he walked closer to the hotel, Junior saw more and more people in clown costumes and makeup. Many wore the white shirts, blue vests, and blue hats with the letters CUT, but a few wore the more colorful baggy attire and floppy shoes typical of circus clowns.

While one of the lobby's two security guards glanced at him as he walked by, neither stopped him. No one was being stopped or questioned. Clowney had announced that any and all of his supporters were welcome at his victory party.

The party, Junior knew, was on the hotel's top floor, so he rode up one of the elevators and emerged into an alcove outside the ballroom. The ballroom doors were open, people were flowing in from the elevators, and Junior was swept along with the crowd into the party.

Music was blasting a mix of Queen's "We Are the Champions," Springsteen's "Born in the USA," Credence Clearwater Revival's

"Fortunate Son," and other rock and roll standards. The room was crowded and the open bars at either end of the room were packed.

Enormous TVs hung on the walls around the room broadcast Clowney sitting in a huge gold throne-like armchair with a woman on his lap. On one of the arms of the chair was a drink. Around him were his bodyguards. He was speaking, and while he couldn't be heard over the music, his words were captioned below him.

But Junior wasn't there to drink or to focus on what Clowney had to say. He wandered through the crowd, but saw only party goers reveling in the night. Wait staff traveled the room with trays of hors d'oeuvres and finger foods. Round tables were set up along the sides of the room, and people sat in groups of eight or ten with their drinks and the hors d'oeuvres on little napkins. People were dancing to the music in an open space at the far end of the room, and just beyond them were two sets of white double doors with gold trim. Junior walked in that direction.

Security personnel in dark suits stood in front of the doors, and when Junior reached for a door handle, one of the men extended an arm to block him.

"This area's off limits," the security man said.

"How come?" Junior asked.

"You can't go in there," the man said.

Junior wandered several steps back into the ballroom and thought about what to do next. Mama gave him the answer.

"Just tell him who you are. They'll let you in," she said, her voice low and with that hint of a threat that had always frightened him every bit as much as her screaming tirades. "You know what I mean," she added.

He approached the security guards again. "Is Clowney in there?"

The guard sighed impatiently. "No one gets in without clearance."

"Tell him his son is here. Tell him Walter Tagill Junior is here to see him." He heard Mama again and added her words to his. "To congratulate him."

The man looked back at him, surprised, then opened the door and went inside. Moments later, the man returned and held the door for him.

"Go on in."

• • •

Sharpe was standing in front of the hotel, looking up toward the penthouse. He was focused on finding Walter Gibson, whom Robin Mendoza had learned through several database searches was the son of Millie Gibson and her first husband, Walter Tagill Sr., aka Clowney.

Walter Gibson had once been Walter Tagill Jr.

He had also seen the news feed and knew that Clowney had Raisa Tolleson with him, and from what he could see, she was being held against her will. Even if she were with him voluntarily, to report a story, she would never be sitting on his lap, and she would never be as out of it as she appeared to be now.

Sharpe was as focused and excited and as driven as he ever was while working on a case, but he suddenly realized that he was not in thrall to the beast. He had absolutely no desire for heroin or opioids or speed or booze or drugs of any kind—and he could hardly believe it.

"Well look who we have here," a voice behind him said. "Great minds, and all that." Judah Hammer was approaching with six of his men.

The two men shook hands.

"I'm going up to get Raisa out of there," Judah said.

"And I followed the guy who killed the three escorts here," Sharpe said. "He's up there now."

Judah looked surprised. "Here?"

"He's here to kill Clowney. I'll explain later." Sharpe started toward the entrance, but Judah grabbed his arm.

"Clowney's in a party room. We need to go up the stairs. Everyone follow me, three paces behind, and spread out so security won't see we're a group."

Judah walked into the entrance and headed toward the elevators, but instead of waiting for an elevator, he continued walking to the door to the stairs. He opened the door and started up the stairs, with his men and Sharpe behind.

• • •

As Junior walked through the door, two large men in clown make-up, white shirts and blue vests fell into step on either side of him. The room, which could have held seventy-five people, only contained a third of that. A dozen men in clown costumes were drinking at the eight tables in the room, pouring themselves drinks at a well-stocked bar along one side of the room, or beers from a keg that sat in a tub of ice not far from the bar. Another dozen people were sprinkled around the room, walking back and forth, snacking on sandwiches from the round plastic party platters that sat at the center of each table beside vases of flowers. Junior didn't know who any of the people were, but they looked rich and important.

At the far end of the room, on a large golden chair on a raised platform painted in red, white and blue, sat Clowney, with a woman on his lap. TVs had been mounted on all four walls, and all showed a live feed of Clowney, from the front, with the woman on his lap.

Junior saw himself in the video, standing in the center of the picture in front of Clowney. He realized that the camera was behind him. He turned and saw it, mounted high on the wall behind him.

Clowney looked at Junior, laughed and said something to the woman. Then he beckoned to Junior and said, "It really is the whippet! This is unbelievable! It's the whippet, to celebrate with me on the greatest night, the greatest triumph of thy life! Come here, Walter. Come here and let me look at you!"

Junior walked to a spot directly in front of Clowney. He was having trouble hearing, as Mama was screaming, "Kill him! Kill the motherfucker! Kill him now, while you have a chance! Kill him! Kill him, goddamit! KILL HIM!"

He wished she would quiet down. He needed to think, to focus.

He looked around, but saw nothing helpful.

No forks. No knives.

He remembered his own knife, and tapped his pocket. It was there, where it was supposed to be.

But half the people in the room were there to guard the man he was supposed to kill.

He stopped looking around and looked at his father, and saw the same man who had left his mother when she'd gotten sick. The man who had ran away when he'd been needed most.

He remembered sitting…had he been on his father's knee? He remembered the stories his father had told him, and the games they had played in the yard and sometimes in the street. Throwing a ball, chasing each other around, playing with Norman, and Mama too. She had played with them before she'd gotten sick.

He remembered the smell of her cooking, which was always different yet always the distinct smell of Mama's cooking. The meals were so good—because they really were delicious and because they were together, as a family.

Funny that he could remember the wonderful smells now. He'd never remembered them before. He hadn't even remembered that her cooking had smelled good.

He'd forgotten so much.

Because he had to.

His father was saying something, talking to him.

"Do you talk to Norman? He's upstate somewhere, isn't he? Ellenville, I believe?"

"We talk," Junior answered. "Norman's good." He was concentrating, thinking hard.

"And I can't imagine you talk to your mother, where she's at. But they must be looking after her, I'd imagine."

Mama was going a mile a minute at the top of her lungs. "Kill that no good piece of shit, now, Junior. Fucking kill him. Kill him! KILL HIM!"

But what could he do with these guards all over the place, including the two who remained on either side of him?

"You look good, Walter—a little scrawny, maybe, but good. Handsome, even. You look a little like I did, way back when." His father clapped him on the shoulder, which was a shock to his system. His muscles and nerves were suddenly energized. Buzzing.

"Hey everybody! Let me have your attention! I'd like you to meet my son, Walter Junior. I call him, or I used to call him, the whippet. An affectionate nickname, if you will. We haven't seen one another in, my goodness, it's been decades, I guess. I cannot tell you all how wonderful it is to have my boy here with me on this greatest of all nights!"

He rose, forcing the woman off his lap. She took a step, stumbled, and then righted herself. Clowney looked at one of the guards and jerked his head toward the woman, who rushed to her side and held her up and firmly in place.

"The exit polls are in," Clowney said, to both Junior and the camera. "And it's safe to say that I'm going to be the new mayor of Towson. By the way, I'm thinking of renaming the city in my honor. Clowneytown has a nice ring to it, don't you think? But we can discuss that later. For now, this is as good a time as any to tell you, Walter, and all of you—" he gestured toward the camera "—a little bit about what's coming next."

He leered at the camera, tilting his head to either side and half singing his words. "I'm going to fire everyone, everyone, ev-ery-one —you're all going to lose your jobs, lose your jobs, lose your joobbss…"

He nodded slowly. "Everyone who works for the city. You're. All. Gone." He waved a hand as though swatting a fly. "There are plenty of jobs out there—waiting tables, delivering food, driving—plenty of jobs. And, by the way, I have a plan to take care of the poor. People say I don't care about the poor. Well, watch. I'll do something about the poor." He thrust his head toward the camera. "Get a job! Ha. See? I just did something for the poor."

He widened his eyes. "You don't think I can fire everyone? Don't think I have the power? Well, I do. You just have to know how to deal with the people who technically are supposed to be the ones to do the firing. A little carrot. A little stick. Know their weak spots, their secrets, their family's secrets, and be willing to go public." He nodded, grinning. "With the right information and the willingness to use it, people will do whatever you want. Whatever you want! They have to, to save themselves."

A glass of something amber was on the arm of his chair, and he took a long pull from it. Junior watched him, then looked around. He saw a glass statuette, a pointy award of some kind, on one of the tables. Could he get to it and use it as a weapon? He didn't see how.

"So, I have a two-year plan—maybe it will take three—to clean up this city, shrink the government, save all you wonderful folks who elected me tonight money on your taxes. We need police. We need firemen. We don't need all the water department people we have. When there's a hose running into a manhole, we don't need six guys standing around staring at it! So we'll turn this ship of a city around and aim it at less polluted waters. I'll bring in my favorite donor, Brandon Fisk, yes, that Brandon Fisk—the cryptocurrency mogul. And I'll put him in charge of all the publicly funded charities, and he'll shut them all down. All that so-called humanitarian bullshit. And then— then, we run for governor. Do the same for the state. It's onward and upward!"

He held up his glass and drained it as a door along the side of the room to Junior's right opened and Judah Hammer burst in, followed by a half dozen men. All were armed. Behind them was Sam Sharpe.

One of Clowney's men promptly shot Judah in the hand, and Judah's pistol fell to the floor.

"Drop the weapons, fellas," Clowney said.

His men had guns trained on Judah's men and Sharpe. Three clowns bearing automatic weapons approached and took their guns, dropped them on the floor and kicked them away.

"Oh look," Clowney crowed in mock excitement, as he peered into Raisa's confused face. "Your man has come to save you." He straightened and glared at Judah. "Well, I'm glad you're here."

He looked at the camera. "I've always said, I could kill someone on TV and not only get away with it, people would agree with it. They'll love it. Watch," he turned to Junior. "And learn."

He turned back to the camera. "By the way," he said in a loud whisper. "None of this is real. It's—" He started to sing. "Hol-ly-wood! Na na na na na, Hol-ly-wood!"

He shot Raisa in the leg as he continued to sing. She screamed and fell.

No one in the room moved, except Judah, who ran to Raisa and took her in his arms. As his men raised their guns, Clowney waved at them.

"Let him go. I mean, what's he going to do?" Clowney giggled and looked at the camera. "See? I'm still here, folks!" Clowney seemed to see his glass for the first time.

"I've long wanted to share a toast with my son. Together, Walter Jr. and I are going to toast all you suckers and losers, and the whippet, excuse me, Walter Jr. is going to join me as we move forward into Towson's future. And, as I said, Towson is just the beginning!"

He stood and looked down at Judah, who was doing his best to hold Raisa to him, while cradling his wounded hand.

"We have here a local criminal who thought he was a threat to me. With a two-minute phone call I put him out of business, took away his gaming license." He smiled and shook his head. "Mess with me and you don't know what you're in for."

He stepped to the bar and poured himself a drink, then poured another for Junior.

Junior thought to say he doesn't drink, but Mama was yelling at him again. He tried to focus. He tried to listen, and then Clowney held his glass up to Junior and to the camera, and brought it to his lips to drink. As he did, his eyes closed for an instant.

Mama saw and screamed. "NOW!"

Junior turned and smashed his glass into his father's throat, then yanked it back and smashed it against the side of his jaw. He dropped the glass and pulled out his knife, flicked it open and plunged it into the big clown's neck.

Over and over and over.

And the bullets hit him, like cars—and in his mind they were cars. Clown cars slamming into his side, as the room faded and was gone.

As Clowney's men began firing at Junior, Rinny Mallach leaped at the nearest man, grasped the wrist of his gun hand, twisted and, using his other hand, snapped one of the clown's fingers. He tore away the AR-15, dropped, rolled and came up firing, taking out the gun-wielding clowns with two bursts of gunfire.

Sharpe rushed to where Judah and Raisa lay together on the floor and examined their wounds. He took out his phone and called for medical assistance.

The main doors to the ballroom opened and Detectives Gold and Cortez burst in, followed by a sea of blue. "Drop it!" Gold yelled at Rinny, who dropped the gun and raised his hands.

Epilogue

The aroma of freshly brewed coffee wafted through the office as Robin handed steaming mugs to Cortez, Gold and Sharpe.

"One for you, too," Sharpe suggested. "After all, you're the one who figured out the connection between Walter Jr. and Walter Sr. aka Clowney."

Robin took Sharpe's suggestion and poured herself a coffee. "That was just one piece of it," she said. "A lot of people contributed to solving this case."

Gold said, "The knowledge that Mildred Gibson used to be Mildred Tagill, and that her husband left her when she was diagnosed schizophrenic was a pretty valuable piece of information."

"What will happen to Walter?" Sharpe asked. "Will he stand trial?"

Gold looked down at his coffee for a moment before answering. "I can tell you what happens in theory; what will actually happen remains to be seen. First, he'd be deemed competent to stand trial, or not. That depends on his ability to understand the charges against him. If he's not competent, no trial."

Cortez sipped her coffee. "But he can always be deemed competent later and stand trial then."

"True," Gold admitted.

"Thank you, Abe," said Cortez, with a grin.

Gold looked at her, annoyed, then continued. "Not guilty by reason of insanity is another thing entirely. It's a decision a judge or jury makes after a trial." He sipped his coffee and bent to put the cup down on the table in front of the couch. "Thank you, Sam." He put out his hand, which Sharpe took. "And you, too, Robin." He shook her hand. "Please know that you provided the public with an invaluable service in stopping this serial killer."

"I only wish we'd gotten to him sooner," Robin said.

"You might want to thank Reuben Hammer, whose therapist had this guy as a client," Sharpe added.

"We might," Gold said, with a smile.

"What about the mayor's office?" Sharpe asked. "It's vacant at the moment, right?"

Gold shook his head. "The office of public advocate is automatically next in line. So the former public advocate is now mayor."

"And there will be a special election as soon as possible," Cortez added, looking to Gold for confirmation. "Right?"

Gold shrugged. "I guess so. Above my pay grade, really."

Once the detectives had left, Robin put down her coffee and walked to where Sharpe was standing between one of the chairs and the couch. She touched his forearm.

"You did a hell of a job in the home stretch—clean." She grasped both sides of his face between her hands, and kissed him on the lips.

Sharpe was too startled to react, but he didn't move away.

When Robin stepped back, still looking him in the eyes, he looked away, in the direction of the window, where the sun was shining and cars and pedestrians were passing by.

"Yeah," he said. "I did, didn't I?"

The office door opened and a woman's voice said, "Sorry to interrupt."

"Can we come in for a minute?" a man asked.

Sharpe turned and found himself in the arms of Harriet Teitlebaum.

"You got him!" She said, starting to cry. "Oh, you got him, didn't you?"

"Thank you," said Jason Hamilton. "Thank you so very, very much!"

• • •

Izzy Hammer placed the chicken cutlets he had coated with egg batter and breadcrumbs into the sizzling saucepan in which garlic and oil were snapping and popping. In another pan, he melted several sticks of butter, then poured in flour and cooked the mixture for just over a minute to create a roux, which he mixed in with a sauce consisting of white wine, lemon juice and chicken stock. He flipped the cutlets, while adding herbs to his sauce and stirring frequently. After another minute he removed the cutlets with a spatula and laid them on two paper towels which sat on a nearby plate. He added new cutlets to the pan and stirred his sauce some more.

He poured three cups of water into a pot, turned the heat to medium, and laid in the asparagus.

In the great room, Judah and Raisa were huddled on the couch. Raisa lay with her bandaged leg extended onto the coffee table in front of the couch. Rachel lay beside her mother, her face pressed against Raisa's side. Judah lay on Rachel's other side, his injured arm, which was wrapped in gauze and tape, curled against his chest while his other arm was around their daughter's belly.

Dinah was seated on an armchair, looking at an iPad. Josh was at her feet, playing a game on his phone.

The door to the porch opened and a woman with curly gray hair came in, followed by Reuben, who led her several steps into the room.

"This is Arlene Dunn, the therapist who had Walter Tagill Jr. as a client, and who had the courage to tell me, so I could tell Jude, and he could tell Sam Sharpe."

Dunn smiled and waved shyly.

"Please forgive me if I don't shake your hand," Judah said.

"This is my brother, Judah, his wife, Raisa, and their daughter, my niece Rachel."

Dunn held out a hand.

Raisa began to lean forward and extend a hand, but Rachel pulled her back. "No, Mommy. Stay with me!"

Raisa looked apologetic. "Sorry, our daughter's going through a bit of a hard time."

"Oh, I understand," Dunn said, sounding as though she did.

At the sound of her name, Rachel pressed her face against her mother's side and tightly shut her eyes.

"She's terrified something will happen to us," Raisa explains.

Reuben turned toward Dinah. "My sister, Dinah, and my nephew, Josh."

Dinah took Dunn's outstretched hand.

"We're having asparagus!" Josh yelled.

Dunn pretended to look concerned. "Just asparagus?"

"Nope! Chicken fun cheese!" he yelled.

"Stop yelling," Dinah said, rolling her eyes. "And it's chicken francese."

"Chays! Chays!" Josh yelled.

"Stop yelling!" Dinah ordered.

"I like asparagus," Josh yelled. "Because it makes my pee smell funny!"

"You are still in my doghouse, Joshua Hammer." Dinah waved a finger at him. "And I'm never letting you out of my sight again."

Josh looked innocently back at his mother. "So, no school?"

Dinah narrowed her eyes and shook her head at her son. "Don't 'no school' me. And don't get wise! No visiting your friends, homework as soon as you get home from school, and that's that!"

"That's that?" the boy whined. "Aw, shit!"

"Language!" Dinah yelled. "Now, go to your room!"

Arlene Dunn raised an eyebrow, as Reuben walked to the head of the long table. "Why don't you have a seat next to me, Arlene?"

She went to him and sat down.

"No!" Joshua yelled.

Reuben shrugged to the therapist. "Life in my house."

Josh yelled. "I'm not going! I'm staying here with Rachel!"

"Let him stay, Aunt Di," Rachel begged in a baby voice. "Pwease, pwease. Pwetty pwease?"

Dinah sighed. "Oh, all right. For Rachel."

The door opened and Lev entered, carrying a large off-white canvas bag by a metal handle that protruded through a slit in its top.

"I have here," he announced, "the answer to the kids' issues. Di, this will help Joshy, and Rai, it'll help Rachel."

"What is it, Uncle Lev?" Josh asked, as the room descended into silence.

Izzy appeared in the doorway to the kitchen. "Whatcha got there, Lev?"

"I thought you'd never ask." Lev set the package down with a metallic clang on the coffee table near Raisa's foot, and slid the canvas bag up and away, to reveal a small cage. Inside the cage was a puppy with a white nose, paws and forehead, brown floppy ears, and a brown diamond between its eyes blending to black on its back and sides.

Rachel gasped and leaped from the couch, her eyes wide, and hands clapping her cheeks. "A puppy! For me?"

"For everyone," Lev said. "I thought he would probably stay here, since Judah and Raisa work, but he's for us to share."

Dinah was staring at Lev.

Judah and Raisa were looking at each other. Raisa was expressionless, but Judah turned to look at Rachel. A smile broke across his face.

"It's not a bad idea, Lev."

Lev was jubilant. "See? I knew it!" He pointed at Dinah. "Hah!"

Josh got to his feet and hugged Lev's thigh. "Uncle Lev, this is the best day ever!"

"So, he's a boy?" Dinah asked, apparently resigned to the situation.

Lev nodded.

The dog had leaned to one side and bent his head toward his bottom, licking.

"Aw, he's licking his asshole!" Josh cried.

"Ewww!" Rachel yelled, gleefully. "He's a dirty dog!"

Josh had sat down next to the dog and was reaching for him. The dog saw him and jumped up, his paws on Josh's chest, and began licking his face.

"Oh, man. Now he's licking my face."

"He's disgusting!" Rachel yelled, delighted.

"He's the best!" Josh agreed. "This is gonna be great!"

Dinah cupped a hand over her eyes. "No," she said. "It's not."

Izzy appeared in the doorway to the kitchen. "Dinner is served," he said.

Once everyone was seated, Izzy and Reuben brought in the food and began serving and passing plates around the table.

"Where's Zebby?" Dinah asked.

"Where do you think?" Reuben said.

"Zeb?" Dinah called.

"Just a minutah!" came the answer from the den.

Once everyone had a plate of chicken, pasta, and asparagus, along with a hunk or two of garlic bread, Zeb came rolling in with his wheelchair.

"How are you going to eat with your computer on your tray?" Dinah asked, as she reached for the computer.

"Leave itah," Zeb insisted. "I have to show you something-ah."

"We've been discussing Zeb moving into a facility with a homelike environment," Lev explained, in Arlene Dunn's direction.

"Look at this-ah," Zeb said, and Dinah bent toward his computer to look at what he was indicating.

"Oh, my God," Dinah said. "It's a letter—well, an email."

"Read itah," Zeb insisted. "To-ah everyone heah."

"My name is Irene Goldstein," Dinah read. "And my son, Warren, is involved in a role-playing game in which Zeb participates. Warren is on the spectrum and has trouble interacting with others. He is frequently bullied at school and in the neighborhood, and has even experienced bullying in his gaming life. Zeb has been a godsend and literally a life-saver. He is deeply involved in this role-playing game and may be involved in others. He spends all of his time supporting and mentoring, not only my Warren, but many others as well. He is the kindest person I have ever known, even if I have never met him, lol. A thousand thanks to you, Zeb, for the love you have shown our Warren." She looked up, her eyes shining.

Everyone was looking at Zeb.

"Oh, Zebby," Dinah breathed, and threw her arms around her brother.

"Wow," Arlene Dunn said, looking at Zeb with admiration. She turned to Reuben. "That's some brother, you have."

He nodded. "Isn't he?"

"And look at thisah," Zeb added, and bent over his track ball, clicking a few times.

Dinah squinted. "Holy crap. Zeb's this month's champion in a fantasy football league!"

· · ·

Judah lay on his side in bed, his bandaged hand pressed to his stomach. Next to him, Raisa lay on her uninjured side. They had managed to get Rachel to sleep in her bed for the first time in a week, and all she'd talked about was the new puppy. She'd spent several hours coming up with names.

Raisa reached out and touched the side of Judah's face. "What are you going to do?"

"About what?"

"Your work."

"What do you mean?"

"Your gaming license."

"Well, Kofi James works as a lawyer in Atlanta, and he and Frank have an uncle down there who is a hell of a golfer, it turns out. And he's played golf with, well with probably the most famous and talented golfer in history. You know who I mean?"

Raisa nodded. "I think I do."

"Well, someone else in their foursome is a man named Horace Maxim, a pretty high-powered lawyer down there, and Horace has a brother named Lionel, who currently sits on the state supreme court here. Those brothers, Horace and Lionel, they've been watching Mr. Walter Tagill Senior—Clowney—and they haven't much liked what they've seen. They won't get involved in our local elections, but they will prevent any of Clowney's people from interfering in the business of any friends of the James family." Judah smiled. "That includes me."

"So you've got your license back?"

"Not yet, but it's coming. Within the week, I'm told."

Raisa was silent for a while. Her eyes filled with tears.

Judah brushed them away with a finger. "What is it? What's wrong, babe?"

"I'm scared—"

"I know, but—"

"No, I'm afraid of losing you because I have trouble handling some of … some of what's going on. I get so freaked out, and I know that in the past that, that you turned away from me because I get scared. I know it's why you left me, back when—"

"Shh." He held his finger to her lips. "Let me tell you something," Judah said. "That was then. For me, you balance all the ugliness in my life. Your beauty, and how…" He searched for a word. "How naive you can be, with all your years as a journalist and all the bad shit you've seen."

She continued as if she hadn't heard. "I'm terrified you're going to stop loving me, if—"

He shook his head. "Won't happen. There's too much to love." He laughed. "Like the way makeup and nail polish make you claustrophobic. And that jewelry and flowers don't impress you." He touched her face in wonder. "You are evidence of God in my life."

She blinked. "You really believe that?"

He nodded. "With all my heart."

"But, the violence—"

"Yeah, I can be brutal, to keep the world from intruding on your gentle kindness and on innocent people's lives—like our daughter's. I'll do whatever has to be done."

She exhaled sharply through her nose and shook her head. "You're one crazy man."

Judah nodded. "True, and I think I'm only now starting to appreciate you for who you are. I'm only just now getting a peek at the real Raisa. You're not what I thought. You've come through so much. Yeah, your fear was a problem for me, because you were afraid to go through things, afraid to live your life. But now, you've gone through things, you're living your life. You've come out the other side this changed and beautiful woman. Sure, sometimes you're still afraid, but there's shit to be afraid of. You'll heal and I'll help. You're this … this sweet and tender landscape, and I love you."

He hesitated, then said. "Marry me."

THE END

About The Author

David E. Feldman, publisher has authored 15 books and ghost-written many more. His significant film work includes 2 film awards and winner of the inaugural Long Beach N.Y. Artist In Partnership playwriting contest in 2022. He has an MLS degree in information & Library Science from Queens College.

David has overcome multiple life and health challenges, which are topics reflected in his books. Now clean and sober more than thirty years, he has surmounted depression, cancer, two hip replacements, an intestinal resection, spinal fusion and a double hernia operation…so far. Rather than seeing himself as a victim of circumstance, he is grateful for the wonderful care and support he's enjoyed and leans into spirituality and his creative work. These have also become inspiration for his characters in his mystery and thriller series and standalone novels.

David's book awards include: *Not Today - Dora Ellison Mystery Series* won Best Mystery, Killer Nashville Claymore finalist; *The Neighborhood* won The Book Excellence Awards – finalist.

Currently he is hard at work on his latest series, *The Hammer & Sharpe Noir Mystery Thrillers*. He also writes essays and articles both digitally and for print.

David also plays piano, sings professionally, and is passionate about painting for both fun and commission. He adores his sweet bride of nearly 40 years, their two sons and their Yorkie.

To learn more about David E. Feldman:
DavidEFeldmanAuthor.com

Books by David E. Feldman:

The Dora Ellison Mystery Series
Not Today: Book 1
A Gathering Storm: Book 2
A Sickening Storm: Book 3
A Biological Storm: Book 4
A Special Storm: Book 5
A Divisive Storm: Book 6

Hammer & Sharpe Noir Mystery Thrillers
Let Thy Children Come: Book 1
Dead Ringer: Book 2
Mama's Boy: Book 3

Additional titles by David E. Feldman
The Neighborhood
Percival
How to Be Happy in Your Marriage
Pilgrimage from Darkness Nuremberg to Jerusalem
Born of War: Based on a Story of American Chinese Friendship

To learn more about David E. Feldman, including his

Dora Ellison Mysteries

and his

Hammer & Sharpe Noir Mystery Thrillers

please visit:

DavidEFeldmanAuthor.com